I0639013

Hush, My Darling

HUSH, MY DARLING

A BENOIT AND DAYNE MYSTERY

WINTER AUSTIN

TULE
PUBLISHING

Hush, My Darling
Copyright© 2022 Winter Austin
Tule Publishing First Printing, January 2022

The Tule Publishing, Inc.

ALL RIGHTS RESERVED

First Publication by Tule Publishing 2022

Cover design by ebooklaunch

No part of this book may be used or reproduced in any manner
whatsoever without written permission except in the case of brief
quotations embodied in critical articles and reviews.

This is a work of fiction. Names, characters, places, and incidents are
products of the author's imagination or are used fictitiously. Any
resemblance to actual events, locales, organizations, or persons, living or
dead, is entirely coincidental.

ISBN: 978-1-958686-58-4

DEDICATION

It doesn't seem for a book such as this that there should be a
dedication to one of the most loyal pets in the world,
but I knew this was the best place to memorialize her.
We lost our most beloved border collie, Belle, to
intestinal cancer during the writing of this book.
She's over the rainbow bridge and in a pain-free place.
To my Baby Girl. I miss you.

ACKNOWLEDGMENTS

There are a lot of people that help in the process of getting a book out there in the world for all the readers to read. Mine are a small contingent, but they are a mighty one.

First will always be the One who has been my Rock and Foundation.

The entire crew at Tule is a fantastic group. I have learned a lot of new things in the past two years, and it has made me grow as an author. I always aspire to learn, write better, and never settle for the same ole, same ole, and Tule has given me the room to do so. It's such a privilege to be an author for Tule. Thank you: Jane, Meghan, Cyndi, and Nikki.

A lot of my skill improvements come from one of the best editors in the biz. Julie keeps me honest. Keeps me straight. Makes me sound smart. And can talk me off the edge. The mark of a great editor/author relationship comes in the fact that the editor can read her author as well as Julie reads me. I'm so glad we continued working together at this level. Julie, you're da bomb!

My beta readers, Rachel and Jenn, *hated* me this go-round, yet still loved me. Both would have such visceral reactions as I sent them chapter after chapter, and it was great fuel to keep going. There were frustrations as work and life sucked writing time from me and left them hanging, but the book did get done and both were satisfied with how it ended. I can't do any of this without either one of them. Love ya both!

My family has grown up, yet they're still here. When I started this journey, they were babies. Now I have young adults out there making me proud to be their mom. I love you all.

Then there is my partner in this crazy thing we call life. My husband, even after a long day teaching, sacrificed some nights of cooking or picked up food, and trying to avoid being around the house on the weekends so I could write. He'd chastise me if I goofed off but then beg me to clean up his schoolwork as he marches ever forward to obtain a master's in education. We've been through hell and back again, and here we still stand as husband and wife. Love you, Shawn.

CHAPTER ONE

Prelude: Saturday Night

G ROWING UP IN the Jackson Park neighborhood of Chicago, Lila Dayne didn't have many good memories. The ones she did have were the nights when it rained. She'd open her curtains and watch the lightning ripple across the sky over Lake Michigan. If it was summer, she'd pry open her ancient bedroom window and let in the smell of electrified air. Storms hadn't bothered her in those days. They were tame compared to her home life.

Years later, her love of rainstorms would forever be tainted.

A crack of thunder had jolted Lila from her nightmare. She slipped from the bed, careful not to disturb the lump next to her, and padded out of the bedroom into the kitchen. She would not sleep as long as it stormed. Hugging herself, Lila tiptoed up to the sliding glass door and peered outside.

Lightning lit up the backyard, creating eerie shadows from the trees and bushes. The momentary bright flash revealed the downpour. Thunder rumbled through the sky seconds later. Swallowing against the panic clawing at her throat, Lila turned from the sliding glass door. She headed toward the soft blue glow emitting from the living room.

Gerry, her pet beta fish, drifted aimlessly through his

temperature-controlled waters. She bent over and peered into the tank. Seeming to sense her presence, he rotated and floated into her line of sight. They stared at each other for a moment, until Gerry got uppity and darted into his Easter Island statues.

"One day I'll get you a woman and she'll put you in your place," Lila muttered at the taciturn fish.

Another crack of thunder left her shuddering. She grabbed a folded blanket from the sofa, shook out the large fleece throw, draped it around her shoulders, and flopped down in the middle of the couch. With her legs tucked up under her, she tried to burrow deep into her covering. At each flash of lightning and crack or rumble of thunder, she trembled.

But Lila refused to close her eyes. Doing so would have her return to that night. Her clenched jaw ached as she prevented her teeth from chattering. She dared to focus on the sound of the rain, but that, too, was a grim reminder.

He had used the storm to mask the sounds of his attack. Breaking into her home, throwing Lila into the fish tank, and thrusting that blade into her body and destroying what little bit of happiness she'd finally come to have. In the end, he hadn't finished the job. He'd been spooked away, leaving Lila bleeding out next to her precious, dying koi.

She'd laid there among the shattered glass and puddles, unable to call out, listening to the rain pellet the front stoop through the open door.

She could still smell the fish tank water mingled with her blood. Feel the blood leaving her body. Sense her life fading as her fish gasped their last breath.

"Lila?"

The male voice slashed through the memories. She yelped, throwing the blanket aside. She bolted from the sofa and ran for the door.

"Lila, stop!"

Her frantic hands couldn't make sense of the locks. She was trapped. He was going to kill her this time.

A hand on hers, and she froze momentarily, until the instinct to fight kicked in. She swung her elbow back, intending to connect with his abdomen, but instead he moved with her thrust and brought her around. The moment she was facing him, he released her and held his hands up in surrender as he stepped back.

"It's me, Lila. Kyle."

"Kyle?"

He lowered his hands. "Yes. Kyle."

Clasping her hands over her mouth, she stifled a sob.

He closed the gap between them and dragged her into his arms. Lila pressed her face into his bare chest and gave in to her grief, curling into his body as if he were her lifeboat. Kyle embraced her tighter, caressing the back of her head, and said nothing.

How many nights in the last few months had he done this for her?

Her grief spent, she sagged against him.

"Is it gone?" he asked softly.

Her throat dried out from her ragged weeping, she merely nodded. Kyle untangled his arms from around her and dipped down. Lila was caught off guard as he picked her up, but instinct had her wrapping her arms around his muscled neck.

"What are you doing?" she asked.

He grunted, then carried her to the bedroom.

"Kyle, I don't—"

He stifled her protest with a kiss. Lila, too exhausted to push her protest further, gave in. After all, he'd seen her at her worst and hadn't run. He broke their kiss to lay her on the bed and crawled in with her.

He pulled her into his arms and kissed the back of her neck as he spooned her body. "Go to sleep. It'll be over soon."

"Why?"

He rubbed his nose against her neck. "Why what?"

"Why haven't you broken it off with me? I'm a train wreck."

"Why are you questioning it?"

She turned her head to try to look at him. "Because people like me scare people like you."

"Guess I'm not that scared." He nudged her head. "Now sleep. We've got a long day tomorrow."

Lila lay there, sinking into the feel of his arms around her and his warmth against her backside. Her tense muscles relaxed, and, eventually, the emotional turmoil dragged her to the cusp of sleep.

As she was drifting off, she realized the storm was over and the patter of rain against her bedroom window was all that remained. Though the residue of her flashback lingered.

Deep in the back of her mind, a voice whispered, "Heed the nightmares."

Lila disregarded it.

SHERIFF ELIZABETH BENOIT watched the downpour from the open doorway of The Watering Hole. The pounding of the rain mingled with the rock beats rolling from the antique jukebox that pumped through the bar's sound system. The bar was deserted except for the owner, Elizabeth's sister Marnie, and Elizabeth's newly appointed undersheriff, Raphael "Rafe" Fontaine, and it had been that way for the last hour. When the first flickers of lightning rippled through the sky, the patrons had vacated the bar with hopes of making it home before the deluge started. Even the de-thorned king himself, disgraced ex-sheriff Kelley Sheehan, had abandoned his seat of honor for home.

The rain had been coming more and more often since the calendar flipped to August. Fields tall with corn and billowing beans were filling with water. Creeks were over their banks, spilling their excess into the rivers, which rose with each hour as the upriver dams allowed more water to escape. Flash floods were a daily threat. And the residents of Eckardt County were in emotional upheaval.

"National Weather Center says it should stop soon." Rafe's rough voice was a balm to Elizabeth's own emotional upheaval.

"For as long and as heavy as this has been coming down, it has done its damage." Elizabeth leaned against the wooden doorjamb and breathed in the wet air that smelled suspiciously like fish and mud. "We'll be getting calls for washed out roadways when the sun rises."

"All the more reason you should go home and sleep," he

said. "You've been here every night this week and getting home later and later."

True. But what Rafe didn't know was that when she got home, she might nap or doze off, but she wasn't getting a full night's sleep. Her brain refused to shut down, swirling with all the stresses that came with being the sheriff and now the problems with the flooding.

So far, they had not had to rescue anyone from flooded homes. Elizabeth's proactive evacuation measures had forced everyone living in the flood plain, along with their pets and any livestock, to higher ground. Rafe's wisdom and soothing tongue helped greatly when most of the residents argued with Elizabeth over the plan. Those who had listened and done what was expected of them were now singing her praises.

But was it enough? What about those who thought they might be out of harm's way, still raising their pitchforks and hollering foul? And others pounding her with questions for things she just didn't have the answers to. Worse, she was sensing a disturbance with her deputy detective, and Lila had begun to withdraw.

"Rafe, the same could be said for you."

"Because I've been here trying to get you to go home."

Elizabeth turned from the slowing rain and patted Rafe's chest. "That's what a good undersheriff is supposed to do."

She moved to the bar where her sister was finishing her nightly cleanup. In a corner, lying on a special bed her second-favorite human had created for her, Bentley, Elizabeth's devoted red border collie, lifted her head from her nap. Elizabeth wagged her fingers and Bentley resettled her nose on her crossed paws.

"He's right, big sis. Go home. Sleep," Marnie said, placing something on the bar top.

When her hand moved away, she left behind a small plastic packet. Inside were two small white pills.

"Are you seriously trying to give the sheriff drugs, li'l sis?"

Marnie scoffed. "As if. Those are melatonin. A natural sleep aid. Take them. You'll sleep."

"I do sleep."

"Liar." Marnie drained the water in the bar sink. "Those dark bags and deeper wrinkles say different."

"I don't have wrinkles."

"Ha!" Her sister disappeared into the back.

Elizabeth picked up the pill packet. If Marnie wasn't lying to her, these were safe. But would they really work?

"Wouldn't hurt to try," Rafe said as he came to stand beside her. "Bentley's ready to go. I'll walk you to the house."

"It's less than a half a block away." Elizabeth pocketed the pills in her jeans. "You go home."

"Ellie—"

She held up a finger like a scolding mother. "If you so much as play that macho card on me, I'll smack you."

"I was just going to say, use the umbrella this time."

She smiled. "Fine." Snapping her fingers brought Bentley to her side. "Come on, baby girl, let's go home. Good night, Marnie."

"Night!" came from the back room.

Elizabeth felt Rafe's eyes on her as she exited the bar.

Five years next month since she'd come home to Juniper, Iowa. Six years last month since she'd finalized her divorce with Rafe's older brother, Joel, a Delta Force operative. In all that time, except for one heated kiss late last year, Elizabeth had not acted on her desire for Rafe. And he hadn't on his desire for her. Even her ex-husband had given her permission to pursue that avenue. A lot of good it did when his own brother wouldn't act on it.

She deployed the umbrella as she stepped out into the steady rainfall. Elizabeth trekked toward her house the next block over from the bar. Bentley, too tired herself, stayed glued to Elizabeth's side. Together, they avoided the large puddles covering the sidewalk and spilling into the street.

Nine months into this job as Eckardt County sheriff and the newness of it had finally worn off. She'd wrangled more money out of the county to hire one more deputy, get Rafe into the position of undersheriff, and hire a nightshift dispatcher. Things were also easier after Elizabeth had put an end to a long-term drug problem in the county. But sadly, by shutting down one problem, she'd opened wide the barn doors on other long-term issues. Those had all taken a backseat when the flooding began.

Sighing, she mounted the steps to her porch. Once under the roof, Bentley shook the rain from her coat, splashing Elizabeth.

"Well, that defeats the purpose of an umbrella." She shook the droplets free and closed the umbrella.

Ignoring her, Bentley trotted to the door and sat, waiting to be let inside. Elizabeth looked back toward the bar and watched as the undersheriff's Charger rumbled to life and the headlights flicked on. A few seconds later, Rafe backed out of the parking space and pulled away, headed east toward his home. Elizabeth stood on the edge of her porch until the taillights faded from view.

Not for the first time in her life, she regretted the code of honor Rafe lived by.

Bentley huffed.

"Alright, I'm coming."

Elizabeth unlocked the door and swung it open. Bentley darted inside. Elizabeth hesitated before entering herself and looked back at the rain. It had slowed to a soft patter. Over the *drip-drip* off the eaves an ominous roar reached her.

A violent urge to vomit hit Elizabeth with the same force as the floodwaters against the river levee. The Mighty Mississippi had wiped out Juniper's last line of defense. She would be pouring into people's homes and businesses and sweeping away anything not bolted down.

Elizabeth turned her back on the sound of rushing water and closed her door. Two little pills wouldn't be enough to make her sleep tonight.

CHAPTER TWO

Day 1: Sunday

L ILA LEFT HER house before Kyle woke. After he'd calmed her, she'd managed only an hour more of sleep. Giving up, she slipped from his arms, showered quickly, dressed in her uniform, and left a note for him that she'd started the workday early.

The gray light of dawn revealed a drowning world. She drove her vehicle at a snail's pace through the streets, stopping when she came to a small bridge over a creek. A creek that had spilled over its banks and was now covering the entire roadway and bridge. From what Lila could see, the bridge was tilting at an odd angle, which could mean a washout. Not good.

She backed her vehicle up and drove to another bridge that went up and over a set of railroad tracks and the creek.

Those tracks were submerged.

The whole eastern side of town was under water. The Mississippi River battered storefronts and abandoned homes. She had pushed cars into buildings and slammed against their dented sides. A few blocks farther, Lila saw that the water had shattered a storefront window, and the merchandise was floating away.

She turned the nose of her car uphill and away from the

devastation. As she left the submerged part of town, she moved closer to the residential areas and eventually the rural side of Juniper. In the nine months she'd been here, Lila had learned and memorized every route and backroad in the county. Having a hill and miles of land between them and the river, the biggest concern for the residents up this way was the oversaturated ground leaking water into their basements and drowning their crops.

Lila spotted a Crown Vic with Eckardt County Sheriff painted across the side. She pulled her car alongside the Vic and rolled her window down, getting blasted with damp, humid air and the stench of rotting vegetation. Her fellow deputy rolled his window down.

"Fitzgerald."

"Dayne. What are you doing out this early?"

Deputy Ben Fitzgerald, along with Undersheriff Rafe Fontaine, were the last of the old guard under the former corrupt sheriff. Fitzgerald was tolerable on a good day and reticent on any other. Since Lila had been sworn in, he had been warming to the sheriff and deputies in the department. But there was still an air of caution around him, as no one was certain which way the man would swing if Elizabeth Benoit ever lost her position.

"Storm woke me up and I couldn't get back to sleep. Decided to get a jump on the day." Lila stuck a fingernail in her mouth and gnawed.

"The levee up by Hendersons' place gave."

"I saw the damage," she said around her nail.

"Gonna have to put the newbie on guard duty."

"That's the sheriff's call."

"You're going to chew those nails to the bone," he commented.

Lila hesitated and pulled her finger from her mouth. She peered at the ragged edge of the nail and grimaced. Four were down to the quick, her thumb being the sole survivor.

"In my experience, people who are nail biters have some deep, dark secrets they're hiding."

She dropped her clenched hand into her lap. "Fitzgerald, not everyone has something to hide. It's a bad habit."

"Born out of a troubled mind."

Lila rolled her eyes. "Suddenly, you're an expert in psychology?"

"Human nature."

What a crock. Fitzgerald was digging for dirt. He always liked to stay one step ahead of the gossip mill.

"Speaking of the newbie," he said. "I noticed I'm not the only one with her on my radar."

"What is that supposed to mean?"

He jabbed a finger at her. "You don't like her either."

Lila shrugged. "I have nothing against her."

"Bull."

The new night dispatcher, Alexis, broke through Fitzgerald's radio, the sound carrying through his open window and over the still air. Lila hadn't turned her radio on, as she hadn't officially reported for duty.

"Deputy Fitzgerald, we have a call for a 10-54." Livestock on the road. Always a fun call.

He muttered something as he grasped his radio. "Have Deputy Young respond."

"No go, Deputy Young is on another call. You're closer."

As Fitzgerald argued his way out of going, Lila tuned him out and peered through her windshield. Through the gray fog of the water-laden air, she could make out moving shadows. She reached up and grabbed the steering wheel, using it to hoist her body forward. The shadows were beginning to form as trotting figures. She squinted, trying to decide if it was real or a figment of her chaotic mind.

"Fitzgerald," she said.

He ignored her, still arguing with Alexis.

"Ben!"

He jolted. "What?"

Lila pointed ahead. "Cows."

Having heard her voice, the cattle picked up speed, running straight for their cars.

"Shit." Fitzgerald ducked down as the cattle swarmed around their vehicles.

Lila gaped at the herd of mothers and calves moving by, acting as if something was chasing them. A few of the heavier cows bumped her car, making it shudder under the force of the impact. She cringed. Once the majority of them had passed, she spotted what was indeed coming after them.

Two lumbering men emerged from the fog, hollering and waving their arms. An older man and a younger one came closer. The older man looked about done in.

"Damn it," Fitzgerald spat as he exited his car. "Bill? Bo? What the hell?"

Lila turned off her car engine and vacated it. With her hand on her service weapon, she followed Fitzgerald.

Winded by his hustle to get to them, Bill, the older man, bent at the waist and gasped for air. "Ben, we tried to stop them. But some dumbass left the gate open, and they were all on the road when we got here."

"You do realize they hit our cars. Those belong to the county, and whatever damage—"

Bill waved off Fitzgerald's tirade, then sank to his knees.

"Oh my God," Bo, his son said, dropping next to his father.

Lila rounded her counterpart and pulled Bo away. "Deputy Fitzgerald, call for EMS. I think Mr. Cullen is having a heart attack."

"Shit." He did as she ordered.

"Bo, get back." Lila eased the old man down on the soggy roadside. "Bill, try to relax. Are you on any heart medications?"

He shook his head, his features turning white. His right hand massaged his chest. "I don't … think … it's …"

"Stop talking. Save your breath for breathing." She looked up at the hovering Bo. "You need to get those cows rounded up, or we're going to have an accident."

"I can't do it alone."

"Ben," Lila barked.

"Damn it. We need horses or ATVs to get those stupid animals back here."

"I'd get it done if I were you."

Bill grasped Lila's hand. "Just help me to a car. I'll be fine."

"You're staying where you are."

"And you'll get ran over by those damn cows," Fitzgerald pointed out.

Glaring at him, she climbed to her feet. "Then the two of

you help him to your car."

Once they had Bill lying on the backseat of Fitzgerald's unit, the two men raced back to Bo's truck and took off after the cattle. Lila stood by the open door, keeping an eye on Bill and watching for the ambulance.

"Something spooked them cows," Bill muttered.

Lila frowned. "Probably all the storms."

He shook his aged head. He took several heavy breaths before speaking again. "That gate was ... wide open." A few more deep breaths. "Someth'n' ... in the ... pasture."

Lila squatted down next to him. "When the EMTs get here, I'll go check it out. Okay?"

Bill gave her a wobbly nod.

Before she forgot, she hustled over to her car and turned on her radio. She hailed Alexis to let her know she was on site and would be aiding Fitzgerald. By the time she ended the radio transmission, a pair of cows and calves trotted past, heading toward their pasture.

Lila stood guard, monitoring Bill's vitals until the ambulance crept up to their position. Lila gave her assessment and let them do their job. As promised, she crawled into her car and drove up to the pasture where a half a dozen or so cattle loitered outside the opened gate. They didn't seem too keen on reentering their home.

Lila exited her car and cautiously approached the black bovines. In her short time as a deputy in Eckardt County, she'd been called out to three other livestock incidents. Roaming farm animals seemed to be a theme for the area. Added to the misery—owners who were all too helpful in teaching her how to manage the beasts.

Talking to the cows—like she had been taught—as she approached made them lower their heads and twitch. They backed away, allowing her to pass. She wasn't about to make them go into the pasture while she was alone. With her luck, they'd probably bolt and run the other direction.

The distinct odor of decay hit her. An elongated lump lay thirty feet left of the gate. The decaying thing was most likely the reason the cattle took advantage of the opened gate. Maybe it was a dead calf? She groaned. She would have to go out there and confirm what had died, since Bill was probably on his way to the hospital and Fitzgerald and Bo were busy rounding up the stray cows.

She eyed the churned mess of mud and grass that was the driveway and then checked her boots, screwing up her face in a scowl. She really didn't want to go into that field. There were times she questioned her sanity of taking this job as a rural county deputy.

The mud's depth caught Lila off guard. Grimacing, she yanked her foot free. The muck clung to her boots. She was going to have to drive barefooted back to the house for a clean pair. Thirty feet through ankle-deep, swampy mud was a workout worthy of the bold and willing who ran in the Tough Mudder races.

As she drew closer to the body, it began to take on a distinct human shape. A cold sweat broke out on her skin. This was not good. This person had been out in the elements for some time, their clothing covered in mud and drenched. The body lay on its side, one leg bent toward the chest and the other stretched out, with an arm flung backward.

Lila was gasping by the time she reached the body.

Drawing in a lungful of air was a mistake. She gagged. Decomposition overpowered the smell of mud and manure. She paid closer attention to the condition of the body, and her muscles tensed.

The clothing was in tatters. The body was missing shoes and socks. The bloated and discolored feet declared advanced decay. The arm was no longer attached to the body, held in place only by the shirt sleeve.

Lila grasped her radio and hailed Fitzgerald. "We've got a DB."

"Whaddya mean we have a DB?" he panted back between muttered curse words. "Is it a cow?"

"No, it's human." Lila tried to get a look at the face, but her angle was wrong, and she couldn't keep her balance in the mud.

"Who is it?"

"I don't know. The body is on its side."

"Roll it over and describe them to me."

She swallowed the bile rising in her throat. "It's pretty advanced decomp."

"Do you need me to radio the sheriff?" Alexis broke in, monitoring their call.

"That would be nice, since there is a dead body out in the middle of a muddy cow pasture," Lila sniped.

"Geesh, Dayne, chill out," Fitzgerald came back. "Alexis, call the sheriff."

What an ass. He had free rein to bitch at Alexis, but Lila wasn't allowed that luxury?

"Dayne, find out who it is."

Battling the fear and the stench, Lila reached out with a

trembling hand. Carefully, she took hold of the mushy shoulder, squelching the urge to snatch her hand back. She gently tipped the body on to its back.

First thing that struck her, the DB was a male. Second, his face was gaunt and riddled with decay. His shirt was unbuttoned, and peeking out from under the haphazardly draped flaps were deep marks. Lila pinched the edge of the ragged and disgusting fabric and peeled back one side of the shirt.

Words.

She flicked aside the other edge.

Hush, my darling.

Lila screamed, throwing her body away. She lost her footing and slammed into the muddy ground. Mucky water sprayed her, peppering her face, not unlike the blood that had spurted from her wounds as he'd stabbed her. The words seemed to pulsate at her, growing larger, coming after her.

He was here. He had found her.

She scrambled out of the mud and scrabbled back from the body. Her hands shook as she grappled with her duty belt—the damn thing was weighing her down. Lila managed to turn around and tried to put distance between her and that message.

Her breath seesawing with every mud-sucking step, she scanned the area for any sign of him. Was he here? Watching? Waiting for her to emerge from this hellish pasture?

He wouldn't get her. Not now, not ever.

She struggled to get her pistol from the holster, succeeding when the dirty strap came loose, and she slid the gun free.

"Dayne?"

She froze.

"Dayne, what the hell?"

He was here. Where was he? Lila searched the gray world and saw nothing.

Suddenly, through the mist a figure approached. Lila lifted her service weapon.

"Stay back!"

"Whoa! Dayne, hold on."

"You're not going to win this time."

"Lila, put that gun away!"

"Go to hell!"

The gray mist parted, and she made out the man, hands up, a service pistol clutched in them, aimed at her. "Lila, holster your weapon, now. Or I will shoot you."

Panicking wasn't going to save her. She regripped her weapon and zeroed in on his chest, right on the name patch. Fitzgerald.

Wait. What?

"Lila. It's me. Ben. Drop your service weapon."

Ben? The name finally penetrated her clouded mind.

"Oh my God." Lila dropped her arms, her gun dangling in her hand. "Oh my God. Ben."

He approached her, never lowering his weapon. "Lila, holster it."

Tears streamed down her cheeks. She bit her lips and lowered her head. Instead of doing as he asked, she held out the gun to him. When he had taken it, Lila collapsed to her knees and sobbed.

Her life in Eckardt County as she'd known it was over.

CHAPTER THREE

Elizabeth exited her SUV and strode toward the chaos.

Rafe fell in step. "You know that conversation we had when she first started?"

"Deputy Fontaine, if you're going to lecture me on today of all days, take your happy butt back to your car and drive away."

He grunted. A sound she'd heard too many times in her years as the wife of a Fontaine. That grunt signaled a temporary appeasement to her demands, but it wouldn't last long. He would have his say.

Elizabeth stopped and faced him. "Another sound out of you and I'll drop you back down to low man on payroll."

Rafe scowled but kept his peace.

Huffing, she resumed her march to the pasture and the three-ring circus. If there could be anything to be thankful about in this whole screwed-up mess, it was that the media had not gotten wind of their discovery. The reporters were all consumed with documenting the historic flooding. Who knew thousands of gallons of water could be their saving grace?

Elizabeth passed the medical examiner's transport van. Just beyond that was an EMS vehicle. She tramped past a parked F-250, heading straight for the deputy manning the gate.

"Fitzgerald, where is she?"

Her taciturn deputy pointed toward the EMS vehicle.

Next to the open passenger side door, covered in mud, with a reflective sheet draped over her shoulders, Deputy Detective Lila Dayne thwarted the advances of a concerned medic. "I don't need anything. Back off."

Elizabeth made a course redirection toward the two before Lila made a bigger scene than she already had. In his details, Fitzgerald had relayed explicitly what Lila did when he found her. In her panicked mind, she'd drawn her weapon and came dangerously close to shooting him, Bo Cullen, and some cows. Once he had her restrained and calmed down, Fitzgerald checked out the body, and the story he told still left Elizabeth wishing she hadn't eaten such a big breakfast.

A hand shot out and grasped her arm, dragging her to the opposite side of the ME van. She glared at the man who'd dared to intervene. "Deputy Lundquist, you better have a damn good reason for this."

"I do, Sheriff, honest. Let me handle Dayne."

She crossed her arms, her raincoat crinkling with the movements. "What makes you more qualified to handle this situation?"

Under that neatly trimmed beard, his face flushed. Elizabeth's sleep-deprived brain took two seconds too long to hash it out. When it did, she wanted to kick her own butt for not seeing it sooner.

"Damn it, Kyle," she hissed. "You have violated so

many … And now I know."

Kyle Lundquist shifted his stance. "It just happened."

"Just happened?" Elizabeth rolled her eyes. "Sleeping with a fellow deputy doesn't just happen."

"Sheriff!"

"I'll be there in a sec, Fontaine." She jabbed a finger into Kyle's vest-protected chest. "You get her settled, then take her back to the department. Meanwhile, the two of you better come up with a damn good reason I shouldn't suspend the both of you permanently."

She turned on her heel and stepped forward.

"That message was for her."

Elizabeth halted.

"He left that body for her."

"We don't know why that body is there. Or why that message set her off," Elizabeth said.

"I do."

She turned back to the former navy man now deputy. "Care to elaborate?"

"She told me he spoke to her only once when she was attacked. And that's exactly what he said."

"Why was I never told about this?"

"Because she never told anyone before," Kyle said, his voice hitching on never.

"Ellie!"

"I'm coming!" She nodded toward Lila. "Get her out of here. We'll talk later." She left him and returned to the waiting party of three.

Dr. Olivia Remington-Thorpe was properly dressed in chest-high waders and a raincoat for a trek out into a muddy cow pasture to examine a body. "I see you didn't sleep a wink again last night."

Elizabeth caught the shared look between her doctor friend and her undersheriff. Those two were in cahoots. She waved Olivia's concern off like an annoying gnat. "Comes with the job description."

"I could prescribe you a sleep aid for a short period of time."

Iowa had a unique setup for its medical examiners and coroners' system, giving each county or district a chance to decide if they wanted to hire an ME or elect a coroner. Eckardt County officials made concessions to have a medical examiner. This measure went into implementation five years ago after a slew of bad coroners and corrupt sheriffs allowed unexplained deaths to be passed off as natural causes when evidence said otherwise. Eckardt residents were tired of having the label "most corrupt county in Iowa" tacked onto their good name. Because the county was mainly rural, Olivia had the rare distinction to still practice medicine and do her duties as an ME.

"Don't bother. I won't even take them," Elizabeth said.

"You should seriously consider it. Lack of sleep isn't healthy."

"I'm all too aware of that. I was married to the insomnia king. Let's get this over with so you can get the body out of here."

"Deputy Fitzgerald, were you able to find any tracks to indicate someone had dumped the body?" Olivia asked.

"No," Fitzgerald said. "Do you honestly believe we're going to be able to tell out here?"

"He has a point," Elizabeth said as their trio set out.

"Too bad." Olivia got a few steps ahead of Elizabeth and Rafe.

"Tell me you didn't know about Lundquist and Dayne."

He had the good sense to not look at her and kept his mouth shut.

"So help me, Raphael Fontaine, I'll make good on my threat."

He glared daggers at her. "What sense does that make if you know too? She needed him, and he's good for her." He averted his gaze. "It's a small department. How the hell didn't you know before now?"

Because she was too wrapped up in her own duties and trying to not make good on her own desires.

"Does Meyer know?" she asked as they drew closer to the body.

"I have no idea."

Brent Meyer, the rookie deputy who'd survived a bullet to the gut, was a few months away from being reinstated to full duty. Lila was working with him to get him back in shape. In the interim, he maintained desk duty. Others had warned Elizabeth on numerous occasions that Brent may have developed a crush on Lila.

Crushes were one thing. Full-out relationships between deputies was another. Elizabeth herself treaded murky waters in that regard.

Olivia was bent over the body.

"Initial impression?" Elizabeth asked.

"He's been dead for a while. How long is hard to tell. The rain, the mud, and the manure have helped the process along. At this moment I can't tell what killed him." Olivia pulled the shirt back to reveal the message. "Interesting. Is this what sent Deputy Dayne into fight-or-flight mode?"

Elizabeth stared at the message. *Hush, my darling.* This was one sick and twisted killer. Kyle's revelation that Lila never told anyone but him about this burned.

"I can tell you right up front, despite the decomp, this man is not a resident of Eckardt." Olivia stood, her dark brown eyes holding Elizabeth's gaze. "You're going to have to do a national database sweep of missing persons."

"If he was reported missing."

"Let's get him to the morgue. We'll see what the autopsy can tell me."

Elizabeth let the message imprint on her brain. "After I have a nice long chat with my two wayward deputies, I'll be making a call to Chicago."

"Why Chicago?" Olivia asked.

"Because Chicago has more answers about this than I do."

"OH MY GOD. You told her?"

Lila threw her muddy uniform into the washing machine and marched into the bathroom.

"I didn't tell her a thing—she figured it out." Kyle followed her.

She jabbed a finger at him. "Not in so many words you didn't. It's what you didn't say that clued her in."

"For God's sake, Lila. She was going to figure it out

sooner or later."

She shook her head and gripped the bathroom door. She stood there in her wet undergarments, her scars and fears laid bare to Kyle. She hadn't meant to go down this path. It was meant to be a quick fling, get it out of her system. Now she'd lost control.

Kyle knew too much about her. She'd revealed it all, from the rough childhood to the attacker's words to the loss of her chance to ever be a mother, and how the father of her baby had turned his back on her. Kyle was privy to every dark secret because she'd gotten too comfortable with him.

"Other than us screwing each other, what else does she know?"

He flinched at her cold words. Lila wanted to regret them, but her anger was a simmering pot ready to boil over. The wound she'd inflicted was quickly banished, and his features hardened.

"Along with us *screwing*, she knows why you reacted like you did to that message."

Lila's nails dug into the wood. "I should have never told you that."

"Like you never told anyone else about it? Not even your therapist. How's that working out for you? What the hell, Lila? You lost your damned mind out there and nearly shot a fellow deputy and a civilian. This is going to be all over town the moment the floodwaters recede. And it reflects badly on Elizabeth."

"Well, maybe she should have thought twice about hiring me."

"Maybe you should have thought twice about reentering

the law enforcement field with a screwed-up head." His face went slack the instant the words parted his lips.

Lila's body shook as the insult took hold. Biting her tongue, she backed into the bathroom.

"Lila—"

She slammed the door in his face and then locked it. She backpedaled to the Jacuzzi-style tub and sat on the edge.

"Lila, I didn't mean it," he said through the door.

She wrapped her arms around her scarred midsection and hugged herself. She bowed her head and let the tears fall.

Why did it hurt so much to hear from him the same things she'd been telling herself for months?

"Open up. Please."

"Leave me alone."

"I can't. I need to take you to the department. Sheriff's orders."

"I'll get there some other way. Leave."

"Lila."

"Leave!"

There was a soft thump and a heavy sigh. Seconds later, she heard his retreating footfalls, then eventually the faded sound of the front door closing.

Lila swallowed the sobs. How had she messed this whole thing up?

CHAPTER FOUR

S HE GOT THE *look*—an upraised eyebrow with a stern line to the mouth and a flash of irritation in the eyes—from Georgia Schmidt the minute Elizabeth entered the department office. Bentley shot into her private office ahead of her.

Holding up her hand to stave off the lecture, Elizabeth bypassed the Eckardt County dispatcher's desk. "I know, and I'm dealing with it."

"Are you now?"

Her steps slowed. "What's that supposed to mean?"

Georgia tilted her head to the side and crossed her arms. "Exactly what it means." She held up a finger and wagged it. "She without sin casts the first stone."

Grimacing, Elizabeth continued into her office. Bentley had taken her usual place in a beat-up armchair in the corner of the room. She sat there, alert and head cocked to the side, staring at the lone male slouching in Elizabeth's office.

"Where is Deputy Dayne?"

Kyle flicked at an imaginary piece of lint on his black uniform pants. "She said she'd find a ride here."

Elizabeth sagged on a corner of her desk. "You left her alone?"

He lifted dulled eyes to meet her own. "Like I had a choice. I opened my fat mouth, inserted my size thirteen foot, and she kicked me out."

Slapping her thighs was the best option at this point, because she was certain strangling her deputy would land her in hot water with an assault charge. "You do realize you left an emotionally unstable woman alone with access to weapons?"

Kyle gripped the armrests. "I'm well aware of that. Had I stuck around, she would have probably committed murder."

"Kyle—"

"Sheriff, what happened, happened. And now that you know about it, she regrets every minute of it. Does that make you feel better?"

Elizabeth deflated, Georgia's admonishment ringing in her ears.

"No, it doesn't make me feel better. It does make me even more concerned than I was in the first place."

A shuffling sound in the doorway followed with a low *woof* diverted Elizabeth's attention.

Lila, wearing jeans, a pale green tee under a gray zip hoodie, and lace-up boots, entered the office. She placed her badge and holstered sidearm on the desk. "You can save the concern for me and just hand me the termination papers. Leave Kyle out of this. I'm the outsider. No one will miss me."

"That's not how this works."

Lila shook her head, the bobbed blonde ends flaring out. "Sheriff, that's how it's supposed to work. It was fraternization. Don't blame him—I'm the one who instigated it."

"Seriously?" Kyle remarked.

Elizabeth slid off the desk, ignoring the discarded badge and weapon. "Deputy Dayne, please shut the door and take a seat."

"How did you get here?" Kyle asked as Lila sat in the chair next to him.

"Brent brought me."

Elizabeth circled her desk and sat in the leather chair. "And does he know why he brought you here?"

"Not exactly."

"Thank heavens for small mercies," Elizabeth muttered.

"Sheriff, don't drag this out." Lila sat forward in her seat. "Cut me loose. It's best for all parties if I just leave."

"And where do you think you'll go?"

She shrugged. "Anywhere is better than here. Safer."

Elizabeth exchanged a confused look with Kyle before focusing on her detective. "I'm not getting your drift, Deputy Dayne."

"He found me. He's ready to finish what he started all those years ago. If I stay here, I might as well hand him the knife and let him end me."

Now Elizabeth understood what was going on. "How does running help your cause any? If he found you here, he'll find you again. And again, and again, until he either kills you or you kill him."

"Sheriff, there's no other way."

"Lila, there's always another way." Elizabeth rapped her knuckles against the desk calendar. "If he's here in my county, I can't stop him without you."

"You don't need me."

"Yes, I ... we do. You know everything about him. And you can help us stop him from killing again."

"Sheriff, you're not listening to me. I can't do this. Call

my old partner. He's got all the case notes on this, and he's been chasing after this guy since he retired. He's your best option."

Elizabeth had experienced this type of bullheadedness from Lila once before, over a traffic violation. The battle that ensued between the two of them ended when, ironically, Kyle had intervened. That episode happened five months ago. Had their affair been going on that long? Longer?

Closing her eyes, Elizabeth slumped into the backrest. Between her exhaustion and Lila's emotional turmoil, this was not a conversation any of them needed to be having when they were stressed and overworked.

"Lila, I am listening." Elizabeth opened her eyes. "I'm doing my due diligence in trying to help you through this as well as come to grips with what has come to light this morning. We are stretched thin because of the flooding, and now I have a serial killer's calling card dropped in my backyard." She let her fisted hand relax. "I don't want you to go."

Lila fingered the hoodie string and avoided looking at Elizabeth. Lila's unoccupied hand rested on the chair, tapping a rapid beat. When Kyle placed his hand over hers, she stiffened.

As much as she knew the couple working and sleeping together was wrong, Elizabeth couldn't object to their relationship if it kept her deputy detective in a mentally good place. Then Lila jerked her hand out from under Kyle's and clutched it to her chest.

Elizabeth lost a spark of hope.

"Okay, let's do this." She stood. "Lila, take the day off.

It's not like we aren't all in dire need of a break right now. Give yourself some time to process what has happened and make a rational decision."

"I don't need time."

"Do this for my sake." Elizabeth met Kyle's troubled gaze. "I want you on desk duty for the day. You can help Georgia and Brent field calls. We'll circle back to you later."

He nodded, sinking farther into his chair. For a man who'd served in the navy, under a strict command structure, his posture left a lot to be desired.

Zeroing in on Lila, Elizabeth waited until the calcitrant deputy lifted her head. "Day off. Think it over. End of discussion."

After a moment of staring, Lila nodded.

"Good." Elizabeth sank into her chair. "Dismissed."

Kyle rose before Lila and remained rooted in place until she pushed to her feet. Taking no notice of her discarded badge and gun, Lila exited the office. Kyle moved to take the items.

"Leave them," Elizabeth said.

With a curt nod, he escaped her office.

Heaving a sigh that expended what was left of her energy, Elizabeth met her dutiful companion's soulful eyes. "Bentley, I want to start the day—no, the month over again."

The border collie huffed, laying her head on her paws.

A rapid-fire knock marked Georgia's entry. "You have a call on line two."

"Olivia?"

Georgia shook her head and held up two fingers as she

returned to her desk to answer the ringing phone.

"Apparently, I need to add mind reader to my dossier." Elizabeth picked up the receiver and punched the blinking red button. "Sheriff Benoit."

"Sheriff, glad to make your acquaintance."

"I'd like to say the same. Who is this?"

"Oh, sorry. I thought your dispatcher would have relayed that to you. I'm Agent Tate McCall with the Illinois State Police investigation division. I understand you have found a body this morning that fits the MO of a killer I have been tracking for years."

"Agent McCall, how did you come by this information already?"

"A former colleague, retired detective Cecil Waterford. Cecil called me soon after he got off the phone with you."

Elizabeth grunted; her thumb beat a steady cadence on her desk calendar. "Well, Agent McCall, we don't have a whole lot of information to impart at this time."

"That's fine. I called to ask that you have your ME refrain from performing the autopsy until after I arrive."

She rapped the desk hard and eased forward in her chair. "Excuse me?"

"Sheriff, I don't relish having to ask you this, but there are things about this killer and his methods that only a select few know about. I want to see and examine the body before any cutting is done."

"Fine and dandy, but I'm pretty sure we have one of those select few people right here who can help us out."

Movement in the doorway caught Elizabeth's attention. Georgia had returned and taken sentry duty.

"Yes," Agent McCall continued. "I'm aware of that. Lila Dayne, correct? She's a deputy there in Eckardt County?"

Clanging bells went off in Elizabeth's head, making the already bad headache into a migraine. Of course, Cecil—Lila's former partner and the man Elizabeth had had many conversations with over the past year—would have relayed this. The way Agent McCall said Lila's name spoke of something more than just a woman in a case file.

"By your sudden silence, I've made you suspicious of my objectives."

"Agent McCall, I'm wary of outside agencies coming and tromping all over my county uninvited. Let me consider your request and speak with my deputy before I extend that invite."

"Sheriff Benoit, I can't stress enough the importance of allowing my assessment of the body before the autopsy. Time is of the utmost importance, as I'm certain you are aware."

"Oh, I'm aware. We have your contact information. I'll call you within the next three hours. Good day." She dropped the phone on its base.

"A real horse's ass, isn't he?" Georgia asked.

"A heads-up would have been nice."

Georgia chuckled. The throaty sound faded as the curly blonde turned serious. "You've got a fight on your hands trying to keep her here. Lila's terrified."

Elizabeth rubbed her aching forehead. "I've never seen her that scared before. I just … I can't …" She cradled her head in both hands. "What am I going to do?"

"Right now, you're going to call Olivia and beg her to

hold off on that autopsy. That agent knows all about this killer, and you need him here. Go talk to Lila and tell her he's coming. And that, dear sheriff, is the extent of my advice to you."

"Thanks for nothing."

"You're welcome." Georgia turned to leave.

"Georgia."

"Yes, Ellie?"

"Be a dear and bring me a cup of the strongest coffee you can make. And send Kyle in here."

"Yes, ma'am."

Elizabeth let her forehead thunk on the desktop. "God help me."

CHAPTER FIVE

VELCRO STRAP CLENCHED between her teeth, Lila jerked it taut and connected the pieces. Flexing her hands inside the fingerless, padded boxing gloves, she felt the worn fabric conform to her fists. Already warmed up and stretched, she ducked under the ropes and strode to the center of the ring.

Brent Meyer, her sparring partner, danced side to side, shaking his arms and shoulders, waiting for her. "You sure you want to do this?" he asked around the mouthguard.

She craned her neck, hearing the pops, then clamped down on her guard. She lifted her fists and beckoned him forward.

"Guess we're doing this." He brought his hands up and moved to the center of the ring.

From the day he'd been released from the doctor's care to now, Lila trained Brent, per his request, to get him back to full-duty status. A bullet nearly ended his life, but he was determined to resume his job as an Eckardt County deputy, using her as inspiration. And she let him.

They tapped fists and stepped back. Brent had been a quick study, and Lila ended up learning a few things from him. She especially liked to spar mixed marital arts with him because he refused to go easy on her. Today, Lila needed to let off a hoard of pent-up energy.

Each took testing jabs at the other, moving in a circle, dancing forward and back. The parameters for their spar were kickboxing only, no grappling. Lila wasn't in the mood to wrestle—she wanted to hit.

She cocked her head to the side.

Brent nodded.

They went at it, trading jabs and kicks. Brent managed to land a hit to her torso. Backing out, Lila smiled around her mouthguard. He had two seconds to breathe, and she came at him. Their strikes were landing hard on the pads covering their vulnerable body parts. Lila avoided any stomach blows on Brent; she wasn't about to set him back in his recovery.

She needed this. Sparring always consumed her mind, exorcising the demons in her head and forcing her to be in the present. She studied Brent's body movements, picking apart his attacks to predict his next move until she was a step ahead of him. When he caught onto her method, he changed it up.

They kept at it. The longer they sparred, the harder the hits came and the faster they began to move. Lila's muscles burned from the exertion. Sweat dripped from their faces and bodies, sprinkling the mat in a ritual that had been going on for centuries. Instead of reliving her nightmares or reseeing that message carved into that body, Lila focused on how to take down her opponent.

Brent was about to make a huge misstep. He cocked his upper body to the side, ready to throw a powerful swing. Lila chomped on her mouth guard, preparing for her counterattack.

His arm shot past her. She grabbed it, spun, and putting her back to him, planted her feet into the canvas, and flipped him over her body. He slammed into the mat on his backside, leaving him dazed and blinking at her. Lila straddled his torso and placed her fist next to his chin.

"And this is how you get KO'd."

Grimacing, Brent groaned. "Seriously?" he spat out his mouthguard. "I had you."

She removed her own guard. "You only thought you had me." She climbed off him and held out a hand to help him up. "A plus for effort, though."

He grunted as he came to his feet. "Another round?"

"Some other time," a gruff voice said from the sidelines.

Lila inched to the ropes as Fontaine mounted the edge of the boxing ring. "What are you doing here? Doesn't the sheriff have you running down leads?"

"She sent me to get you." He nodded at Brent. "Lookin' better, Meyer. Got to keep your guard up more. She's finding your weak points."

"Thanks, I think."

Lila removed her gloves. "Why is she summoning me? I'm supposed to have the whole day off."

"To make a decision. I know. We ran into a snafu, and you're the one with the knowledge on the matter."

"If this is about that body, I told her to call my old partner and leave me out of it."

Fontaine crossed his arms on the top rope and stared her down. "Already done that. Seems he passed the buck on to someone else."

Lila's mouth went dry, her body seized. *He better not say it.*

"Does an Agent Tate McCall ring any bells?"

The gloves slipped from her hands, slapping the taut canvas mat.

Those blue eyes bore holes deep into her soul. Fontaine missed nothing; it was why he deserved the undersheriff position. It was the main reason Lila couldn't stand working with him. The weight of his judgment suffocated the victim. He had this tendency to strip her bare of her deepest, darkest secrets.

Just like he was doing now. The prick was plucking her strings to his own tune.

"Lila?" Brent's query broke through the roar in her head.

She felt his stare, but she refused to break eye contact with Fontaine.

The grizzled sheriff's deputy's gaze darted behind her. "Meyer, shower up. You've got some work."

"More desk duty?"

"Would you rather have no work?"

"I'll take what I can get."

A moment passed before Lila heard Brent slip through the boxing ring ropes. At the door's bang, she pounced.

"He called her, didn't he?"

"He did. Ellie's none too happy to be blindsided by this."

"She's read the report on me and that case. How is she not aware of who he is?"

"It's not about who he is. It's what he was to you."

"He was the state police agent investigating the murders."

Fontaine's features soured. He could not like her answer all he wanted—it was the answer she would forever give. If Tate blew the whistle, then his head would roll.

"Right," Fontaine said slowly. "Clean up. Sheriff wanted to talk with you."

"Not today." Lila bent over and snagged the gloves from the canvas. "She said I had the day to myself."

"She also said you needed to make a rational decision about your place here in Juniper and Eckardt County."

Lila scowled. "She tells you too much."

"I'm the undersheriff. It's my right to know."

"Not when it fringes on personal boundaries."

"You seemed to have forgotten that when you took up with Lundquist."

Lila lunged at the ropes. "She crossed the line to tell you that."

Fontaine stood his ground, glowering back at her. "I figured that out a long time ago, and I kept my damn mouth shut about it."

Flinching as if he'd slapped her, she leaned back. "You did?"

"Nearly everyone knew except Ellie and possibly Meyer. Does he know?"

"I have no idea. I think he does." She hung her head. "I hope he does." Because if he didn't, and if her instincts about him crushing on her were on the money, he was about to lose what little bit of trust he had left. After what Brent's family had put him through, this was the last thing he needed.

"Lila."

Her head snapped up at Fontaine's strident tone. He never called her by her given name.

"Just talk with the sheriff. Air this out before this Agent McCall gets here."

"He's coming?" Lila's sweat glands went into overdrive.

"Not only is he coming, but he insisted that the autopsy wait until after he arrived and he had a chance to examine the body. The sheriff is trying to deter him. That's why you need to talk with her."

"He won't accept anyone turning him away. Not when it deals with the I-80 killer."

"Then make sure the sheriff has a full arsenal when it comes to this agent." Fontaine stepped down. "She has one hour left to give him an answer. After that, I think he'll be here whether we like it or not." With that said, he quit the gym.

Lila stared into the darkened void where Fontaine disappeared. Her past, the one she had tried so hard to put behind her, was coming at her full throttle. Nothing she said or did would change its course.

Letting out a guttural shout, she threw her gloves across the ring.

She refused to be a slave to the machinations of those who held the strings.

THE RAIN STARTED again. Lila sat, alone, in her car. She and Brent had each taken their own vehicles to the gym and left at separate times, something she was grateful for at this moment. She wasn't in the mood to explain herself.

Lila watched the raindrops pepper the windshield, bead up, and race down the slick glass. Beyond the water barrier, Eckardt County sheriff's department loomed large. The towering red brick and limestone block building also housed the courthouse, the DMV, licensing department, and in the structure's bowels, the holding cells. Hung beneath the bell tower, a Victorian-style clock kept precise time, chiming at the eight a.m., noon, and five p.m. hours every day except Sunday. Juniper's town clock kept better time than Chicago transit.

In her short period of residency in Juniper, Lila had adjusted to the slower tempo and simple, rural ways of the people who had inhabited the area for a century or more. At first, some of the folks had held it against Lila for being from Chicago. They worried she'd try to impress upon others— especially Sheriff Benoit—her big city ways and further corrupt their small community. Mostly the residents were biased because Lila was an outsider, someone with no family, no roots, and no sense of community. She would always be looked at with circumspection, and she accepted that.

Lila had adapted. Put the idea that she would belong out of her head and did her job to the best of her capabilities. Befriending Pratt Meyer, the town's golden boy, had boosted her standing. Brent's father was a local bigwig, and he'd had taken a bit of a shine to Lila over the time she'd spent with Brent during his recovery. At times, Elizabeth exploited that connection, even though she herself had become somewhat of an ally to Pratt. Saving the life of the man's only son and ending a decades-long feud might have had a lot to do with it.

Lila sighed, adding to the building condensation on the interior side of the car windows. She should go inside and face the sheriff instead of sitting out here writing her own eulogy.

She scrubbed her face with a groan. None of this was supposed to follow her here. Her past did not belong in her future.

And yet, here it was.

She grabbed the door handle and shoved the car door open, forcing her body out of the seat and into the drizzling rain. Ignoring the dinging reminder she had left her keys in the ignition, she pushed the door shut. With her hood up over her head and her shoulders hunched against the rain, she trotted up the sidewalk and inside the building.

Lila hesitated in the entrance, swiping off the hood. During damp, humid days like today, the ancient odors of cigarette smoke, old wood varnish, and dust seeped out of the walls. It was an odd, cloying scent, but one that always felt like home to Lila. An ache deep in her chest gave her pause.

Home.

What a foreign and outrageous idea. In all her years on this earth, Lila couldn't name one single place she'd called home. No, scratch that. There had been one place. It was the last place she should have ever considered a home. Naivety and stupidity could be blamed for her decisions at that time. Lesson learned.

She headed for the hallway entrance to the sheriff's private office. Lila wasn't up for small talk with any of the others in the department who might happen to be in the bullpen.

Her soft knock was answered with a "Come in."

Entering Sheriff Elizabeth Benoit's domain brought more of that homey feel to it, right down to the wet dog smell. Lila lingered in the doorway. Her boss was closing the door that opened into the bullpen. Perched in her usual spot, Bentley lifted her elegant head and blinked at Lila. All was as it should be. Just the three of them. Shut off from the outside world.

Elizabeth gestured for Lila to take a seat as she sat in the chair's mate. This would not be a boss-to-employee discussion.

Girding herself for an unknown battle, Lila joined Elizabeth. Behind them, Bentley let out a satisfied huff. Lila settled deep into the chair's piddly cushion and met Elizabeth's steady gaze.

They stared at each other, which gave Lila some time to study her superior. Last month, Elizabeth had chopped her hair six inches shorter and gave herself bangs. The new do looked good on her but had also revealed a smattering of gray hairs. Lila tended to forget that Elizabeth was nearly a decade older than her own thirty-six years. A sea of freckles, brought on by sun exposure, blanketed Elizabeth's nose and cheeks. Her dark brown eyes shone with an intelligence earned with age and a drive to always learn. Those eyes were also world-weary and bracketed by deep crow's feet. Elizabeth exuded exhaustion. The fatigue was affecting Lila.

Earlier, lack of sleep and high emotions only led to them

talking in circles instead of resolving the issues at hand. Lila had a sinking suspicion this conversation would be the same scenario.

"How much time do you have left before you give him your answer?" she asked.

Elizabeth glanced at her clock. "Fifteen minutes."

"Don't bother. He's already on his way."

"So certain of that?"

"I am."

Lila shifted in the chair to relieve the pressure on the thick scar tissue along her left side. Brent had managed to land a wicked hit there.

"Tell me about him, Lila. I need to know who this Agent Tate McCall is before I must deal with him."

"There's not much to tell."

Elizabeth frowned. "Cecil told me you liked to play hardball when it came to this man."

"Yet Cecil said nothing more." It was a fact. Never a question. Lila could trust her former mentor to keep his silence.

"Correct," Elizabeth replied. "He said, and I quote, 'It's not my story to tell.'"

"And Agent McCall? What did he say?" Lila asked.

"Nothing more than what your connection to his ongoing case was."

"Then you have you answer. All I can tell you is that he knows these cases inside and out. My advice? Cooperate with him. Sooner he gets what he wants, the sooner he leaves."

Elizabeth leaned back into her chair and steepled her hands in front of her. "That's all?"

Lila pushed to her feet. "Pretty much."

"Lila, please sit."

"I told you what you needed to know."

"Please. Sit."

The silence dragged between them. Soundlessly, Lila sat. She might be as stubborn as a cement post, her mother had always said, but she barely scratched the surface of stubbornness when it came to Elizabeth.

With a nod, Elizabeth placed her hands in her lap and seemed to sag in her chair. "I know this is hard for you. I can't begin to imagine the nightmares you live with every day. But I am trying." She tilted her head. "It's different for you, but I have been well versed in all forms of post-traumatic stress. It came with my marriage to Joel."

When she first arrived in Juniper, Lila had the fortune of meeting Elizabeth's ex-husband, Joel Fontaine, a former Delta Force operator and now instructor in their training program called Selection. While she liked the guy, Lila got why Elizabeth and Joel were divorced. It was the same reason her and Tate's relationship—could it even have been considered that?—had ended badly. PTSD was messy and ugly.

"Then you'll understand why I can't stay here any longer," she told the sheriff.

"This is not Chicago. This is not the place where the killer attacked you."

"Yet he still decided to find me. The only reason he'd deviate from his typical pattern was to mock me. He wanted to remind me that I won't be the one who got away for much longer. Juniper, Eckardt County aren't safe for me anymore."

"Lila, let me put it to you bluntly. Nowhere is safe. We live in a world of danger, from the microscopic to man-made objects to Mother Nature herself. Birth is terminal." Elizabeth shifted forward, her stare boring into her. "How we choose to live our lives is what separates us from the animal kingdom. And to be frank, I think we let fear rule too much."

Rapid knocking punctuated her statement.

"What?" Elizabeth asked.

The door opened and Georgia poked her head around the edge. "You know who is on the line."

"Tell him I don't have an answer for him."

"Sorry, Sheriff, but it's not you he wants to talk with." Georgia nodded at Lila. "He told me to tell you it's the bottom of the sixth, three runners on, and Thomas is up to bat. Said you'd know what he was talking about."

Lila pinched the bridge of her nose. Of course he'd bring *that* up. If she rejected his call, he'd deploy his little blackmail.

"Sheriff, would you mind if I used your office to take this call privately?"

Elizabeth stood. "Take all the time you need. I'm going to check on progress with the flooding and see if our whipcrack crew has any leads."

"Thank you."

"Any time." Elizabeth ushered Georgia out.

"Line three," Georgia called back.

Alone with Bentley, Lila eased out of the chair and shuffled around the sheriff's desk. She picked up the handset, punched the blinking button, and prepared for the fallout.

CHAPTER SIX

E LIZABETH LIED. SHE didn't check in with her on-duty
deputies. She didn't observe the current status on flood
damage and control. Nor did she bother to tell Georgia
where she was going.

No, she lied herself right into Olivia's office, where she
discovered her friend bent over the pile of files Elizabeth had
sent over hours before.

"What have you found?" she asked.

Olivia held up her hand, then set it down next to the
document she was studying.

Elizabeth wandered over to a plush chair and sank onto
it. She scooted deeper into the seat. It was like sitting on a
pile of blankets, comfy and reassuring. Guess one needed
these types of chairs in their office when they were a doctor
about to impart distressing news. Elizabeth really needed to
reconsider those crappy chairs in her office.

Olivia continued reading—perhaps memorizing—the
material in front of her. She had forgone her usual hair
straitening and let her nearly black hair go *au naturel*. She
did have the mass of curls corralled with a sash of bold
orange, green, yellow, and blue. Gone were the hip-waders
and muck boots and in their place, she wore dark green
scrubs. Olivia and her husband, Dr. Dominic Thorpe, an ER

doctor and a general surgeon, were two of only a handful of Black Americans in the county, and neither of them had grown up here.

"I'm almost done," Olivia said as she scribbled on a notepad next to the file.

"Take your time." Elizabeth examined her battered fingernails. Why didn't she trim them on a regular basis?

"Done." Olivia looked up as she set her pen down. "Can I do the autopsy?"

"Nope. Agent Tate McCall of the Illinois State Police is coming, and he's going to get first crack at the body."

Olivia muttered something that Elizabeth couldn't catch, but she was certain the good doc was cursing Agent McCall.

Elizabeth propped an elbow on the armrest and supported her head on her fist. "He called my office and insisted on talking with Lila. They were on the phone when I left."

"Wonder what that conversation was about."

"He was probably trying to get the lay of the land. He doesn't know what Lila has told us."

"Which equals exactly squat," Olivia butted in.

"True. But there's something more to their connection than just having worked the I-80 killer case and Lila being a victim." Elizabeth's eyelids were growing heavy.

"Ellie, you need to get some sleep."

She waved her friend off. "What's your take on those autopsies?"

"Forget it." Olivia pushed to her feet. "You are going to take a nap. Right here, in my office." She rounded her desk and beckoned for Elizabeth to stand.

"I don't need a nap."

Olivia hooked her hand under Elizabeth's arm and tugged. "Yes, you do. I will hear no more excuses. After you've slept, I will have a better idea of what I need to look for when I finally get to do the autopsy."

Allowing Olivia to haul her upright and lead her into a private room beside the office, Elizabeth conceded maybe a thirty-minute nap wouldn't hurt. But only thirty minutes.

"You can't let me sleep too long," she said as she plopped down on the comfortable sofa.

Olivia handed her a light blanket that hung on the back of the sofa. "You'll sleep as long as it takes. No arguing." She pushed against Elizabeth's shoulder. "If something comes up, I'll wake you."

"Promise?" Elizabeth settled on the sofa cushions with the blanket draped over her shoulders.

"Yes." Olivia closed the door in her wake.

Elizabeth laid there, staring at the opposite wall adorned with paintings from African artists whose names eluded her fatigued brain. She kept reminding herself to sleep a short time. As her eyelids fluttered, the drab grays and blues of the paintings began to run and meld. The blanket on her shoulders seemed to gain twenty pounds. For the first time in a week, Elizabeth's mind shut down. She closed her eyes. The exhaustion pulled her under, and she knew only oblivion.

OLIVIA RETURNED TO her desk chair. She stared at the closed door to her private room. A minute ticked past, then a sense of calm came over her. Ellie had fallen asleep. The first time Olivia had mentioned her uncanny ability to know what someone was feeling or going through, she had weirded out Dominic. Her husband had long gotten over that particular quirk.

She picked up the legal pad with her extensive notes and read through them. Hell would freeze over before she allowed an out-of-state police agent to outrank or outthink her in her own morgue.

Ellie had given Olivia ten autopsy reports. Of the ten, only six were identified. The other four unidentified bodies had been beheaded, which made IDing them difficult. Five males and five females, nothing extraordinary about the victims to make them stand out to the investigators, so the killer didn't have a particular type. All who had been IDed were not from Illinois; presumably the four unidentified victims were missing from another state and they hadn't been able to match them up with any missing persons reports.

Each victim bore the same pattern of stab wounds. Two to the left kidney—the left side could indicate the killer was righthanded and reaching around to do the damage—and three to the abdomen, generally hitting the liver, the stomach, and at times the intestines. Death would have been excruciating, in some cases slow, others quick. Either way, the victim suffered.

There were no other indications of death being caused by anything other than exsanguination. Every victim showed signs of dehydration and starvation prior to their murder. The decapitations happened postmortem. As were the removal of fingertips, teeth, and any other marks like tattoos, birthmarks, or scars that could make recognizing the victim easier. One victim had a leg amputated above the knee with surgical precision. Olivia suspected they had had some type of medical-grade rod or work on the knee that would have pinpointed their origins.

This killer was thorough and smart.

For Olivia, this was a challenge that demanded her full attention. She had already asked her colleagues to cover some of her appointments if they had room in their schedules. Those patients who could wait were rescheduled.

She lifted her head and blinked at the office. She needed to spread out the reports and create a murder board of sorts for herself.

For the next hour and a half, using her walls, desk, and any flat surface available, she laid out the evidence and autopsy reports by date of discovery. When she was satisfied with her system, Olivia peeked in on Ellie. Her friend snored away. Good, she needed the sleep.

Standing in the center of her office, Olivia surveyed her handiwork. Now she had a better scope of the cases and a way to see the photos clearly. With a fresh notepad in hand, she moved from the first IDed victim and notated similarities and differences. She'd reached the third victim when there was a knock on the door. It opened before she had a chance to acknowledge the visitor, and Dominic stepped into the office.

Her husband gaped at her walls. "What in the world is all of this?"

"That big case Ellie gave me." Olivia arched her back to

ease the aches. "Dominic, this thing is ... fascinating."

He stood before one of the beheaded victims. "My God," he muttered.

"I know." She moved to his side. "The cut was clean. The killer used an exceedingly large, sharp blade to do it. The ME that did this autopsy feels it was some type of butcher's blade."

"Could have been an axe."

Olivia tapped her pen against her chin. "Maybe." She jotted down Dominic's thought.

"Dear, your enthusiasm for this is more disturbing than your other quirks."

She kissed his cheek. "You say the sweetest things."

"He's not wrong, you know," said a sleepy Ellie, who emerged from Olivia's private quarters. "You let me sleep too long."

She glowered at her rumpled friend. "I bet you feel loads better."

Ellie snorted as she looked over one of the victim photos and report. "I can't get over how he removes anything that could ID the victim. Why behead them?"

"For those, there had to be a special reason. Maybe extensive dental work or plastic surgery." Olivia watched her husband as he read through an autopsy report. There was a worrisome wrinkle in his forehead. "Dominic, did you need me for something?"

He lifted his head. "Can I speak to you about a patient?" He looked pointedly at Elizabeth.

"Don't mind me," she said holding up her hands. "I'll just"—she pointed at the door—"go use the restroom. Out in the hall."

Once they were alone, Olivia gave her husband her full attention. "Who is the patient?"

He returned the report to its rightful spot in her sequence and moved closer to her. "What I say stays between you and me. Understood?"

She frowned. Dominic wasn't one to consult with her about his patients, and she did likewise. As a general rule, they avoided referring between each other to keep the other doctors from calling foul.

"Dominic, what's this about?"

"The stab wounds on these victims. I've seen this same exact pattern."

"How? We haven't had one of these types of victims here until now. I know you haven't seen the body that was found this morning."

"Actually, I have, but the person was living." He picked up a photo of a female victim and placed it in Olivia's hands. "It's Lila. She has extensive scarring in all of these places." He pointed to each spot. "She's had a nephrectomy to remove the lower half of the left kidney and a hysterectomy. She told me that the surgeons were able to repair her liver, and they didn't have to remove any portion that was lacerated."

Olivia blinked, her mind not fully comprehending what he was telling her. "Does Ellie know?"

"Yes. She had to or Lila would have never gotten the job."

Olivia shook her head. "Dominic, are you trying to tell me that you think Lila was a victim of this killer?"

"That's exactly what I'm telling you."

"It's improbable. This killer is highly organized, meticulous in his work. He would have never allowed a survivor."

"But he did. Lila is proof."

"How do you know that? She has never said anything to me. Neither has Ellie."

Dominic sighed. "I only know because the first day she started her job, she was injured in that old Barrett place. Remember? I was the attending physician in the clinic that day. She had to tell me before I could treat her."

"No one has thought to alert me?"

"She never gave us permission to do so. I'm sorry."

Olivia was interrupted by a knock on her door. Dominic gave her a pained look.

"Yes?"

The door opened, revealing the topic of their discussion. With Lila was a disheveled man with wild brown hair, wearing a pair of tan slacks and a black polo with an embroidered yellow shield on the left shoulder that stated Illinois State Police Investigator.

"Deputy Dayne?" Olivia asked.

"Hey, Doc. Uh, Dr. Thorpe, I didn't know you were here."

Dominic nodded. "Dr. Remington-Thorpe and I were discussing some things."

Lila frowned, her gaze bouncing around the office, and then she glanced at the man next to her. He stood only an inch taller than Lila, but his presence filled the room. "This is Agent Tate McCall with ISP. He's here to see the body."

The agent just walked right in without being asked. "Interesting," he said as he wandered from victim board to victim board.

"Excuse me," Olivia snapped. Lila rolled her eyes and shrugged.

Agent McCall pointed at the board for the fifth victim. "I've never known an ME to do something like this before. Good on you."

Was that supposed to be a backhanded compliment?

"What is going on here?"

Thank God, Ellie had returned in time.

Agent McCall left his perusing and strode over to Ellie. He thrust out his hand. "Sheriff Benoit, I'm Agent McCall."

Ever the consummate professional, Ellie took his hand and shook. "You're here already?"

He smiled. "That I am."

Lila made a low sound and crossed her arms as she leaned against the doorframe.

Olivia's nerves prickled. There were too many people in her office. She glanced at Dominic.

He gave her a curt nod and handed her the photos he held. He placed a kiss on her cheek. "I'll talk with you later," he said in her ear.

"I'll call when I'm on my way home."

Dominic excused himself from the group.

"I didn't scare him off?" Agent McCall asked, looking at each woman.

"No. He's a surgeon and has patients to see." Olivia set aside the photos and her notes. "Agent McCall, I had to put off this autopsy to wait for your arrival. You are here now. Might I suggest we proceed with your assessment so I can do my job."

"Right." He stepped to the side. "If you'd show me the way."

"That's my cue to leave," Lila said, pushing off the frame.

"Deputy Dayne," Ellie said in a low voice.

The two stared at each other a moment. Lila's face reddened. She shook her head and turned.

"Sorry, Sheriff," she said as she disappeared.

Olivia looked sharply at the agent, who grunted. The deep furrow of his brows and the severe downturn of his mouth was enough to make Olivia study the man harder. There was a hint of something more than just the disdain of a cop backing away from an investigation. Agent McCall and Deputy Dayne had a history. Olivia turned her attention to Ellie. Her friend was glaring at Agent McCall. She knew something.

"Dr. Remington-Thorpe, let's get on with this," Ellie said, her voice gruff.

"This way." She gripped Ellie's elbow and led her out. "You have a lot of explaining to do, my friend."

"I'm not the only one."

They looked at each other. Through the fatigue and anger, Olivia saw the worry in Ellie's eyes. Lila was not telling her something and Ellie was taking it to heart. Olivia loosened her hold on her friend's arm. She peeked back at Agent McCall, who followed at a discreet distance but kept a steady gaze on them.

"They're both hiding something from everyone," Olivia whispered.

"And I aim to find out what it is," Ellie stated matter-of-factly.

LILA WAS CLOSE to making her escape from the hospital when Kyle turned the corner in the hall and stopped. They hadn't spoken since their little meeting with the sheriff about the fraternizing. She didn't want to talk with him.

He glanced around and then strode toward her. His stride and bearing exuded navy man and professional law officer. She stared, frozen in place. It looked like she was about to have that conversation whether she wanted it or not.

"What are you doing here?" she asked past a tight throat.

"Sheriff told me to come." He reached for her.

She stepped back. "No."

"I'm sorry about what I said. It was stupid."

Lila crossed her arms. "It might have been stupid, but you meant every word of it."

"You don't exactly make it easy to get close to you."

"There are reasons for that. What went on between us was supposed to be nothing more than to let off steam. That was it."

Kyle remained silent, staring at her. The look unnerved her, as it always did. He had this way of looking at her and seeing deep to her soul. She hated it.

"He's here, isn't he?"

Lila bit her lips and avoided his gaze.

"I'll take by your lack of a verbal confirmation that he

is." Kyle stepped around her. "Good to know."

She rotated to watch him walk away. He didn't look back. Once he rounded a corner farther down the hall, Lila resumed her escape from the hospital.

The rain had stopped. She wound her way around large puddles as she trekked through the parking lot. At her vehicle, she hesitated before opening the door. Tate had parked his state-issued car next to hers, a move that irritated her. There were plenty of open spots in the lot, but he still had this need to push her buttons.

Hidden under Tate's scholarly appearance and overbearing personality was a calculating mind with a penchant for geek humor. At one time, it had been enduring to her. In comparison to every man Lila had grown up around or worked with, Tate was the complete opposite.

She yanked open her car door and rammed herself inside. She started the car, shifted into reverse, and kept her foot on the brake. She slammed the gear shift back into park and let her head fall against the steering wheel.

Tate's visit was doing everything she feared it would. Tears pooled in her eyes; her throat burned.

God, how she hated him. His coldhearted wrenching statement the day he left her still echoed in her mind.

"I can't be with you anymore. I can't be with someone who lies and hides things from me."

Hot tears dripped from her cheeks. Tate had blamed her for the loss of their child. Blamed her for bringing attention to herself by pursuing the I-80 killer case, putting herself in his crosshairs. She was supposed to do her job as he saw fit, except she refused Tate's demands, and in turn she became a victim. Then he learned about the baby, a child he was never told about and would never have been. Instead of standing by her, Tate threw her away, never to talk to her again until today.

Lila let loose with the soul-tearing yell, banging the sides of her fists against the wheel. Her frustration spent, her hands throbbing, she sat back against the seat. She stared at the building looming on the other side of the windshield. Tepid air blew through the vents, stirring the humidity around more than taking it away.

She'd let Tate jerk her strings, and bowed to his insatiable need to be in control. Again. She reached for the gear shift, hesitated, then turned the key, silencing the engine.

Running was what made her think safety was found in the lull of opioids. As long as the little white pills did their job, she lived in a blessed state of numbness. She never had to face the loss of her unborn child and how she'd never be a mother, or relive Tate's horrible breakup, or a sadistic killer's attack.

Lila pulled the key from the ignition and stuck it in her hoodie pocket. Elizabeth was right.

If she ran again, the killer would just find her. He wasn't done with her. She had her warning.

She exited the car and marched back to the hospital. She was done running.

CHAPTER SEVEN

Silence greeted Lila as she approached the morgue. Kyle, arms crossed, leaned against the doorframe, blocking the entryway. He must have sensed her presence, because he looked over his shoulder and did a double take.

Lila crept along the hall, looking through the row of windows that ran the length of the autopsy room. She paused at the third pane and watched Tate as he methodically examined the naked body, a sight she still could not make herself face yet. She let her gaze drift first to Elizabeth—standing with her feet hip-width apart, her attention zeroed in on Tate—then to Dr. Remington-Thorpe, who was stationed at the end of the table, her arms clasped behind her back as she, too, watched Tate. He was in his element and in the zone. No one and nothing would deter him from his single-minded mission.

Kyle's scent, cedar and cold air, just like his Viking ancestors, pulled Lila from her scrutiny. She looked up at his looming form next to her. He was Tate's polar opposite. Tate was passive-aggressive, a borderline control freak, overly health conscious, and geek to the bone. Kyle was a military man with an uncanny scientific mind who liked college football, Busch beer, medium-rare venison steaks, and letting her have her way with him sexually. Tate wanted to fix Lila.

Kyle just wanted Lila to open up and be herself.

She tore her gaze from Kyle and continued watching the process inside the room.

"I thought you didn't want to have anything to do with this?" he said softly.

She didn't answer him.

"How long does this take him?"

Lila crossed her arms and shrugged. In the room, Tate, his back to the window, carefully lifted the body and rolled it so he could see the backside. He was looking for the stab wounds to the kidney.

His shoulders jerked, his head came up, and he lowered the body. "This isn't the I-80 killer."

Lila dropped her arms, gaping at the window.

"What makes you say that?" Elizabeth asked.

Tate rotated, removing his surgical gloves. "This body has no stab wounds in the specific areas that are the I-80 killer's known MO. In fact, he doesn't have a single stab wound. This man died by other means, and someone used his body as a message board."

"He's missing his teeth," Dr. Remington-Thorpe insisted.

"Which means nothing," Tate rebutted. "A lot of killers will remove the teeth to delay identification. There are no marks indicating his prints were burned off his fingers, either. This is not the I-80 killer."

Lila pushed past Kyle and marched into the room. "That's not possible."

Tate gave her a passing glance. "Look for yourself, Deputy Dayne. My assessment remains the same."

"Bullshit!" She stomped over to the autopsy table and pointed at the crudely carved words. "That!" She jabbed her finger at the message. "That was meant for me. He said that to me right before he stabbed me."

This time Tate looked at her more closely. "What?"

Lila glared at him, her shoulders rising and falling with each heaved breath. "That's right. I didn't tell you that. I made no mention of that to anyone investigating what happened to me. Especially you."

His eyes narrowed. "You kept vital information to yourself about that attack? Why would you do that?"

"Because it was one less thing to be *accidentally* leaked."

"I never allowed anything vital to be leaked."

"Always under control. Right? But you weren't."

Tate made a threatening step toward her, and suddenly Kyle's hulking form was between them.

"Get out of my way. Wait. Who the hell are you?"

"The new guy I'm screwing," Lila lobbed at Tate.

The room went deathly silent. Lila gave props to Kyle, as he didn't even twitch.

Elizabeth cleared her throat, shattering the silence. "Deputy Lundquist, please step outside. Dr. Remington-Thorpe, if you would join him, please."

Lila braced for the full force of Tate's fury the moment Kyle removed himself as a barrier. The jackass wanted a fight, she was about to bring it. With a curt nod, Kyle about-faced with military precision—he didn't look at Lila—then exited the room behind Dr. Remington-Thorpe, closing the door in their wake. Lila curled her hands into fists and held them at ready. Tate's face was mottled with dark red spots.

She smiled. Point one for her.

"Deputy Dayne, there's no need for violence," Elizabeth said as she came to stand next to them.

"Just preparing to protect myself, Sheriff. Agent McCall here doesn't like to be reminded of his failures."

"Not true," he spat out. "You allow fraternization among your ranks, Sheriff Benoit?"

"That's not a topic of discussion I will be having with you, Agent McCall." Elizabeth placed her hand on Lila's raised fist and pressed it down. "However, it's abundantly clear that the two of you had a past relationship, one that you both elected to keep from me. There seems to be a lot of deep-seeded animosity because of it. So, I'll give you each a chance to come clean with me, then we'll figure out how to continue on."

"I did not come here to be put through a therapy session on relationships." Tate threw his gloves aside and removed the paper gown. "This man is not a victim of the I-80 killer. That is my final assessment. I will be returning to Illinois."

"Go ahead," Lila said. "We don't need your kind of help."

He dropped the gown with the gloves. "You think you're capable of handling this investigation? With all of your hang-ups and mental trauma?"

"Not happy to see me back doing what I'm good at? Did you expect me to just find some dark hole where I'd drug myself into oblivion and die?"

"Last I saw you, that was the path you were running down full throttle."

"Lila," Elizabeth warned.

"Don't worry. His arrows don't bother me anymore." Lila headed for the autopsy room door. "Let him go. Like I said, we don't need his help. I've got this." She flung open the door and gestured for Tate to exit.

He stood there like a statue, resentment pouring off him in waves. "What happened to you?"

"A serial killer and a prick who couldn't stand to have his perfect life ruined happened to me."

Elizabeth interjected herself between them. "I think we're done here. Lila, I'll handle this. Why don't you and Deputy Lundquist return to the department and begin the preliminary steps in this investigation."

Lila stared at the sheriff, the suggestion warring with her desire to personally see to it that Tate was kicked to the curb. A light cough from the hall made her stiffen. She should go with Kyle. Elizabeth was right—she could handle Tate.

"That man is a victim of the I-80 killer," Lila said. "He's outsmarting you. And he's coming for me."

ONCE LILA HAD left with Kyle, Elizabeth had Olivia return to the autopsy room. Agent McCall had taken a seat on one of the rolling chairs. Elizabeth remained standing, staring down at the now-composed state policeman.

"You should have never hired her to be a deputy," he said. "She's one bad murder investigation away from a return to her addiction or someone getting killed."

Elizabeth's blood ran cold. Lila had come extremely close to doing the later this morning. But the former, her addiction, this was news to Elizabeth. Oddly, in her tirade against Agent McCall, Lila had outed herself on the drugs.

"What drugs are you talking about?" Olivia asked, the attending physician side coming to the forefront.

"You don't know? After the attack and all the surgeries, Lila got hooked on the oxy they prescribed to her."

"Lila does not show any indications of drug use," Olivia said. "I would know."

"She might be clean now, but she's teetering on the edge of a relapse. It was one of the reasons I disassociated myself with her."

Elizabeth shifted her weight to her left leg and hooked a hand on her holster. "Disassociated yourself? Do you hear what you're saying?"

He gave a limp shrug. "Would you rather I say I dumped her?"

"You question me on fraternization, yet you're guilty of it."

"It's not fraternization when the people involved are from entirely different departments. I'm state police; she was a detective with Chicago PD. I'll be the first to admit it never should have happened."

"Yet it did," Elizabeth said. "In the wake of your *disassociation*, a woman was shattered, and for what? Is it like Lila said? You couldn't have a black mark on your perfect life?"

Agent McCall sighed, placed his hands on his knees, and pushed to his feet. "I did what I came to do, made my assessment, and now I'm leaving."

Elizabeth stepped aside as he moved past her. "What if you're wrong?"

He halted.

"What if Lila is right? That the killer has switched up his strategy simply to force your hand and bring her out in the open. Then what, Agent McCall?"

"What if I'm right, Sheriff Benoit? What if this case or any other turns terrifying? Can you trust Deputy Dayne to stay clean and not run?" At that, he left.

Olivia groaned. "Ellie, this could go bad. Very, very bad."

"I'm well aware." Elizabeth approached the autopsy table. "From your professional standpoint, how long would you say he's been dead?"

"Without doing the proper testing and factoring in the elements and conditions, I can't nail down an exact timeline. But my experience and the rate of decomposition, he's been dead for days."

"How long do you think he was out in that pasture?"

Olivia shook her head. "What did Bo Cullen say?"

"I have yet to talk with him. With Bill in the hospital and their cattle scattered to hell and back, he's been a bit preoccupied. I'm going to talk with him next. Have you had enough time to go over those reports from the other victims?"

"Yes."

Elizabeth backed from the table. The deceased wasn't getting any more deceased. Somewhere on his body was the proof, other than the message, that he was another victim of the I-80 killer as Lila insisted. If anyone would find it, it would be Olivia.

"Prove he's an I-80 killer victim." She met Olivia's steady

gaze. "Prove Lila right."

FIVE MINUTES AFTER following Kyle out of the parking lot, Lila veered off the path and circled back to the hospital to park her car along the street and wait for Tate. She didn't have long to sit and stew. He stalked out of the main entrance, heading straight for his car.

Lila beat her thumb against the top of the steering wheel, her right foot mimicking the same jig. The taillights on the state-issued car lit up, then the reverse lights came on. Lila put her car in drive. Tate pulled out of the lot and put his car in the direction to leave town, and she followed.

She kept a comfortable distance as he picked his way through the town streets. Because of the flooding, Tate would have to drive toward Iowa City and get on I-80 to cross back into Illinois. That stretch of road just outside of town would be the perfect spot.

Ten minutes into her tail, Tate left Juniper. Three minutes outside of town, he hit the brakes and jerked his car off the road. Smiling, Lila did the same. By the time she had the car parked, he was out of his vehicle. Lila exited her car.

"What the hell are you doing? Did you honestly think I wouldn't spot you tailing me?" he barked as he stalked toward her.

Lila met him between the cars. She landed her punch square to his jaw.

Tate staggered but didn't go down. Massaging his face, he turned back to her. "Feel better?"

She shook her throbbing hand. "A little."

He worked his jaw, grimacing. "Now that we have that out of the way."

Her pent-up frustrations spent, Lila stumbled backward to her car and sat on the hood. They stared at each other.

"I was under the impression you wanted me to leave," he said.

"You didn't have to stop on the side of the road."

"Have you follow me all the way out of the state? No." He shook his head. "You wanted me to stop."

With all of their brewing bitterness out in the open, Lila knew it was time to be rational. "That body came from the I-80 killer, and you know it. Why are you discrediting it?"

"Why did you keep that message from me? Damn it, Lila. You are the sole survivor of this monster. That information would have been a key element to these cases."

"What good would it have done to know it? It's not like the other victims could tell us what he said before he stabbed them."

Grumbling, Tate rammed both hands in his hair, and he did that weird scalp massage he was known to do when he hit a brick wall. "I think your attack was done by a copycat."

"Yes, it's always been a possibility. Which doesn't discount that this new body isn't another one of his and he's just changed his MO."

Tate glowered at her, his hands falling to his side. "The I-80 killer doesn't change up his MO."

"You're so stuck on what he can't and won't do, you're missing the point. Killers modify. Especially when their methods become public knowledge." Lila slapped the car hood. "We had too much information leaked to the press."

"Still sounds like you're blaming me for that."

"Who should I blame? You were the one with the most knowledge, so it only makes sense."

Red fused his cheeks, matching the blotch on the left side of his jaw. "I wasn't alone with the intimate details of how the I-80 killer worked."

Lila let his meaning settle between them. She would not give in to his baiting this time. In Tate's world, he was blameless, flawless in his work and skills. If there were problems, that was someone else's fault. She made the perfect scapegoat.

Like a flipped light switch, Tate's anger flicked off and he was calm and collected, the rational one. "Everything aside, there were still major points never leaked. A copycat had the rudimentary knowledge to do as much damage as he could. With all that we knew about what he did to his victims, it made no sense to just go after you. You weren't weakened by starvation, and you were at home where you could fight back."

"I'm not saying you're wrong. Lord knows, I've had two years to dwell on every aspect of the attack."

"A good portion of that time you were stoned. How did you manage to even think about anything?"

Hot sparks flared to life deep inside Lila's chest. Here he went again. Trying to one-up himself in the asshole department.

Nope. Don't let him. Not even one word.

Lila stared at a distant tree over Tate's right shoulder and let the anger go. He could bring up her biggest mistake all he wanted. Sobriety had a way of changing one's mindset.

"I managed to think of a whole lot of things. Cecil was right there with me."

Tate blanched. "Yeah, Cecil. Always the hero of this story. There to save you before you died. To help you dig yourself out of a hole. If not for Cecil ..."

"Yeah, thank God for Cecil."

Sighing, Tate sat beside her on the car hood. They sat there, listening to the world pass by on its slow rotation.

Lila felt like she was in a surreal loop. This was not how she planned to confront Tate. She should hate him. Despise him. Want to throttle him for ripping her heart from her chest and tearing it up before her eyes. Maybe she'd grown wiser in the years since their separation.

Right. That wasn't it.

She just didn't have the energy to fight all these battles. The battle with Tate was the least of her worries.

The warmth of his hand covering hers sent a shiver through her. She stared at their connection. Earlier today, Kyle had tried to do the same and she avoided his touch. Why couldn't she withdraw from Tate?

He squeezed her fingers. "I've missed you," he said softly.

She slipped free of his hold and tucked her hand under her arm. "You should probably get going. It'll be dark by the time you cross the state line."

"I don't have to leave yet."

She gave him a sideline look. "After the show you put on with the sheriff, you're going to renege on your declaration?"

"My command expects me to stay for a few days because I was certain it was an I-80 killer victim." He lifted a shoulder. "Maybe you're right. I shouldn't discredit the fact he's on to me and ready to play games. Then there is the threat to you."

"I'm more than capable of taking care of myself now."

He rubbed his jaw. "I noticed." Tate stood and faced her. "You have a nice hotel here?"

"There's a bed-and-breakfast not far from the sheriff's place. I'll show you the way."

"Just give me the address and I'll go. You need to do what your sheriff ordered." He frowned. "Are you really sleeping with that scruffy deputy?"

Lila gave him a half smile. "Yeah. I am." She gave him the address and got into her car.

She waited for Tate to get into his car before she drove back to town. A semblance of peace settled over her.

It was something she hadn't felt in … forever. With it came a clear path.

The time had come to confront her demons.

CHAPTER EIGHT

Elizabeth stood on the edge of the field where the unknown victim had been left. She heard the lowing of the cows—Bo had moved them far from the crime scene to prevent any disturbances. She let her gaze drift over the swells and humps of the pasture and then followed the line of a distant hill. Far back as she could remember, this field had belonged to the Cullen family. It was nothing special. It did not border any state or federal highways. The access to it from those major points meant a long, meandering drive. This was land that only the locals knew about.

How did the killer know Lila would be here and discover the message? How could he have predicted the timing?

Olivia had called Elizabeth after she had finished speaking with Bo. The ME confirmed the unknown man had died days ago, and his corpse showed signs of starvation. She prefaced her assessment with it was an initial exam. From Elizabeth's quick reread on the files concerning the cases in Chicago, this was modus operandi typical of the I-80 killer.

It still didn't explain why here? Why now? And how?

Lila had lived and worked here in Eckardt a total of nine months. Elizabeth squinted at the spot in the pasture where the body had lain. Bo swore up and down it hadn't been there two days ago when he came to check on the cattle. Best guess, it had been dumped in the last forty-eight hours. Yet, the victim's cause of death was unknown. The date unknown. And the identity unknown.

She bit back a curse. This was not her forte. This was Lila's. She was the investigator. The inquisitor.

Sighing, Elizabeth buried her hands deep into the pockets of her rain jacket. This all reeked of someone familiar with Eckardt County. Someone who either lived here or had spent a lot of time here lately and got to know the lay of the land. Someone who had been watching and waiting weeks or even months for the right time to let their presence be known to Lila. Considering all the factors, Lila was right about one thing. This was all about her.

Convulsions racked Elizabeth.

The steady purr of an engine made her stiffen. She peeked over her shoulder and gritted her molars at the black Dodge Ram. Just who she didn't need to deal with today.

She tried to ignore the clap of a closed door and the crunch of soles crossing the gravel-laden shoulder. It was all for naught. She recoiled as he joined her.

"You shouldn't be here. This is an active crime scene," she snarled.

"So I heard."

The crinkle of his rain jacket snagged her attention. He reached inside his jacket and withdrew a packet of gum. He offered her one—she refused.

"You've got a big mess on your hands, *Sheriff*." He shoved a cinnamon-flavored stick into his mouth. It had to burn a thousand times over for this disgraced sheriff to pay her proper respect.

"A mess it might be, but it's mine to deal with. Some measure of mercy can be said for that."

He grunted. "When I was sheriff—"

"Stop right there, Kelley." She shifted to face him. "You weren't given permission to relay any story about how you'd take care of this." Elizabeth inched closer—noting the heavy odor of bourbon on his breath now mingled with the sweet/spicy scent of cinnamon—and looked him dead in the eye. "This is my county now, and I'm going to do things by the book. So help me God."

Ex-sheriff Kelley Sheehan stared at her, a slight lift to the corner of his mouth. He may have slithered his way out of criminal charges months ago by assisting in the apprehension of a murderer, but Elizabeth would get him one day on something more solid. Her deepest hope was that the charges would stem from the death of her best friend over twenty years ago. Whether he had done it himself or was covering for the person who had, Elizabeth didn't care. Sheehan was as crooked as Burlington's Snake Alley. In her zeal to pin something solid on him, she had learned of backroom deals, not unlike the one she'd made with him months before, and transactions to make him look the other way. But nothing that could be proven.

Those who were willing to talk about Sheehan could only give her conjecture, because most of these people were second- or third-hand accounts to the man's exploits. None of that was evidence enough to send Elizabeth after Sheehan with an arrest warrant.

If their little wink-wink, handshake agreement to expose the criminal behavior of a family that had been suspected associates of his was any indication, Sheehan made it look like he had nothing to gain except to keep his hide out of prison. He would slip up, and Elizabeth planned to be there.

"You're going to need all the assistance you can get for this, Elizabeth. Your reserves are stretched thin as it is dealing with all the flooding."

"I will never lower myself to ask for your help. Ever again."

His slick grin made her feel oily. "We'll see about that."

He lingered, staring at the pasture. Elizabeth's blood boiled at his lack of personal space and that cavalier attitude he was well-known for.

Since his fall from power, Sheehan had been a thorn in her side. Stuck his nose where it wasn't wanted. Voiced his displeasure on Elizabeth's job or lack thereof, in his opinion. He'd sit on his throne, a spot he'd commandeered in The Watering Hole, and verbally berate the sheriff's department to anyone who bothered to listen, his biggest target being Ben Fitzgerald—one he was overheard stating was a traitor to the cause—and his second target was Rafe. For some unexplainable reason—one Elizabeth hadn't been able to get out of Marnie—Sheehan spent a lot of time in her sister's bar. Despite the obvious dislike of the man, Marnie never kicked him out, even at his drunkest, nor did she refuse him his expensive taste in bourbon. Elizabeth was certain but had no proof that there was no exchange of money between the two for services rendered. That raised her suspicion levels to a new high.

So far, customers ignored him. But one day, their lack of interest could end when she did something they disapproved of, and Sheehan would be there crowing his reasons to call for Elizabeth's removal as sheriff.

Rafe and the rest of the deputies assured her that she was doing a fine job with what she'd inherited when she won the election last November. But a little nagging voice in the back of her head—one that sounded an awful lot like her ex-husband's—was beginning to gain strength. The flood situation and now this apparent arrival of the I-80 killer could be just the thing Sheehan was looking for to discredit her.

"I don't recall asking for your company," Elizabeth said.

"No, you didn't," he replied.

She jerked her raincoat about her and spun on her heel. She marched back to her Ford Interceptor.

"If I were you," he called after her.

She paused and turned back to him.

"I wouldn't be delegating any of this."

She scowled at him as he walked back to his truck.

"Not that I really care about your opinion, but why the hell shouldn't I?" she threw at his backside.

He stopped walking and looked over his shoulder. "You trusted me once before, Elizabeth, and it saved several lives. I'd trust me on this one too."

"Doesn't answer my question."

He dipped his chin and walked on.

Huffing, Elizabeth climbed inside her SUV and slammed the door shut. Bentley straddled the console and laid her muzzle on Elizabeth's shoulder. She scratched her dog's head and watched Sheehan leave.

"That man really gets my goat."

Bentley sighed in her ear.

The dispatch radio squawked. "Sheriff Benoit." She picked up her radio from where she'd deliberately left it in the passenger seat and cued the mic.

"This is Sheriff Benoit, 10-5, over." She had gotten a handle on all the codes in the last nine months.

"Sheriff." It was the newly hired night dispatcher, Alexis Zachery, a second-generation Korean-American transplant from Iowa City. She had moved to Juniper, a place that reminded her of where her grandparents had lived, to get away from the stresses of big-city life. "Deputy Young has called in a 10-37 and is requesting your presence, over."

Deputy Corey Young was another one of Elizabeth's newest additions to the force. A capable cop but one who had rubbed a few of the others the wrong way. Others being Deputy Fitzgerald, who was consistently irritated by anyone outside of his favored people, which was a tiny selection. And Lila, for some unexplainable reason.

"10-4. Where is the location, over?"

Alexis rattled off the address. "Also, Deputy Lundquist is here. He wanted to let you know Deputy Dayne has not returned to the department."

Elizabeth closed her eyes. "Damn it!" She took a quick breath to center herself then cued the mic. "10-4. I will handle that situation after I see Deputy Young. Over."

Elizabeth dropped her handset on the passenger seat and scratched Bentley's ears to ease the irritation flooding through her.

"Lila, where the hell did you go this time?"

IT WAS EARLY evening now. Lila's stomach gave a loud rumble, reminding her she hadn't eaten all day. Instead of returning to the department as ordered, she'd diverted to home.

As she drove along the street, she spotted a dark gray, four-door sedan with Illinois plates parked street side in front of her place. She pulled into the short drive and saw a lone figure camped out on the porch steps. After parking her car, she sat there, staring at her visitor. He waved at her as he stood and took a step down.

Of all the things that had gone wrong today, he was not one of them. Thank God for small, or in this case, obstinate miracles.

Lila smiled and bailed out of her vehicle. She crossed the yard in quick time and was enveloped in his strong arms.

"My God, Lila. It's good to see you." Cecil Waterford thrust her back and gazed at her. "This fresh Iowa air has done you some good."

She poked his bulging middle. "Retirement has grown on you, old man."

He grunted, pushing her hand away. Cecil reminded Lila of a more wizened, wider, and more gray-haired version of Denzel Washington. He had been more than a mentor and a partner to her when she was a CPD detective. Cecil had shown her the one thing she'd never received growing up—the care and respect of a father.

"I didn't know you were coming," she said.

"After your sheriff told me what happened, I knew I

should be here. Is that asshole McCall here?"

"Of course. Does he know you're here?"

"Doubt it, and let's keep it that way." Cecil grunted, his head bobbing with the noise. "Figured when the two of you came face-to-face again there was bound to be bad fallout."

Lila shrugged. "Done and over with, and he's still alive. Don't worry about it." She moved up the steps. "I came home to get something to eat. Let's get out of this humidity."

Gerry was waiting, floating above his Easter Island statues. The moment Lila approached the tank, he darted for the top.

"You still have that fish?" Cecil asked.

Lila shook a few flakes of food to the uppity fish. "Yep." She lowered the cover and checked the water temp. Everything was good.

She turned to Cecil. "Do you want—"

He held up a men's blue tee with NAVY in white block lettering across the front. One eyebrow lifted in silent question.

Lila marched over and jerked the tattletale shirt from his hand. "This is ... mine."

"Uh-huh, sure."

She wadded up the shirt and tossed it on the sofa. "Are you hungry?"

"I could eat."

Lila caught Cecil eyeing the shirt as she walked into the kitchen. He eventually followed. Damn Kyle for leaving that shirt out in the open. He'd been wearing it in bed last night and must have tossed it on the couch while he watched the morning news before he showered and came to work. Damn him.

She went straight to the fridge and pulled out two individual-size containers. "What do you feel like? Lasagna or—"

"Lasagna sounds good."

She put back one of the containers and pulled out a second one with lasagna, then popped them, aluminum foil lids and all, into the countertop convection oven and set the temp and timer.

Kyle had suggested they keep meals like this ready to go. One weekend out of the month, they'd spend their off time prepping the meals for single servings. Most of the food stayed at Lila's since Kyle lived with his sister, and neither of them wanted her knowing about their relationship.

"He a cop too?" Cecil asked.

Lila stared at the oven window, watching the coils turn orange red. Her face felt as hot as the metal.

"Oh, Lila, didn't you learn your lesson with Tate?"

She faced her old friend. "Tate was different."

"It's never that simple. Relationships between law enforcement officers don't end well. Ever."

"Just because all of your relationships failed doesn't mean it holds true for everyone."

"Because I speak from experience, I'm warning you," Cecil said.

"As long as we agree you are only warning."

Her cell phone vibrated in her hoodie pocket. Lila had forgotten she had stashed it there. She pulled it out and winced at the fifteen text messages and eight missed calls.

Kyle and Elizabeth.

"Shit," she muttered.

"Problems?" Cecil asked.

Shaking her head, she stuck the phone back in her pocket. They could wait. Her stomach demanded food, and she wanted one-on-one time with Cecil. A luxury she wouldn't have long. He came to Juniper for her, yes, but this was the I-80 killer. A case that haunted Cecil as much as it did her. Though he wouldn't come right out and admit it, Cecil blamed himself in part for the attack on her. Nothing she said convinced him otherwise.

The phone vibrated again. Nope, not gonna answer.

Without asking, she made a pot of coffee. They were going to need it tonight.

"You don't look like you've been sleeping," Cecil mentioned.

"It's been raining."

"I noticed the flooding."

She grabbed two mugs out of the cupboard and placed them on the table. Cecil settled in a chair. Before Lila could return to the coffeemaker, he grabbed her hand.

"Sit. It'll keep."

She stared at their joined hands. Once strong and sinewy hands were now crooked and pudgy. They were still as warm and caring as the night he lifted her from the floor and carried her out of that hellish nightmare. Those same hands had helped nurse her through the recovery, both from surgery and drug addiction.

Lila eased herself into the chair across from him. Cecil patted her hand and released it. They sat in comfortable silence, something that didn't come easily for her these days.

When she had been alone with Tate back in Chicago, she had felt an insane urge to keep up a steady stream of chatter, in part to deflect his passive-aggressive moves and another part to keep herself from thinking too much about how their relationship was going to shit. Now, when she was alone with Kyle, she kept herself with washing dishes, cleaning the house, laundry, running five miles on the Nordic Trac, or sex. No chatter, despite his attempts to draw her out.

"The storms are bringing the memories out?" Cecil asked.

She shrugged.

"Nope. You don't get to brush it off. When was the last time you spoke with a head doctor?"

"Haven't had time."

"Make time. You've got a good thing here. This Sheriff Benoit took a risk hiring you on as a deputy. You can't afford to let anything slide, especially when it comes to the psych stuff."

"You're a fine one to talk."

"I was never attacked by a serial killer and nearly died."

Lila slumped in her seat. "Doesn't mean you get to preach at me when you've got your own demons."

"I'm also retired. I don't have others to worry about when it comes to my hang-ups."

The comfortable silence was long gone.

She shifted her gaze to the full carafe sitting on the warmer. "Sheriff told you what happened this morning?"

"She had to. She's concerned for you. It's why I'm here."

Her reaction this morning, pulling the service weapon on a fellow deputy and a civilian, that's why he'd come. Not because of the I-80 killer.

The timer on the oven dinged. Saved by the bell. Lila hopped up and hurried to the counter. She turned the oven off and pulled out the lasagnas.

"Lila, it's time to face the facts. You blow this opportunity and you're done."

She set the dish down on a hot pad and thrust out a fork to Cecil. "Now you sound like Tate."

He took the fork and pointed it at her. "You know I'm right."

Harrumphing, she turned to get her own food and a fork. She brought the coffeepot with her and dropped down on her chair.

Cecil had already taken his first bite. "Who made this?"

Lila brought her fork to a halt, letting it hover over her food. "What's wrong with it?"

"Nothing." Cecil's eye twinkled. "This is too good to be something you made."

"Excuse me? I'm a fine cook."

"If by cook you mean it came out of a box."

She scowled at him. "I'm a better cook than that."

Cecil chuckled. "Says every horrible cook in the world."

"I'm not that bad."

"Believe what you want." He forked another portion.

"Cecil—"

The front door opening put a stop to her biting remark. She bolted out of her chair. Cecil grasped her forearm before she could run, the gesture steadying her in her moment of fear.

Kyle barged in and skidded to a halt under the arch separating the living room from the kitchen-dining area.

"Who is this? Why is he eating my food?"

"This must be Navy," Cecil said and rose from his chair. He released Lila and held out his hand. "Cecil Waterford. Lila's old partner."

Kyle frowned, then came closer to the table and took Cecil's hand. "Deputy Kyle Lundquist. I work—"

"Don't bother," Cecil interrupted. "I know what you are to her."

Lila flinched at the confusion on Kyle's face.

Cecil resumed his seat. "Pull up a chair. Lila and I were just getting started."

Oh, they were getting started all right. Now she was about to finish it before it got bad. Very, very bad.

Cecil tugged on her hoodie sleeve, and Lila plopped down on her chair. Kyle found the spare and straddled it. He stole her fork and took a bite of her lasagna.

"Hello?" Lila stole her fork back.

"You can share," he remarked.

Cecil chuckled again. "Like a married couple."

"Not even," Lila protested.

"What?" Kyle blurted out at the same time.

Their mutual outburst made Cecil laugh.

Lila stabbed her silverware into the pasta, and she loaded up her fork then shoved that into her mouth. Okay, yes, she sucked when it came to cooking. It wasn't as if she had any role models in that department. Kyle had made most of the food. His mother hadn't slacked off when teaching her son the culinary arts. Something about 4-H projects and all that.

"Why are you here?" she asked him.

"Looking for you. When you don't answer texts and calls, it worries people."

Worried? She scooped more pasta onto her fork. Why would they be worried about her? She'd made clear her intentions at the morgue. Had Tate said something?

"I was coming. I wanted food." She ate the lasagna.

Kyle reclaimed the fork. "Where did you go after you pretended to follow me from the hospital?"

Lila glanced at Cecil, who was watching their conversation intently. "Here," she said.

Kyle swallowed his food. "Try again."

She confiscated her fork, cradled the lasagna dish out of his reach. "How about none of your business."

Cecil coughed.

Kyle eyed her, his face a blank slate, but his eyes said everything. He was going to find out what she did, slowly and methodically like he did with every crime scene when he was on evidence duty.

Joke was on him. That would be a cold day in hell before she told her current fling she'd had a frank conversation with her ex-fling. Lila had been more open with Kyle than any person in her life save for Cecil.

It had been a mistake.

"I think I've had enough to eat." Cecil pushed his dish forward and stood.

"Wait. Where are you going?" Lila bolted from her chair.

"Your sheriff suggested this nice B and B while I'm here."

If she hadn't been using the table as support, Lila would have collapsed. "Really?"

Cecil scrutinized her. "Is there a problem with it?"

"Uh, no."

"It's a nice place," Kyle butted in.

One of Cecil's eyebrows went up and understanding dawned on him. "He's there."

She cringed.

"Who's there?" Kyle asked.

Making a noise in his throat, Cecil shook his head. "I should have figured. All right. I promise to behave."

"Lila, what is he talking about?" Kyle persisted.

"Don't worry about it."

Cecil gripped her shoulder. "You've got work to do. I'll check in with your sheriff tomorrow." He nodded at Kyle. "Deputy Lundquist, you stepped in it. Nice meeting you, just the same. Lila, I'll see myself out."

She remained rooted in place as he exited the house. Once the door shut, she sank into her chair.

The oxygen bubbling in the fish tank was the only sound in the house. Lila cupped the back of her neck and massaged the tightening tendons and muscles.

"It's McCall," Kyle said softly.

She sighed. "I don't want to talk about this with you." She moved to stand.

Kyle grasped her arm and squeezed, bringing her to a halt. She slumped in the chair.

"You don't have to. I'm going back to my place tonight." He released her and vacated his seat. "I'll let the sheriff know you needed to decompress. Be at the department early tomorrow." He headed for the door, his boots echoing over the hardwood flooring. "Good night, Lila."

She flinched at the sharp clap of the door. He wasn't the one who had stepped in it.

She was in the proverbial shit up to her neck.

CHAPTER NINE

E LIZABETH PARKED ALONGSIDE Deputy Young's depart-
ment-issued SUV. They were on a gravel road, miles
from the nearest paved surface, where the only traffic came
from the farming families who lived along here. The fields of
corn and beans were turning a sickly shade of yellow,
repercussions of too much water and not enough sun.

"Stay," she commanded Bentley as she flicked on the Interceptor's emergency lights.

She exited the SUV and ensured the door closed to keep
the interior cool for Bentley, then Elizabeth joined her
newest hire.

Corey Young was a tall woman, a former Iowa basketball
star who decided fame was not for her. She kept her long,
thick, dark-brown hair wrapped in a bun just above her
uniform collar, and she never wore makeup. Being a cop was
in her blood, as she came from a long line of first responders
and military members. Hailing from the Sioux City area, she
was of Sioux descent. She had responded to Elizabeth's job
opening almost the moment she posted it.

"What do you have?" she asked.

Young pointed a Slim Jim stick at the nineties-era green
Ford Taurus with no plates. "Not sure how long it's been
here. It's abandoned. Locked. And it stinks."

"Stinks how?"

"Like roadkill. A lot of roadkill."

Elizabeth grimaced. "Was it parked over or near something? Is there a deer body around?"

Deputy Young shook her head. "I checked. Nothing in the ditch either. This isn't the smell of rotting plants. It's straight up decomp. I wouldn't open up the car until you got here. Just in case."

Just in case there was a body. Yeah, Elizabeth understood that.

"Were you able to see if there was anything left inside that could cause the smell?"

"Nothing up front. There's a ton of crap in the backseat—clothes, boxes, and plastic bags. With all that mess compacted together, I couldn't make out anything through the windows."

"VIN number?"

Deputy Young shook her head. "I couldn't stand breathing that foul air long enough to locate it."

"Okay, we'll try again later." Elizabeth took a deep breath of moisture-ladened air. "Let's get this over with."

As they approached, she was struck by the sharp, sickly sweet odor of decomposition coming from the car. Young wasn't kidding when she said it smelled like roadkill. It permeated the air around the vehicle.

"Unlock it," she ordered.

Young made short work of the lock on the driver's side. Elizabeth covered her mouth and stepped back as her deputy opened the door. A wall of stench hit them. Elizabeth swallowed her gag.

"Let's get all the doors open and air it out."

"Yes, ma'am."

Together they got all four doors open and gave the odor time to dissipate.

"That's way too strong for something like a fast-food joint burger," Young said.

"I agree." Elizabeth eyed the trunk. "We better check in there before digging through that pile in the backseat."

Young gave her a sidelong look. "I'm not crawling in that car to find a latch button or keys to open it."

"Get a crowbar. Whatever is dead in there has ruined this hunk of junk for good."

"If you say so." The deputy headed back to her unit to get the crowbar.

An approaching truck rumbled down the road toward Elizabeth. No doubt one of the few families that lived along here heading home. She waved at the farmer. He slowed his vehicle as if to stop, but she gestured for him to continue on. One aged farmer with a medical emergency was about all she could handle for today. After a few seconds hesitation, the man drove on.

Young returned, brandishing the crowbar. She marched up to the Taurus's trunk with authority, rammed the flat end of the bar under the lid, and pried. A couple of wiggles and grunts and the lid popped. She used the crowbar to lift the lid.

"Oh, God!" She heaved and turned away.

Elizabeth, mouth covered by her raincoat, moved closer and peeked inside. Curled in the fetal position was the soupy mess of a human being.

"For the love of God." She backpedaled and struggled to get her cell phone out. "Deputy Young, get away from my crime scene," she barked at the dry heaving woman.

Once they were clear of the makeshift coffin, Elizabeth was able to yank her phone free of the raincoat. She dialed Olivia's number.

"Radio this in. Get Lundquist and Dayne down here. Now," she ordered her deputy.

While Young hailed dispatch, Elizabeth waited through eight rings and was directed to Olivia's voicemail.

At the beep, she left her message. "Olivia, I need you. We've got another body."

OLIVIA LIFTED HER head from the male victim's exposed cavity. "What the hell?"

She grabbed her voice recording device. "Upon further examination of the unidentified male, it is my determination that manner of death was caused by a ruptured heart valve. The victim shows signs of severe malnutrition and dehydration. Due to the victim's weakened condition, it led to a heart attack. Tox screens and blood tests are yet to be done. Time of death is undetermined. Decomposition is advanced but no indications of when it happened."

"Interesting."

Olivia cried out, backing away from the autopsy table. She turned off the recorder and dropped it on a tray, rattling the unused utensils. "Agent McCall, knocking would have been a nice way to announce your presence."

"Apologies, Dr. Remington-Thorpe. I did not want to disturb you as you dictated."

"What are you doing here? I thought you were going back to Illinois."

He entered the room. "Lila convinced me otherwise. I'm glad I didn't go. I wanted to see what you had learned. This"—he gestured at the exposed body—"revelation was unexpected."

A discoloration on the edge of his jaw gave Olivia pause. She squinted at the reddish abrasion. "Did something happen to you, Agent McCall? You have a bruise right there." She pointed to the spot on her own jaw.

"I'm fine. Just a love tap." He leaned over the body. "A heart attack? You're certain?"

"If you look at the heart, you can see the damage done by the rupture. The part that has me baffled is the damage to the connective tissues and the valves. I think the victim had an underlying health condition that led to the rupture of his heart. As he became dehydrated, it would have worsened the situation, leading to the weakened point and a blowout. I've asked the lab to test for a specific set of diseases."

"Such as?"

"Ehlers-Danlos syndrome. It's a disease that effects connective tissues, the skin, and blood vessels."

Agent McCall frowned. "I'm not familiar with that."

"Not many are. I'm running on a hunch here, but it's a good one. The victim possibly knew about the disease, but the killer would not."

McCall nodded and continued to study the body. "He never stood a chance with the I-80 killer's procedure. It explains why he was never stabbed. But he made for a great message board."

Olivia scowled at the state police investigator. "Explain to me why he's called the I-80 killer when the files I have state that the bodies weren't all on I-80."

"In Chicago, he did deviate a bit off I-80, but for the most part the bodies were on or near the interstate. However, from as far east as Pennsylvania and as far west as California, there have been bodies fitting the same MO found along the interstate. The files you were given pertained to Lila's investigation in Chicago. The case files I have are more extensive."

Olivia gaped at him. "How many?"

"Confirmed deaths that can be connected to the I-80 killer, forty-three."

"My God," Olivia choked out.

"Of those forty-three, only twenty-eight have been IDed. The ones not IDed have been beheaded. Genders, ages, time of discovery are all over the map. He has no preference or type, which makes him exceptionally dangerous."

"And why have you told Elizabeth none of this?"

McCall sighed, wandering over to the chair he had occupied earlier and sat. "Lila knows. Cecil Waterford, her former partner, knows. I did not want to alarm the sheriff until I was certain."

"Forty-three?" Olivia leaned against the evidence counter. "That makes him ..."

"The worst type of serial killer," McCall finished for her. "I worked with a few behavioral analysts from the FBI, and they all came to the same conclusion. This man is a hunter.

He's a loner. His methods are his own. Due to where the bodies were found in proximity to the interstate, they firmly believe he is either a long-haul trucker or works in some kind of job that requires a lot of highway travel."

"The manner of death for all the victims is the same? Do they have a theory on that?"

"Best guess, he wants them to die a slow death. Probably watches it happen. It's a control thing. The fact that they have been deprived of water and food for a period of time suggests he's keeping them somewhere before he kills them. He could have many places for this along his route. Or he keeps the victims with him while he travels."

Olivia let what Agent McCall said sink in. She sorted this information with what she'd surmised on her own from the case files in her office. What didn't fit into place was Lila.

"You're trying to fit Lila's puzzle piece into this scenario," McCall said matter-of-factly.

"I am."

"Olivia?" Dominic entered the autopsy room. Her husband's footsteps faltered when he saw Agent McCall. Frowning, Dominic approached her.

"Where is your phone?" he asked. "Ellie has been trying to call you, and so have I."

"It's right ..." She turned around and scanned the evidence counter. "It was right here." But it wasn't. She picked up a few items, but it wasn't hidden under them. "I set it down on the counter before I started. I know I did."

"Is this it?"

She turned to Agent McCall, who was holding up her green-cased phone.

"Yes." She took it from him and entered the passcode. Ten missed calls from Ellie, Dominic, and Eckardt County dispatch. "What's going on?"

"You're needed at another crime scene." Dominic grabbed her equipment bag hanging on the back of a closet door. "Ellie said you need the wet gear for this one."

Agent McCall moved to the door. "I'm coming with you."

"Agent McCall, I doubt this has anything to do with the reason you're here," she said as she removed and tossed her examining gown and gloves in their special bin.

"One never knows, Dr. Remington-Thorpe." With that, he exited.

Dominic handed her the bag. "Why didn't you answer the phone?"

"I didn't hear it." She slung the bag over her shoulder and checked her phone closely. "The ringer was turned off." She swiped through the settings. "So are the notifications. What the heck?"

"Are you sure you didn't do it on accident?" he asked.

"No. I never turn them off. Never." She scowled at the place where McCall had been seated. Behind the chair was a small desk she used for paperwork. Had he found her phone there? But why would it be on that desk? She never set it down there.

"Maybe one of the others moved it before they left," Dominic suggested, reading her thoughts.

"But how did the ringer and notifications get turned off? And why?"

His pale brown eyes sparked. "I don't know." He kissed

her cheek. "You better go. Ellie's in a panic."

Olivia moved to the door, stopped, and looked back at her husband. "You said wet gear, right?"

"Yes."

"Why?"

"Ellie said the body is ... mushy."

Olivia wrinkled her nose. "Ooooh, this is going to be one of those skin and fat melting off the bone types. I haven't had one of those since the body farm."

Dominic grimaced at her enthusiasm. "I'll lock up the room so no one can tinker with your cadaver."

"Thank you," she called back as she headed out the door.

Her body hummed with anticipation. She pulled out her phone and dialed Ellie. Her friend picked up on the second ring.

"Give me the address. I'm on my way."

CHAPTER TEN

S O MUCH FOR her having the day off to regroup and think about her decisions.

Lila exited her car on the fringes of the other gathered vehicles. She'd passed the roadblock manned by Brent. He told her that the sheriff had found another body and it was all hands on deck. Not what Lila wanted to hear.

As she approached the abandoned Ford, the ME van pulled up, followed closely by an Illinois State Police car. Lila halted and faced Tate's car, crossing her arms as she glared at him. Olivia hopped out of the van, gave Lila a finger wave, and headed to the van's back end. Tate extracted himself from his state-issued vehicle. He remained next to the car, staring back at Lila.

"Deputy Dayne."

Gritting her molars at the strident tone, she let her arms drop. "Yes, Deputy Young?"

The younger woman cocked her head to the side, her dark brown eyes flashing with ire. "Sheriff wants you over there before the ME gets to the body." She held up an N95 mask. "You're going to need this and some VapoRub."

Lila took the mask. "Got it." She moved past Young.

"The body looks and smells bad."

"I'm sure it does," Lila threw over her shoulder.

She wasn't sure what it was about Corey Young that got under her skin. Maybe it was because the woman carried herself with a swagger that irked Lila. Or that she was here because Brent wasn't ready for full duty. Or perhaps it was because Lila believed the woman lacked field experience. Whatever it was, Lila did her best to be civil, more for the sheriff's sake than her own.

The cloying odor of decomp was suffocating as she drew close to the car. Lila pulled the mask on. It couldn't keep everything out, but it helped cut down on the overwhelming stench.

"Hey! You can't go over ... Sir!"

She checked on the commotion coming from Young. Tate was marching toward her. Lila lowered the mask and waved off the pursuing deputy, then she intercepted Tate, grabbing his arm and propelling him backward.

"You can't be here."

"No, you shouldn't be here," he countered.

She gave him a slight shove before releasing his arm. "Opposite is true. This is my job. My jurisdiction, not yours. How did you even know about this?"

"I was with Dr. Remington-Thorpe when she got the call."

Lila was about to ask why, then rethought it. She didn't need or want to know.

She noted the bruise on his jaw. Guess she hit him hard enough to leave a shiner. Should make him think twice about being an ass. He now had a clear idea that she was not the Lila he knew.

"Tate, you need to return to your vehicle and stay there.

Whatever is waiting for me in that car has nothing to do with why you came here in the first place."

"You don't know that," he said.

"No, I don't. Until the ME and I have a chance to look over the body, you go nowhere near that scene. Return to your car, Agent McCall." She signaled Deputy Young to come forward.

Tate lifted a finger and shook it in her face. "You put on a good show, Deputy Dayne," he said in a lowered voice. "I'm sure he's impressed."

Lila narrowed her eyes as Tate was escorted away. She didn't put a show on for anyone, especially Kyle. Let Tate think what he wanted; he was in jerk mode. She pulled the mask up over her mouth and nose. Was Kyle even here? He should be. She turned back to the crime scene and headed in that direction.

Elizabeth, a mask covering her face as well, stood beside a masked Fontaine, who watched a figure moving behind the car's front right side.

Kyle.

"Deputy Dayne." Elizabeth nodded. "Before Dr. Remington-Thorpe does her thing, I want you to examine that body."

"If it's as badly decomposed as you say it is, I doubt I'll be of much assistance."

"Please try. I need your assessment."

Lila caught Fontaine's furrowed brow on his normally stoic features. He was still doubting her. Did she blame him? Not really. Deep down, she still wanted to hit the trail. But she had promised herself she was done with running and hiding. She would face this head-on. How could she do so with assurance when her biggest detractor stood right next to her number one ally?

"As always?" she asked Elizabeth. The always being to allow Lila to examine the body and the scene, take her mental notes, and let her digest what she'd seen before she gave her report.

Elizabeth nodded, then broke from their small group to intercept Dr. Remington-Thorpe.

Lila met Fontaine's steely gaze. *"Don't screw this one up,"* he seemed to say.

Sticking her tongue out behind the mask gave her a thrill. Childish, yes, but so satisfying. Especially when he couldn't see her do it. God, he was such a dick.

She chanced a look over her shoulder in the other dick's direction. Tate was obeying her orders, leaning against the hood of his car. How long he planned to abide by her demands was questionable.

She circled to the Taurus's rear end. Enough daylight remained to do first assessments on the car, but the evening shadows were creeping closer. Dispersed about the perimeter were tall tripod stands mounted with LED spotlights ready to ward off the night.

Even with the mask filtering what it could, the putrid odor made Lila's eyes water. How could she assess the body through a sheen of tears? She pulled a pair of crime scene gloves from her jeans pocket and wiggled her hands into the tight, protective vinyl. Stopping within inches of the bumper, she peered inside. The lid blocked what little light remained.

Kyle joined her and flicked on the light positioned right beside the car's backend.

"Thanks," she said.

He didn't answer. Ever the silent Viking. He damn sure made a point to keep a professional distance between them.

Lila grimaced at the sight inside the trunk. She couldn't tell if it was male or female. By the way the body was contorted, it was certainly someone as young as their teens but most probably an adult. The jeans and a T-shirt, maybe, were degraded by the chemical reactions as the body broke down and putrefied. The clothing was plastered to what could only have been the skin, which was a liquidized and soap-like mess. Maggots swarmed the body. The sight made her normally strong constitution waver. Flies buzzed the body and dive-bombed Lila. She swatted at them.

"Been here for a while," Kyle said with his low rumble. "Even without the sun, the heat and rain made it worse. And the insect activity, well, you can see. The fluids are leaking out of the bottom of the car."

Lila glanced down and spotted a dark stain forming near the toe of her boots. "Gross." She took a small step back. "We're not going to be able to tell when death occurred and how long it's been here."

"Sheriff talked with a few people who live along this road." He continued his normal evidence collection and assessment. "Everyone says they first remember seeing the car parked here two days ago."

"And no one reported it until today?" she asked.

"Probably wanted to give the owner time to retrieve it. Folks around here are known to do that." Kyle squatted behind the car, disappearing from her view.

"Two days isn't enough time for the body to reach this stage, even with mitigating circumstances. It has been in this trunk longer than that." Lila shook her head. "I can't tell anything with this mess. ME is going to have a helluva time getting this out of here."

He reappeared, sealing a brown paper evidence bag. He tossed that into a small plastic tote with other collected evidence. "Then why are you even here?"

His gaze flicked to the far-off man loitering on the edges of the crime scene. Kyle didn't have to say it, she could read it in his eyes. Why was Tate even here?

Lila swallowed hard and directed her full attention on the car-trunk victim. Normally, she and Kyle had a comfortable working relationship, one that hadn't been skewed by their sleeping together. They had a peculiar way of bouncing ideas off each other or reading the other's mind when it came to evidence and crimes. Which would come in real handy right now, but he was making it difficult to even carry on an intelligent conversation.

Lila liked working alongside Kyle, because he treated her with respect. Something she'd gotten only from Cecil, and none of it from Tate.

Frankly, she had no one but herself to blame for Kyle's distance. She was the one who pushed him away.

Lila turned away from the mess. "I'm going to let Dr. Remington-Thorpe handle this." She headed back toward the sheriff.

"I'll convince her to have the car towed to the hospital, and she can figure it out from there," Kyle said as he fell in step with her, still keeping an arm's length between them.

"DCI needs to process that car." DCI was Iowa's Division of Criminal Investigations, brought in when the crime scene went beyond Kyle's and Lila's resources.

"Already called. They'll be down early tomorrow. We need to get the body out as soon as possible."

They paused next to the sheriff's SUV while Lila removed her gloves and mask. She let her gaze drift to her ex. Tate was standing a few feet in front of his car, watching her. Lila practically felt the annoyance and impatient energy coming from him. He could keep on waiting.

"What was his reason for coming here?" Kyle asked.

Lila twitched at his unexpected question. "A poor one. He came because he thought it might be an I-80 victim."

"From the looks of that scene, it would be hard to tell."

Harder still to prove.

Lila tossed her gloves. "I'm going to send him packing."

"Then what?"

She stilled. "Then we're working this scene."

"Just checking." He walked away.

Guess she deserved that. She trudged over to Tate.

"Go to the bed-and-breakfast," she interrupted him as he opened his mouth. "The body is in a stage of putrefaction. There's no way to tell what happened to the victim, much less know what gender it is."

"You're sure?"

"For the love of God, Tate. I saw it. There's nothing there to find at this point. The ME needs to get it back to the morgue. I don't even see how we're going to get the body out of the trunk and keep most of it intact."

He nodded. "I'll trust you on that."

"If that's all it takes to make you go away, then fine."

"Thought we had an understanding."

She shrugged. "I asked you to rethink your assessment of that body, and you agreed to stay and do so. That's it."

"He had a heart attack."

She blinked then frowned. "He who?"

"The victim. Dr. Remington-Thorpe had just discovered it before she was sent out here. The victim died of a ruptured heart valve. That's why he had no stab wounds. He expired before the killer could inflict his damage."

Her shoulders sagged. "It could still be him?"

"You're certain that he said those exact words to you?"

His doubt straightened her spine and poured liquid heat through her veins. "I have never been more certain of anything in my life. Those three words haunt my dreams."

Tate held up a hand. "Okay, certainty noted."

"He has unfinished business with me. He's coming for me."

"I won't let that happen." He reached for her.

Lila sidestepped his hand and shook her head. "Go to the B and B. I've got work to do here."

"You'll let me know if something changes?" he asked.

She gave him a weak wave and continued toward the crime scene.

There was still time to change her mind. She could still run. Start over. Give up this deluded idea of continuing to be a police officer. She could be anything or anyone she wanted.

As she passed the sheriff, their gazes connected. The

woman's exhaustion glared back at Lila like a neon sign at the bar and made her stumble in her step. Elizabeth was out of her element here. She had taken on the role of sheriff because she, too, had demons to slay, but she had no formal training as a law enforcement officer. That was where deputies like Lila, Kyle, and even Corey Young came into play. Elizabeth deferred to their training and experience. That trust was a burden Lila struggled to carry. She looked away.

With Elizabeth counting on her, how could she abandon ship?

ELIZABETH WATCHED LILA speak to Olivia. While she needed to hear what her deputy detective had to say about the body in the trunk, Elizabeth wasn't in any hurry. Lila's demeanor relayed that she needed space. Something that was in dire need when Agent Tate McCall made an unexpected appearance.

Speaking of the man, Elizabeth checked the parked cars. Whatever Lila had said to him ensured he'd left. But given Lila's stricken expression, something had passed between the two when they conversed. What had Agent McCall told Lila?

"Sheriff?"

Elizabeth turned. "What do you have for me, Lundquist?"

He held up a plastic evidence bag. In the beam of the spotlights, Elizabeth made out a pink chip.

"What is that?"

"A piece of a fake fingernail. Found it under the floor mat on the driver's side. Might be the victim's or someone connected with the victim."

"Did you see anything like that with the body?" she asked.

He shook his head. "Couldn't tell. I've alerted Dr. Remington-Thorpe to watch for it."

"Good." Elizabeth zeroed her attention on Lila. "What's Deputy Dayne's take?"

"A big mess. No assessment other than what we all suspect. The car has only been here a short time, but the body has been in that trunk longer."

Sighing, she nodded. "Finish with whatever you need to do. Until DCI gets here and we get that car out of the elements, there's not much more we can do tonight."

Right on cue a wreaker, rumbled up.

"I'll get the car secured for transport," Lundquist said and walked over to direct the driver.

Elizabeth took the opportunity to corner Lila. "Deputy Dayne."

She stopped writing in her notepad. "I don't have much to tell you, Sheriff. It's up to Dr. Remington-Thorpe."

"I gathered as much from Deputy Lundquist. No, what I'm needing from you is an explanation as to why Agent McCall is still in Juniper after he claimed he was leaving. And why you disobeyed my order to return to the department earlier."

Deep lines formed around Lila's mouth, and a slight tick started in the corner of her right eyelid. Elizabeth knew that look. Lila wouldn't lie, but she wanted to. Usually, she resorted to the silent treatment. It was a tactic Elizabeth had experienced many times over the years she was married to her ex. He might have sucked at lying, but he couldn't say with the best of them. Lila was just as good.

"Before you dig in with whatever you refuse to tell me, hear me out," Elizabeth said.

Lila tucked her notepad and her hands in her hoodie pocket and jutted out her chin.

"I don't care what you had to do or say to him to get him to stay, it was the right choice. Even if I think he's a brash ..."

"Prick," Lila provided.

"That. I believe you when you swear that John Doe is one of the I-80 killer's victims."

Lila flinched. What was that all about? She reached up and rubbed the side of her nose. And there was the little tic where she'd rubbed away any sign of emotion.

"Why did you not return to the department?" Elizabeth asked.

"I needed food. I hadn't eaten all day. When I was finished, I was going to go in, but Ky—... Lundquist found me and told me not to bother. Then the call came about this body."

A reasonable answer. Elizabeth could confirm this with him.

"Cecil is here," Lila stated.

"He is? He gave me the impression that he wasn't coming. It's why Agent McCall is here."

A shrug was the lone response. With each passing hour, Elizabeth was watching Lila go into lockdown. She hadn't exactly been the most open and talkative person when she arrived in Juniper, which could be chalked up to her painful past. But since finding that body, she was spiraling out, and Elizabeth feared a breakdown was coming and Lila would do the unthinkable.

Elizabeth was being outmaneuvered, plain and simple. Best to end it here, be glad she got what she did out of the stubborn deputy, and focus on the problems currently laid before her. Sometimes the best way to get the answers you wanted was to go around the obstacle.

"Is he staying here in Juniper?" Elizabeth asked.

"At the B and B on your street. So is Agent McCall."

"Good to know."

"Is there anything else you need from me?" Lila asked.

"We're shutting this scene down. I think that's it for now."

"Then I'm heading home." Lila made to leave.

"Alone?" Elizabeth asked.

The blonde hesitated. "Alone," she said. With that she ambled to her car.

"Ellie." Olivia held out a clipboard.

Elizabeth took the board with the signoff sheets and a pen. "What's the plan for the autopsy?" she asked as she scrawled her name on the appropriate lines.

"Tomorrow sometime. I'm not even finished with our other victim."

Elizabeth handed the items back to Olivia. "Any news on that front?"

"Agent McCall didn't talk to you?"

"No. He seemed more concerned with Lila than speaking

to me. Why?"

"Well, I can't conclusively state one way or the other that the man was or was not the victim of the I-80 killer. What I can say for certain is that he died of a ruptured heart valve."

"A heart attack?"

"In a manner of speaking, yes. I can only speculate at this point that the significant signs of dehydration and starvation contributed to it. Those markers are similar to the other I-80 killer victims. However, that's where it ends. I need more time with him and the lab results."

"Hopefully, DCI can process them in a timely manner."

"Cross your fingers but don't hold your breath," Olivia said.

"Why does Agent McCall already know this?" Elizabeth asked.

Olivia tucked her clipboard under her arm. "Because the man made a surprise visit to the morgue before I got your call."

Elizabeth frowned. "He seems to like making surprise visits, doesn't he?"

CHAPTER ELEVEN

LILA TOOK THE long route home, unwilling to face the empty house yet. From the moment they had started their secret relationship, Kyle had spent many nights at her place when they weren't working the night shift. She hadn't been alone once since the storms had rolled in and never left. How would she get through tonight?

She drove past the elementary school, the security lights illuminating the playground equipment. At the next street, she whipped the car around and returned to the school, parking under a light and killing the engine. She stared at the playground as the ticking engine cooled.

On her second day on the job, Lila had panicked when she was faced with telling a victim's parents their child had been killed. She abandoned a fellow LEO and her post. When she finally came out of her fog, she was parked across the street, watching the children play.

Of its own accord, her hand slipped beneath the seat belt and cradled her abdomen. Just like that day, she mourned what she would never have. For as long as she could recall, Lila had wanted to be a mother. In part, because she wanted to rectify the wrongs her own mother had committed. The other reason—misguided and selfish though it might have been—was to have someone who loved her. In her naivety, she'd thought Tate did.

When Lila learned she was pregnant, she'd kept it from Tate. Finding the right time to tell him never came. The attack and the subsequent lifesaving surgeries brought the revelation to light. Tate made it clear that he wanted nothing to do with a woman who kept secrets, especially when they had a bearing on his career and his life.

She hadn't been sure then, and to this day still wasn't, if Tate was mad at her because he wanted the child or because that a child could mess up his carefully laid career path. His words and actions didn't make it clear.

Lila couldn't sit here in the car, mulling over the past any longer. She released the safety belt and exited the vehicle. She ambled over to the merry-go-round that looked more like a Christmas tree than the playground joyride she recalled from her youth. She sat on the edge and pushed off. Leaning her head into the intricate netting, she closed her eyes and enjoyed the lazy rotation.

How was she going to resolve the problem of Tate? His presence was putting a kink in her working relationship with the sheriff and the rest of the deputies, especially Kyle. Lila was well-versed in his methods and how he liked to railroad an investigation when it best suited him. When it came to the I-80 killer case, he was a real ass to deal with.

The merry-go-round came to a halt. Lila pushed off again, this time giving it another boost to spin a little faster. She grasped the plastic-coated cable wire bracketing her body, leaned forward, and watched her boots skim over the circle of dirt carved out by dragging feet.

Managing Tate would be a challenge. Lila could do it to

an extent, but that usually required blackmail. With the others, he would see them as roadblocks to his final goal. If he didn't get his way, he, too, would utilize the blackmail tool, just as he did when revealing her past drug addiction.

Cecil was the ace in the hole for this whole situation. Tate didn't dare cross the retired detective. Some kind of truce had gone down between the two men after Lila's attack. Cecil refused to divulge what it was, but whatever they'd agreed to meant Tate left Lila alone. This was the card Lila might have to play if things reached a point of disaster.

The clap of a shutting car door brought her head up. She planted her feet to stop the merry-go-round. The dark world spun a bit until her eyes adjusted to the stillness. She made out the hunched figure walking toward her.

"I thought you were in for the night."

Cecil shrugged. "I still have these urges to drive around at night to check things over. Nice little town they've got here."

"Nothing like Chicago. Why I picked it."

He cocked his head. "What are you doing out here all alone?"

"Needed to clear my head." She patted the spot next to her. "Go for a spin?"

"I don't think that thing was designed for adults."

Lila chuckled. "I don't think we're going to break it when wild kids have jumped all over it when it's spinning out of control."

With a shrug, he sat down next to her. Together they put the merry-go-round in motion. The night hung heavy with humidity and unspoken truths between them.

"Ran into Deputy Lindquist," Cecil said after they'd spun around a few times. "Told me about the new body."

"It's a bad one. Not sure what we're going to learn about this one."

"I-80 victim?"

"If it is, he's changed up his MO again. This was left in a car trunk. That's not his style."

Cecil sighed, hooking his arms around the plastic-coated cables. "I know you never wanted to talk about the case after the attack, and after you moved here. But there are things you need to know."

The whirl of the playground lights cast shadows in weird angles on his face, making it hard to read him. She shifted her legs under her to sit cross-legged on the edge of the merry-go-round and gripped her knees. "How many more have been found since me?"

"None in the Chicago area. After your attack, he stopped dumping in the city and the suburbs." Cecil brought the merry-go-round to a stop. "More bodies were found along the I-80 corridor. Two of them were dropped off in Iowa, one near Omaha, the other near Davenport. I-80 killer didn't have dump sites in Iowa before."

Lila met her mentor's hooded gaze. "He's been closing in on me."

"You're unfinished business."

Exactly. She grasped the cable and scooted to the edge of the platform. "Do you still have the copies of the files you pilfered from Tate?"

"I brought everything I have with me. And new ones. Out-of-state forensic teams were able to ID a few the bodies left in their jurisdictions."

Lightning rippled across the darkened sky. Lila stiffened, preparing for the rumble of thunder that followed. If it rained all night, she wasn't getting any sleep. Why waste the time?

"Feel like an all-nighter?" she asked. "My place?"

Cecil tilted his chin up. "Thought you'd never ask."

OLIVIA CIRCLED THE autopsy table, studying the body she had sewn together. Fingerprints were intact. Teeth were still in the victim's mouth. Distinguishable features—the large birthmark on his right thigh and the faint scar where he'd had an appendectomy—were still on his body. She did a dental imprint and managed to get a few good prints from his fingers. All these and more would be added to the national databases for missing people and the system for criminals with the hope that something would pop to give them an idea of who this man was.

She paused at his head and lowered the bright examination light. She had gone through what was left of his hair with a fine-tooth comb, pulling most of the debris from the strands, then bagged and tagged it. Any insects, casings, or larva were placed in sealed containers and labeled. Those would go to the entomology experts to study.

Everything was done by the book. To a *T*. Yet Olivia still felt like something was wrong. Missing.

She pushed the lamp higher, turned it off, and rolled the stretcher into a locked cooling unit. With the victim safely tucked away, she sat down in the rolling chair.

The car trunk victim had been carefully extracted and placed in a containment area to preserve what was left of the remains and slow insect activity. The car had been sealed and stored in a special garage for Deputy Lundquist and DCI techs to go over tomorrow.

The clock above the exit stated it was coming on eleven. Dominic had long gone home and was probably sleeping by now. Olivia should wrap this up and join him. There was nothing more she could do tonight.

She yawned. If that wasn't a sign to leave, then what was? She spun the chair to face the small desk and sorted through her notes and reports. Frowning, she shifted aside the autopsy diagram. Below that should have been copies of the toxic screen, serum tests, and disease mapping request forms. They were gone. Olivia flipped through each sheet of paper on her desk and came up empty.

"What the hell?" She smacked her desktop as she pushed to her feet.

The originals had gone to their specific departments, so there were no worries that things would be delayed due to misfiling. But she always made copies for her files and for state and federal filing in the event of trials. Who the hell would take them?

Dominic had locked up the room when she left, and he would never touch, move, or sort through her notes without her knowledge. Those requisition forms were not filled out until after Elizabeth and her crew left the autopsy room. The only other person who had been in here, had sat right here and found her "missing" phone, had been Agent Tate

McCall.

Heat filled her veins. Olivia rarely lost her cool. When she did, she had a viable reason. If that man was tampering with this investigation, she was going to nail him to the wall.

She located her phone and put in a call to Elizabeth. As she suspected, her friend was not sleeping, answering the call on the second ring.

"Did you find something I need to know?" she asked by way of greeting.

"Ellie, we need to talk. Now. Not over the phone."

"Meet me at Marnie's."

"Not there. Somewhere more private. Your office."

"I'll be there in fifteen."

"Make it ten," Olivia said and ended the call.

She sorted her paperwork, placed it and her tablet in her leather laptop case. The evidence boxes were already locked up and the room cleaned. All that was left was to lock the room and head to the sheriff's department.

Olivia paused in the doorway and glared at the desk and chair. "You just messed with the wrong woman."

ELIZABETH RECEIVED A worried frown from Alexis when she returned to the department for the umpteenth time today. Was it still Sunday? Elizabeth checked the time on her phone. Quarter 'til midnight. Yep, still Sunday. God, this day had just gone on forever. Her phone's battery level was dangerously low.

"Sheriff, is everything all right?" Alexis asked.

"In a sense it is, but not really. Dr. Remington-Thorpe should be here soon. She'll just see herself into my office."

Alexis's frown deepened. "Okay."

Elizabeth hesitated in her office doorway and turned back to the young woman. "Remind me who's on duty right now."

"Fitzgerald, Young, and Fontaine."

"Thanks." She wandered into her office.

She had left Bentley with Marnie at the bar, much to the cat Luna's disgust. Before Olivia called her away, Elizabeth got her sister to relay scuttlebutt on Sheehan. What little Marnie did say was that the disgraced ex-sheriff had not come into the bar at all today. A first as far as Elizabeth knew. His warning about not trusting outside sources still rang in her ears.

Elizabeth plugged her phone into the charger cord permanently left in her office, then sank her sore and weary body into her chair and bent over to unlace her work boots. Her two-plus hour nap in Olivia's office had partway recharged the human batteries, but she was still running on fumes. If she didn't get a full night's sleep, bad things were going to happen.

She toed off her boots and wiggled her hot and sweaty feet. Ahh, cool air felt good. With her socked feet propped on the edge of her desk, she rocked back in her chair and let her eyes drift shut. Catch a few winks until Olivia arrived.

"Doctor," Alexis said.

"Ms. Zachary."

Elizabeth peeled open one crusty eyelid to spy Olivia entering the office. Her friend closed the door and hustled to a chair.

"Okay." Elizabeth swung her feet to the floor and scooted forward. "What's going on?"

"Someone is meddling with my autopsies."

"How?"

"My copies for my test requisitions are missing."

Elizabeth tilted her head. "They're what?"

"Missing. Someone took them. Also, the reason you and everyone else couldn't reach me earlier was because someone had moved my phone and turned the ringer and my notifications off."

"Don't you have your phone on a passcode? How is that possible?"

Olivia's eyes narrowed. "Don't ask me. I'm just telling you what I have discovered."

"Does Dominic know it? Maybe he did it."

Her friend shook her head. "Dominic does not touch my work, and he has no reason to mess with my phone settings. He had to search me out to tell me you were trying to contact me. After he tried calling me."

"Do you have a suspect in mind?"

"Agent Tate McCall."

Elizabeth rocked back in her chair. "That's pretty damn specific."

"He's the only one I can place in the vicinity and timeframe when these things occurred or went missing. You and your deputies wouldn't tamper with my work. None of you have a reason to touch my phone."

"Olivia—and don't take this the wrong way—are you sure you didn't misplace the paperwork? Maybe you turned off your ringer?"

If Elizabeth could spontaneously combust from one look, the heated one she was getting from Olivia would do it.

"Ellie, don't take this the wrong way, but do you hear yourself being stupid?"

"Ouch." Holding up her hands, Elizabeth surrendered to her friend's expertise in this matter. "Say he is the one. What would his motive be to do so?"

"I don't know. My phone makes no sense. It's not like I wouldn't allow him access to the paperwork. This is why I wanted to talk to you in private about it. It could be something completely innocent."

"Except it's probably not." Elizabeth tapped her thumb against the desk calendar. "Lila might be able to tell us if he has a history of doing things like this since she's worked with him before. But I'm not bothering her tonight about it. She's been through enough today."

"Agreed. In fact, we all have. It's been a trying few weeks, and this day hasn't made it any better. How are things on the flood front?"

Elizabeth rubbed her face. "Not good. I had to put Rafe in charge of overseeing details on that. With these bodies being dropped in the county, I can't split my time. We have a killer out there who is a threat to one of our own and others. If I can keep this on the down low as much as possible, it'll be a miracle."

"Ellie, believe me when I say I didn't want to put more on you, but you know me. You know my methods. I don't misplace things or make changes without reason, especially when it comes to my work."

"Believe me, I know. I just wish he hadn't been so damn on the nose about it."

Olivia's forehead wrinkled. "He who?"

"Who do you think? Sheehan. He cornered me at the first crime scene and blabbed on about not trusting outside sources and we should use his special skills on this one."

"That man is a menace to society. He should be in jail."

Elizabeth gave Olivia her best deadpan expression. "Don't remind me." The devil's bargain Elizabeth made with Sheehan months ago sat like a hot coal in the back of her mind. But at this moment, she was too damned tired to care.

Olivia scooted forward in her seat. "You should go home and sleep."

"I will."

"I mean it, Ellie. Go home. I'm going home, and I need to know you're not going to ignore me."

Elizabeth wagged her fingers to shoo her friend out the door. "Go. I promise, I'm going home right after you."

"By the way you look, I think Rafe should drive you home."

"It's not that far. I'll be fine."

"Ellie."

"Olivia."

Sighing, Olivia stood. "I'm having Alexis call Rafe here. Good night, Sheriff."

"Night, Doc."

Elizabeth heard Olivia order Alexis to radio Rafe back to the department. Seriously, she didn't need all this mother-henning. Damn it, she was a grown-ass woman.

She went to stand and was hit by a dizzy spell. Flopping

hard into her seat before she fell over, Elizabeth reconsidered the fight to keep Rafe away. A smart woman knew when she needed assistance.

Fine. He could take her home. Just this once.

So, while she waited for him, she'd just lean back in her chair. Close her eyes and catch a few winks before he got here.

Yeah, that's what she would do.

CHAPTER TWELVE

Day 2: Monday: wee hours of the morning

LILA TOSSED THE file on the mound and scrubbed her face with a groan. "I'm so over this." She slapped her hands down on the pile of folders in front of her. "We were never able to get anywhere last time when there were fewer victims. If Tate hasn't been able to make any more headway, what do you expect me to do?"

Cecil picked up his mug, took a drink, and grimaced. "I need more coffee."

As he ambled over to the coffeemaker, Lila slumped in her chair, her head cradled in the curved backrest. She stared at the ceiling, listening to Cecil make a fresh pot and the air pump in Gerry's tank push out oxygen. The rumble of air bubbles and the clatter of his movements faded as her eyes drifted shut. Gawd, she was exhausted.

The storms had long since passed. She could catch a few hours before she needed to be at the department.

A heavy hand on her shoulder jolted her. Lila snapped upright with a sharp gasp.

"Get some sleep," Cecil said, looking down at her.

She shook her head, her hair brushing against her oily face. "I just need a wake-me-up." She rose from her chair. "I'm going to shower, and that should do the trick."

He gave her that stern fatherly expression. "Lila."

"Don't *Lila* me. I'll be fine." She moved to the cabinet hiding the washer and dryer unit to check the status of her twice-laundered uniform. "If anyone should be catching some sleep, it's you, old man."

"Joke's on you. My old age keeps me up at night."

She chuckled, tossing her clean-smelling clothes in the dryer and turning it on. "Keep the coffee hot; I'll be done in fifteen."

Cecil grunted as she entered the walled-off section to her bedroom and bathroom. Door closed, she headed to the dresser for clean clothing. Items tucked under her arm, she turned for the bathroom and froze. The bed was neatly made, the light quilt smoothed to tactical precision. Kyle went OCD every time she left a mess around; the bed was his biggest complaint. He remade it every morning half expecting a naval instructor to come barging in to inspect his work. Lila teased him, asking if she could bounce a quarter off the top. He'd just growl some response and move along.

Grinding her molars, she turned from the bed and escaped into the bathroom. She didn't have the time nor the energy to spend pining over a man. It was her own fault Kyle was mad at her.

Stripped of her clothing, she stepped into the shower, turned it as hot as she could stand, and flipped the showerhead to the massage setting. She stood under the spray, letting the water pound against her neck and shoulders. Clouds of steam billowed inside the glass walls, coating them in a thick layer.

Alone with her thoughts, she let them drift to memories.

Back before the I-80 killer ripped her soul from her, to a time when Tate trusted her enough to give her all the information. To a point before they became lovers.

He had been so enamored with the cases. He loved the thrill of the chase. Picking the killer's MO apart, piece by piece, thread by thread, to get into his mind. Figure out how the man worked and why. Lila had been impressed and starstruck by Tate's way of thinking. She wanted to be that kind of investigator, analytical and thorough, psychological in how to conduct an investigation. She should have never gone down that path.

Lila grabbed her shampoo and squirted a palmful, then worked the overabundant amount into her hair, massaging her scalp and the hairline on her neck.

Now that she was on the opposite side of this investigation, as a survivor, there were things she was beginning to see. She tilted her head back under the spray to rinse her hair. Things that she'd been ignorant about where Tate was involved. Bits of their conversations came back to her. Not a lot, just the morsels that she'd forced herself to retain. She smoothed a pea-sized amount of conditioner into her hair before lathering up with her favorite body wash.

Tate firmly believed the killer was a long-haul trucker. They had visited some of the truck stops, asking people if they saw anything out of the ordinary, someone who seemed off. But the consistent answer was always *they drive trucks for a living—who doesn't look out of the ordinary?*

Every single victim that had been IDed had the same thing in common—they were going somewhere the last time family members or friends had talked to them. Whether it was just to the store or to another town or state, they were traveling. Some of the victims' vehicles had been found abandoned months before or after their bodies had turned up. Others were never located, which led all involved with the cases to believe that they were sold off or sent to the junkyard.

Lila rinsed away the bubbles and conditioner, then turned the showerhead to a gentle spray and let the water tap against her uplifted face.

"It was a copycat."

Tate's instance when she had been released from the hospital reverberated in her mind.

"The I-80 killer does not go to his victims' homes."

"You don't know that," Cecil had shot back.

"It does not fit his MO," Tate snapped.

Lila stepped out of the spray and rubbed the excess water from her face. She blinked at the fogged walls.

"The man who attacked her is a copycat."

A copycat. Someone who admired the killer. Who knew about his style of killing. Wanted to be just like him. Had the I-80 killer garnered an apprentice?

She turned off the water and exited the shower stall. After towel drying, she hurriedly dressed and wrapped her wet hair in another towel. She banged out of the bathroom and rushed into the kitchen.

"What if there's two of them?"

Her outburst startled Cecil from his stupor. He glared her. "Come again?"

She riffled through the pile of folders and located the one set aside for her case. She flipped it open and laid it on top of the stack. "We all know that everything about the attack on me didn't fit with the prescribed MO for the I-80 killer." She jabbed a finger at her incident report. "What if some admirer of his attacked me under his supervision? Or under his instructions?"

"Come on, Lila, not you too. Bad enough Tate believes and spouts that crap about a copycat. But a teacher and an apprentice? That's too farfetched."

"Not really. There have been plenty of serial killer pairings, and a lot of them started out with an admirer of the original."

Cecil shook his head. "Together? Like Leonard Lake and Charles Ng? Are you hearing yourself? Tate's claim of a copycat makes more sense than two of them working together. Other agencies leaked enough details for a blueprint criminals could follow without paying membership dues."

Lila held up a finger. "Just listen. We both know there are depraved people out there who want attention from the sickest and most twisted killers in the world, and they'd do anything to get it. *We*, Chicago PD, never released to the public those little tidbits about where the killer stabbed his victims, or that he had weakened them with starvation and dehydration."

"True. And so far no one else has either."

"Everything about my attack was disorganized and sloppy. It was like he wasn't sure what exactly he was supposed to do and just winged it. If he was looking to get the I-80 killer's attention, that would be the way to do it. The attack on me was a way to get an introduction."

Cecil frowned. "If you're right, what would he hope to accomplish?"

"Recognition." Lila braced her hands on the table and leaned toward her mentor. "I always said, there was an ego to the I-80 killer. If someone screwed with your handiwork and tried to claim it as your own, what would you do? My attacker wanted his hero's attention. He got it."

Leaning back in his seat, arms crossed, one hand lifted to stroke his chin, Cecil regarded her. He was in his thinking pose. "Okay, let's run with this thought. We've got the I-80 killer, and we'll call the copycat Number Two. Somehow his message reaches I-80, and through some weird events, the two start working together. First, how do we prove it's two separate guys?"

Lila dug through the pile and pulled out three files that felt off to her. They were bare bones—reports and newspaper clippings Cecil had cobbled together after getting wind of new victims in the years after she had been attacked. She laid them before her mentor.

"These victims were left in the same manner as all the previous I-80 victims. But two of them were left here in Iowa."

"You're rehashing things I already know." In other words, tell him what she found off about the whole situation.

Lila pulled out the newspaper clippings that had triggered the niggling in her head. "The killer left behind some way to ID these victims. Did you notice how soon after the bodies were discovered they were able to figure out who they were?"

Cecil's hand dropped and he sat forward, taking one of

the articles. He reread it, then another, and then the final one. "Shit."

"If the I-80 killer had done these, there would have been no way to ID those victims that quickly. We still have four unidentified. It's not possible to ID these three that fast unless something was left behind."

"We need to see the autopsies on them."

Lila smiled. "How much you want to bet Tate has them here with him?"

"Not much of a bet when we both know he goes everywhere with those boxes." Cecil returned the clippings to their rightful files. "I think we need to catch some shut-eye for a few hours. Then we tackle him right away. You're on to something, and I want answers."

They left the files scattered all over the table, too exhausted to bother with packing them away.

"There's one thing troubling me," Cecil said as he lumbered over to her sofa. "Why didn't you tell me about the message before now?"

Lila sank into the suede recliner, the only other furniture she had in the place—no way was she sleeping in the bed with Kyle's ghost hanging around—and tucked her knees under her body. "I was worried that information would leak."

"You didn't trust me with it?"

"I didn't trust anybody at that time with anything, Cecil. You saw how I was. You knew what I did to myself. What he said to me ... that couldn't go out to the public."

He shook his head. "You just let it become a part of your private hell."

"Not on purpose." Lila pulled a blanket about her body. "Everyone knows now. Ultimately, it's what he wanted."

"Now he can finish what he started with you."

"Exactly."

CHAPTER THIRTEEN

OLIVIA SIPPED HER morning tea while reading the online newspaper that covered Eckardt County. The headlines were about the flooding that plagued every town and county along the Mississippi on the Iowa and Illinois sides. Olivia scanned the entire daily paper and blessedly didn't find a single article, blurb, or mention of the two bodies discovered yesterday. For now, they were safe to deal with this without the three-ring circus the media would bring.

The steady cadence of footfalls alerted her to Dominic's approach. She smiled as he entered their large, airy kitchen— a must they insisted on having when they bought the house but a room they barely used.

"You came home late." Dominic gave her a kiss, then moved to the Nespresso machine—the one appliance getting a daily workout.

"I didn't wake you, I hope. I slept in the guest bedroom so I didn't disturb you."

"Only briefly. Long enough to check the clock," he said and pressed the brew button. He was wearing blue scrubs today. Mondays and Thursdays were his designated surgery days, but he was always on-call for emergency surgeries twenty-four seven.

"That's good. I don't know what the rest of my week is

going to look like, and I don't want you to lose sleep over my erratic schedule. I've got a new body that is nothing more than bones and tissue to autopsy today. And this John Doe is becoming something of a mystery I want to crack."

Dominic lingered near the counter, waiting for his coffee to finish filling his cup. "Mystery how?"

"He doesn't fit the MO of this I-80 killer I told you about, but then he does. Almost everything was left intact to be able to ID him, something the killer never does. I don't understand it." Olivia sipped more of her tea.

The Nespresso machine beeped its completion and Dominic took his cup. He joined Olivia at the breakfast bar. "You'll figure it out. You always do."

She shook her head, setting her cup down. "How? Multiple medical examiners and coroners before me have not."

"What do you mean multiple? How many MEs does Chicago have?"

Flinching at her slipup, Olivia grabbed up her cup and drained the last of her cooled tea. The information about the other victims across the country that Agent McCall relayed to her yesterday was something Elizabeth had yet to learn about. Olivia wasn't about to spill the news to her husband before the sheriff heading up the investigation was informed.

"Liv, love, what aren't you telling me?"

She set the cup aside, then took her husband's face in her hands. "I spoke out of turn. Never mind what I said." She kissed him. "I better get going."

After taking the cup to the sink, she gathered her tablet. "Liv."

She turned back to Dominic.

"You'll be careful," he said.

"I'm the ME. What could happen to me?"

"That doesn't reassure me. With the way things have been going around here lately, it worries me."

Olivia hugged her tablet to her stomach. "What do you mean?"

He stared into his coffee, rotating the cup.

The niggling suspicion Elizabeth planted in Olivia's head last night that Dominic had misplaced her forms and tampered with her phone whispered in her mind. Could he actually be behind the two incidents? He did have access to her phone and was in her office with her before she went to the autopsy room. He had plenty of time to alter with it while she'd been distracted by Agent McCall's arrival. And Dominic had locked up the autopsy room when she rushed out to the new crime scene.

But, as she'd pointed out to Elizabeth, Dominic didn't have a reason to mess with any of that. Or was she wrong about her husband?

"D-man?"

He looked up from his cup and met her gaze dead-on. He had the bluest eyes she'd even seen in a Black man, and she loved that about him. He was happy. Wasn't he?

Dominic was unassuming, brilliant, and the hardest working surgeon in Eckardt County. He loved a challenge—the more difficult the surgery, the better. To be fair, he was the most skilled person just this side of a mortician to be the medical examiner. But he hadn't been interested in the position, claiming that he'd rather work to save the living than deal with the dead. Olivia, with her odd penchant for the macabre, was a perfect fit for the job and qualified by passing the ME training.

In the last few months, she'd noticed subtle shifts in his demeanor. Olivia chalked it up as stress. He was right, there was an uptick in tragedies, some of which he had to spend hours saving. When they moved here, they were well-informed on the corruption that ran rampant through Eckardt County. It wasn't uncommon to have a victim of an overdose or self-inflicted gunshot come into the hospital. Since Elizabeth took over as sheriff, a lot of those incidents went down dramatically. Still, Dominic didn't seem like himself.

"Something weighing on your mind?" Olivia asked.

He gave her a smile that looked suspiciously like it was forced. "Just work. Seems I'm spending more time in surgery patching up our aging population than anything else."

She returned to his side and cupped his cheek, smoothing her thumb across his clean-shaven skin. "After I help Ellie wrap up this case, we should go on vacation. It's been long overdue."

"I don't know, Liv." He took her hand in his. "There's so much to do. I don't know if I can make the time."

"Make it. We haven't spent near enough time alone in the last few years. We're both due for some personal time."

His eyes darted about as he clearly tried to read her face. Eventually, he relaxed his hold on her and kissed her palm. "I'll think about it. I can't make any promises."

She leaned closer to him. "Think very hard on that. I'm wanting a piña colada on a beach somewhere."

This smile actually reached his eyes. Olivia warmed at

the sight. Her husband needed to smile more. "I'll seriously consider it. You better get going. You have a difficult autopsy to do."

"Yes, yes I do." She kissed him once more on the lips, then left the kitchen.

Those pesky reservations about Dominic being connected to yesterday's incidents chased her heels. She would not give them attention. There was no reason to doubt her husband. He was not the type.

Olivia would lay those suspicions at Agent McCall's feet. He had the most reason to tamper with her work. She'd make sure it stayed that way.

LILA LET CECIL treat her to breakfast at the B and B since he hadn't bothered to sleep there. The owner was more than grateful to even have guests after the historic flooding, so she didn't mind serving an extra customer.

It didn't pass Lila's notice that Cecil's main reason to take her to the B and B was for the two of them to waylay Tate. While Cecil took a quick shower and put on a change of clothes, Lila waited on the screened-in porch that served as the breakfast nook. This whole section of the house had been closed off and paneled with windows for the customers to see out into the gorgeous butterfly gardens. Right now, there was a thick fog hanging just above the tops of the flowering bushes. Somewhere in the back of the house, the owner was cooking a meal fit for a gaggle of farmers. The aroma of maple-cured bacon made Lila's mouth water.

The creak of the stairs drew her attention. She peered through the open areas that had once been the outside windows and watched a well-groomed Tate descend the stairs. His dark hair was neatly combed and laid flat to his scalp—that would not last long. He wore blue jeans and was adjusting the collar of a desert-tan polo void of any logos. He also wore hiking shoes, as if he expected to be out on the trails of Eckardt County. In his left hand, he carried a dark gray jacket. He hit the floor with a bit of a skip and sauntered into the breakfast nook.

Lila pulled her gaze from him and back to the gray scene outside. Her muscles tensed in anticipation of Tate's entrance. No. She wasn't about to let him get to her. Closing her eyes, she drew in a deep breath.

"Mrs. Miller, breakfast smells delicious," he called to the kitchen.

Behind her lids, Lila rolled her eyes. *Smarmy ass.* Gawd, he was such a suck-up.

"Sit yourself down, Agent McCall, and I'll have it out right here in a jiffy," Mrs. Miller chirped.

Oh, he'd wrapped the unsuspecting woman around his ring finger. Bet he had her giggling like a schoolgirl back there in the kitchen.

Lila sensed his hesitation when he stepped into the room. Her body was relaxed, and she was ready for the tornado that was Tate McCall. She opened her eyes.

"I see you've become more of a perky person in the morning hours."

"What are you doing here?" he asked as he circled the table to face her.

She picked up her mug of hot coffee, liberally ladened with some of Mrs. Miller's finest creamer, and gestured at it. "She makes the best cup of joe in the whole county."

Tate glanced toward the kitchen, then the hallway and stairs, then back to Lila. He leaned down, draping his jacket over the back of a chair. "We both know that's a line of bull. Why are you really here?"

"Cecil invited me to breakfast."

Tate blanched. "Cecil is here? Where?"

"Getting ready for the day. You didn't know he was here?"

He grumbled something she couldn't make out and glanced at the doorway. Good on Cecil for keeping Tate off his game.

Lila sipped her coffee and set the mug down. "Seeing as we, me and Cecil, burned the midnight oil going over all those old case files, it only seemed fitting for him to provide breakfast."

The pops and cracks of the floorboard announced Mrs. Miller's arrival. Tate leaned away from Lila.

"Now, Agent McCall, this is some of the finest coffee in the whole county." She placed a matching mug to Lila's on the table in front of him. "I have that shipped to me from a dear friend who moved to Costa Rica." Mrs. Miller wiped her hands on the apron tied to her waist. "Go on, try it."

Lila took up her own cup and sipped, watching over the rim as Tate did as he was ordered. His features brightened and he smiled. Yep, suckered.

"Mrs. Miller, you are correct. This is one fine cup of coffee." He canted his body closer to her. "Think I could sway you into convincing that friend of yours to send me a package or two?"

She flapped her hand at him. "Oh, go on with you." She turned to Lila. "How you doin' there, Deputy Dayne?"

"Just fine, Mrs. Miller. Can't wait to see what you've got planned for us."

The older woman gripped Lila's shoulder and squeezed. "Let me know when you're ready for a refill."

Lila nodded as the woman departed to return to her cooking.

Tate dragged his chair out, the legs scraping across the floor, the noise grating on Lila's nerves. A move that was classic passive-aggressive Tate. But she kept it all bottled inside. He would not see that he could get to her. He sat and drank more of his coffee.

"Thought I was pulling your leg about the coffee, didn't you?"

He set his mug down. "Shoot straight with me, Lila. What are you and Cecil up to?"

"I'd rather wait until he's down here. Let's not have Mrs. Miller accidently overhear something she shouldn't be overhearing."

Right on cue, the stairs creaked with Cecil's approach. "What is that delicious aroma I'm smelling?" he asked as he entered the nook.

"An old-fashioned farmer's breakfast. You guys better loosen those belts. You're gonna need the extra room," Lila warned.

The moment Cecil took a chair next to Lila, Mrs. Miller returned with platters of bacon, scrambled eggs, French toast, sticky pecan rolls, fresh fruit, yogurt, and crocks of fresh butter and maple syrup. After setting the platters in the center of the table, Mrs. Miller hustled back to the kitchen for more coffee and extra drinks.

Lila stared at the sticky pecan rolls, remembering the one she'd tried on her first day on the job, in a kitchen miles from here. The baker had, sadly, lost her life, and Lila had not tasted another roll since. Would it be the same?

Mrs. Miller returned with a tray of drinks for all. The men were digging into the piles of food. Lila just stared at the big, fat pecan rolls.

"You ever have one of Neva McKinnley's pecan sticky rolls?" Mrs. Miller asked.

Lila looked up at the B and B owner. "I did. Right before ..."

Mrs. Miller's smile wavered, her eyes glistening. "I surely miss her." She dished out one of the rolls and placed it on Lila's plate. "Go ahead. I make them just like she used to. It was one secret recipe that did not go to the grave with her."

Lila took the woman's hand and gently squeezed it. Mrs. Miller urged them to eat their fill and then excused herself.

"What was that all about?" Tate asked.

Ignoring him, Lila tore off a hunk of the sticky roll and shoved it in her mouth. Heaven.

Somewhere in the back of the house, a door closed. Cecil twisted around, leaning back in his chair, then righted himself, staring down a chewing Tate.

"Time to come clean."

Lila filled her mouth with more of the sticky roll, watching the man across from her continue eating while he frowned.

Tate swallowed and dabbed at his mouth with a napkin. "About what?"

"We know about the other victims," Cecil volleyed back. "We're also fairly confident you have all the case files with you. So cough them up."

As she drank her coffee, Lila studied Tate's facial tics. He might be able to fool others, but he'd never been able to hide anything from her. Right now, Cecil was going for Tate's balls, and that would piss him off.

He set his napkin aside, then carefully arranged his silverware on his plate. "Detective Waterford, one, you don't have the authority to order me to do any such thing. Two, no."

"You've told the ME." Lila laid her hands on each side of her plate, her fingers rubbing the edge of the butter knife blade. She was shooting in the dark. "Do you plan to tell the sheriff?"

"What I do is of none of either of your concerns."

Ah. That non-answer was confirmation enough.

Gripping the butter knife, she leaned forward. "It does concern the investigation at hand, of which I am working. All it takes is putting a bug in the sheriff's ear about the correct person to contact and you will have no recourse." She sat back, smiling. "It's in your best interest to cooperate."

Tate remained impassive, but she noticed the tiniest twitch of his fingers. "A lot has changed in the last two years, Deputy Dayne. That threat is of no consequence to me."

"Isn't it?"

"Bluffing will not work with me." He glanced down at

his half-eaten food. "This meal held so much promise. Then the two of you had to ruin it." He pushed to his feet and downed the last of his coffee. "I think I will just get my day started." With a tilt of his head, he moved to exit the room.

"One way or another, we'll see those files, Tate," Lila said, keeping her gaze fixed on the spot he had vacated. "When I do, you will have many questions to answer."

"If that moment comes, Deputy Dayne, I gladly welcome you to try."

He left the house through the front entrance, making him walk past the wall of windows and their prying eyes. Lila noted with glee his stiff and jilted walk. They had gotten to him.

"Think it'll work?" Cecil asked as he continued eating.

"I know it will. He thinks Dr. Remington-Thorpe is the only one intelligent enough to trust with his investigation. His arrogance has always been his weakness."

"Lila, what did you ever see in that guy that made you want to sleep with him?"

She peeled off another large portion of her sticky roll and rammed it into her pie hole. That was the million-dollar question.

CHAPTER FOURTEEN

E LIZABETH STUMBLED INTO her kitchen at well past ten a.m. furious with Rafe for letting her sleep so late and herself for allowing it to happen. They were in crisis mode, for God's sake—she didn't have time to be lounging around like some nineteenth century aristocrat who had been the belle of the ball the night before.

A rustling from the living room brough her to a jolting halt. She twisted about.

Rafe rose from the sofa, Bentley at his side.

"What are you doing here?" Elizabeth demanded.

"Waiting on you," he said.

Bentley left him, curled around her owner's legs, and sat down on Elizabeth's feet. She bent down and greeted her companion with a loving rub behind the collie's ears.

"Shouldn't you be out checking on the flood situation?" she asked Rafe.

"Already done. National Guard is en route. National Weather Service is saying we will have a day of reprieve from the rain today. The flood control center has been giving me hourly updates via text. They're planning to release more water from the lakes, and it's going to make the Des Moines River and all the smaller rivers rise."

"And what about the Big Muddy?"

"Mississippi is holding steady at twenty-five feet. She's taking her problems down south, but we've got more coming from up north. Rain is drenching Davenport and Moline."

Elizabeth sighed. "Fine, you've got it under control. But you don't have to be here."

"I do if you want to get to the department. Your car is still there. Remember?"

"Ugh." She gave Bentley one last rub. "Let me get my coffee and we'll go."

"Take your time. Get some breakfast. Things are running smoothly," Rafe said as he followed her into the kitchen.

"Running smoothly, you say? Did shift rotation go over as planned?"

"Like clockwork. I have Meyer and Lundquist working desk detail, which made Lundquist happy because he's going over the physical evidence."

"Where's Lila?"

"She contacted me to say she's working with her old partner, the retired detective, on some things with the cases. She planned to be in the office by noon."

"She has Cecil working with her on this?"

Rafe nodded.

"Well, good for us. What about our two bodies?" Elizabeth plunked all her paraphernalia down on the counter by the coffeemaker.

"Dr. Remington-Thorpe is finishing her report on the first body and told me she'd be starting the process with the second. She brought in a forensic anthropologist for the second due to the advance stages of decomp."

"What does that mean for us?"

"It means the flesh will have to be removed and the exam will be only on the bones."

Elizabeth stopped what she was doing and faced Rafe. "They can do that?"

"All the time."

She shuddered. "Somehow I should be repulsed by that."

"And yet you're not."

"I'm not." She got the coffeemaker going.

As she moved about the kitchen to prepare her breakfast, she was keenly aware of Rafe's looming presence. For years they had denied their growing attraction. First it was because she was married to Joel. Then because she'd just divorced him. Now it was because she was the sheriff and Rafe the underling. It was a dance they would continue because Rafe refused to give anyone a reason to have Elizabeth removed as sheriff.

Much as she'd like to tell the gossips of Eckardt County to suck it, she couldn't argue with his logic. The moment she gave those with the biggest voices and grudges any fodder for their cannons, she'd be out of a job. That was not why she became sheriff. There was history that needed rectified, and she vowed to see justice.

"Have you decided what you're going to do with Lila and Kyle?" Rafe asked.

He had cornered her between the stove and the fridge, sending her senses into overdrive. She leaned into the fridge to look up at him. She was tall compared to most women, but the Fontaine brothers towered over her.

"No. I haven't." Elizabeth pushed past him and shook

free of those fritzing nerves. "As I was indelicately reminded yesterday, pot meet kettle. I have no room to judge."

"Georgia, no doubt."

"Does it matter?"

"In the scheme of things, no. That being said, neither of us have done anything remotely close to fraternizing."

Elizabeth paused in her cooking process and gave Rafe the stink eye. "Just because no one saw it doesn't mean it didn't happen."

"Just the same, you need to do something with those two," he said. "If word gets out you let what they did slide, it'll go bad for you."

"Frankly, I don't care. Wasn't it just yesterday you said he was good for her?"

"I did, but that doesn't mean it makes it right. These are things you need to consider as sheriff, and me as undersheriff."

She wagged a finger at him. "Yet, you didn't say anything to me. None of you did."

Rafe lifted his shoulders. "It was stupid of me not to."

"Punishing Lila at a time like this is not a wise move." Elizabeth turned back to her bubbling oatmeal. "We need her focus and skills. And we need Kyle's intuition. They complement each other on the job. Believe me, it didn't escape my notice that he makes her comfortable. God knows, she's deserving of that after the living hell she'd been through."

"Ellie, your heart is too soft for a sheriff."

She pointed her oatmeal-covered wooden spoon at him. "That is precisely what a sheriff needs at times to do this job.

Or woe to the people if they don't have that."

Rafe shook his head. "What are you making?"

Elizabeth stared at her pot and frowned at the distinct odor of burnt oatmeal. "A mess."

He took her spoon, turned off the stove, and removed the pot. He dumped the contents into the trash and placed the pot in the sink, running water into it. "Let's go get food."

"I'm not in the mood to do that outside of the house."

"Neither am I, but the residents of Eckardt need to see you out and about. It's one thing to have me handle flood management, but the people being affected by it are going to want some answers from their sheriff. The mayors are pushing to have a meeting with you anyway."

"I don't have time to be dealing with them right now. We have two bodies in the morgue that scream we have a serial killer on the loose in the county."

Rafe capped off her travel coffee mug and thrust it out to her. "You don't have a choice. This is the job you won; this is the job you do. You, first and foremost, are a politician, Ellie. Kiss the babies and all that crap. Don't forget it."

"I make a piss-poor one when I'm the walking dead."

"You'll be fine. You got almost eight hours of sleep."

Elizabeth huffed. "Fine. But if I slip up, it's all your fault."

"You won't slip up," he assured her.

SHE DID. ELIZABETH slipped up big-time.

She would have to choose the one restaurant—far from

the river's wrath and still doing business—where every Tom, Dick, and Betty came to get their senior discounted brunch and lunch. The same demographic that had made sure she was voted into the sheriff's office by a landslide. And the same bunch that tended to be the ones to not give two damns about critiquing anyone and everyone on their job performance, or lack thereof.

This was the lot she chose.

Elizabeth, with Rafe and Bentley in tow, ambled up to the hostess station. The ancient woman seated behind the antique casher's desk smiled.

"Welcome to The Haven, Sheriff." She slid off the stool and stepped around the corner to stroke Bentley's face and ears—the dog being the lone animal ever allowed in the restaurant. Only God knew why, but Elizabeth didn't question it. "Today's specials are eggs Benedict and hash browns, or pork and noodles, or chicken and noodles with all the fixin's." She looked up at Elizabeth and Rafe, who towered over the elderly woman. "We have only a few seats open—better get 'em while the gettin's good."

"We'll do that, Mary."

The trio circled the old wagon wheel leaning against a thick wood rail pulled from a long-defunct grain mill and stepped into the wide expanse that was the main restaurant seating area. The Haven was a former glove factory that had been converted into this unique eating establishment back in the seventies. The original proprietor of the factory had been a founding member of Juniper, but his family had long passed away or moved on.

Elizabeth and Rafe wound their way through the hand-

crafted tables and chairs made by the local Amish community. As Mary had promised, most of the tables were filled with
the early lunch crew, but there was one lone table Elizabeth
had her eye on at the back near the hall leading to the
restrooms and an outdoor exit. She tried to make a beeline
for it, but she was hailed with greetings from her constituents
and Bentley was waylaid by pets and coos. Elizabeth did her
best to acknowledge each and every call, but her stomach was
beginning to howl.

Finally making it to the small round table, Elizabeth sat
with her back to one wall, and Rafe sat with his to the
opposite wall. Bentley plopped down right at Elizabeth's feet,
her tail thumping the scuffed wood floor.

Their waitress set down a glass of tea with a lemon wedge
for Elizabeth and a Pepsi for Rafe, then placed a bowl of
water on the floor for Bentley.

"Hey, Kat, how's it going?" Elizabeth asked.

"Busy. Mom and Grandma have been making meals for
the flood workers and keeping things going here, too."

"Remind your grandma she needs to take it easy."

"We're trying. Mom even made Dad and Bub come in
and help." Bub being Kat's uncle.

Elizabeth nodded. "Good for her. What's our choices for
pie?"

Kat rattled off the five different selections—her mom was
known far and wide for making the best pies in the state of
Iowa, and she had the blue ribbon from the Iowa State Fair
to prove it. Elizabeth and Rafe gave Kat their orders, along
with a small plate of scraps for Bentley, then Kat headed
back to the kitchen.

The mood in the dining area shifted. Elizabeth scanned the room while mentally ticking down the time. Movement in the far-left part of the restaurant caught her attention. First one man then a second rose from their seats, hitched their pants up under their ample guts, and meandered over to her table.

Rafe stiffened. Elizabeth tapped his thigh and settled her interlaced hands on the table as the men approached.

Orville Patterson and Jim Thurnhall were two of the most vocal opponents to Elizabeth's "takeover" of the sheriff's office. They liked to think they were some of Sheehan's closest pals, but word was, they were just pains in the asses. No one was quite sure what the two did for a living, but it wasn't farming and they didn't own a business and they always seemed to have just enough money to keep them afloat. Neither were married, and not a single respectable female would be caught dead with them. Both men were on Elizabeth's radar, right behind Sheehan.

"Good"—Elizabeth checked her watch—"afternoon, gentlemen."

"Sheriff," Orville drawled. "Mind if we ask a few questions?"

She cocked her head to the side. "I might if it has any bearing on you two coming between me and my lunch."

They glanced at each other, Jim shrugging. He was more the follower, letting Orville do all the mental heavy lifting. Elizabeth was not fooled by Jim's passiveness. The man was shrewd as a fox and just as deadly. You never turned your back on him.

"Well." Orville shoved his beefy hands inside his pockets

and rocked back a smidgen on his heels. "We heard quite the story last night."

"Did you now?" Rafe said, leaning forward.

"Shore did. Seems Bo Cullen was all shook up over a body being found in their cow pasture." Orville rocked forward, seeming to enjoy the attention he was drawing their way. "A body he says that sent your deputy detective into a tizzy fit. A fit so bad, she about shot one of your deputies and Bo himself."

Elizabeth had warned Bo to keep his mouth shut. Why did it surprise her he hadn't? Gossip was gospel in this county, and the dirtier it was, the better it became, particularly when it pertained to an outsider. Most especially if alcohol was applied to grease the wagging tongues.

"Seems to me"—Elizabeth lounged back in her chair and gave both men a dead-eyed stare—"that if the two of you applied as much gumption into helping with the flood situation as you do with digging up rumor and slander, we'd nearly have this flood beat back. What say you, Undersheriff Fontaine?"

Bentley stepped out from under the table, her body in a stalking position and her hackles raised. Jim took a step back, his gaze riveted to the dog.

"I say, that about sums it up, Sheriff," Rafe said.

Kat emerged from the kitchen with their plates of food in hand. "Out of the way, bums," she snapped at the troublemakers.

Orville and Jim side-shuffled out of her way. Bentley made a chuffing sound that came from deep in her throat— it wasn't a growl, but it was a threatening noise just the same.

It startled the two men away from the table.

"Well, gentlemen, it appears my food has arrived and you two are out of time. Good day, sirs." Elizabeth touched her forehead in salute.

"I know what I heard, *Sheriff.* That woman deputy of yours is a menace to our fair county."

"Orville, the fact that you even know how to use the word *menace* properly should worry us all." Elizabeth picked up her butter knife and stabbed it into the pat of butter provided for her thick slice of homemade bread. "We are through here." She spread the softened butter across her bread. "If you continue to bother me, I'm certain Beth and Kat will be glad to file disturbing the peace and disorderly conduct charges that will grant me the right to haul you into the county jail."

Bentley followed up Elizabeth's threat with a bark that made the two men jump and haul ass right out of the restaurant.

Kat laughed. "Good thing Mary got them to pay before they finished their meal." Her humor fled. "Sorry they bothered you, Sheriff."

"Don't worry about it. Deputy Fontaine and I know how to handle disgruntled customers." Elizabeth took a healthy bite out of her bread.

Kat moved onto her other patrons. Bentley, her bowl of scraps wolfed down, laid her head on Elizabeth's thigh, earning a head stroke for her good job.

"I don't like that Bo is talking," Rafe said between forkfuls of his pork and noodles over mashed potatoes.

"I'm no more happy about it than you are. I'm going to

have to corner him and have a nice long chat with him."

Rafe drank his Pepsi and set the glass down. "You're not going to like this, but you need to sideline her until this thing is over."

"I can't do that. She's invaluable in this ..." Elizabeth glanced around, satisfied that the other restaurant patrons were busy with their meals. "S.K. case."

He frowned, then his face relaxed as he apparently picked up on her abbreviation. "Invaluable or not, she's a liability. One more move like yesterday morning and I don't think we'll be warding off rumors. She could actually do serious harm to someone."

Elizabeth sighed and stared at her congealing chicken gravy. What was she going to do with Lila? She stroked Bentley's head and ears, her fingers dancing over the silky hair.

"Finish your lunch, Ellie. We can hash this out after pie."

"Promises, promises."

CHAPTER FIFTEEN

OLIVIA, TOGETHER WITH the forensic anthropologist, examined the trunk victim before starting the macerating process. By the end of the examination, Olivia was no closer to figuring out what happened than before. What she did learn from the clothing left behind was that the victim was female, and she was missing her teeth and the lower half of her left leg.

The removal of the teeth and the left leg indicated the handiwork of the I-80 killer.

The forensic anthropologist decided to go with a chemical process for the maceration, to speed things up for Olivia and the Eckardt County team. It was now an hour into the potentially two-day process, and the anthropologist had gone to get some food.

Olivia sat at her autopsy room desk, fiddling with a pen as she reread both postmortem reports. She had yet to hear back from Deputy Lundquist on whether he had pulled anything useful off the clothing from the victims. The chipped nail he found in the car did gain a mate. Both had ragged edges from breakage that could be contributed to the female fighting her attacker or the killer fracturing the nails.

If there was any trace of the killer on the larger piece found in the car, it might give them an advantage no one else had before. Olivia did not hold out any hope on the portion found on the body, thanks to the chemical reactions during decomposition. The problem lay in the fact that they were dealing with a highly sophisticated killer. Finding any trace evidence in his wake might prove impossible.

Olivia just hoped the victims' DNA would produce a solid hit. In the day and age of ancestry kits every human being could access, there could potentially be some record of each victim. This little trick would put a huge damper in the I-80 killer's method of preventing quick identification. Or— and this made Olivia sick to her stomach—he'd wised up to this problem and decided to change up his MO. Which would explain why the first body showed up as it had.

Sighing, she pulled her phone closer and checked the stream of texts. Most were from her colleagues giving updates on her patients that needed care. There was a single message from Dominic, asking that she call him as soon as she had a free moment. She tapped the corner of her phone against the stack of file folders and reports. Should she call him now?

A quick triple rap on her autopsy room door made her drop the phone on the desk and swivel. Agent McCall stood in the doorway. His dark hair was as wild as it was the day before. Did the man ever keep a hair in place?

"Dr. Remington-Thorpe, I see you've completed the autopsies."

"Acute observation, Agent McCall."

Her snide comeback was met with a lifted shoulder and a bland expression. "The second body, the one found in the car trunk yesterday evening, what are your findings?" he asked as he waltzed into the room.

Olivia wanted to be annoyed with this man. She wanted to accuse him of messing with her. But she had no logical proof. Confronting him about it would get her nowhere. A conversation with Lila was in order. Olivia wanted a better understanding of this man, and who better to give her the insight she needed than an ex-lover and a detective at that.

"Mine and the forensic anthropologist's findings indicate that this victim in all likelihood is another I-80 killer victim."

"Your reasons?"

Olivia explained to him about the missing teeth and lower leg.

"That's it?" he asked.

"We weren't left with much of a body to examine, Agent McCall. Her flesh has to be removed, which is in process as we speak. Once the bones are ready, the anthropologist will examine them, and he should be able to give us more details about this victim. DCI is running the DNA. Because of the state of the tissue, if she was stabbed as the I-80 killer is want to do, there is no way of telling."

"No marks on the bones?"

Olivia cocked her head to the side and crossed her arms. "What did I say?"

He frowned, his eyes narrowing in that way children were apt to do when cornered about their misbehavior. How odd for a grown man to resort to such an immature action.

"Dr. Remington-Thorpe—my, that's a mouthful."

"It's my name."

He grimaced. "Yes." Agent McCall found a spot in front of her immaculately clean evidence counter and leaned against it. "I know it sounds redundant to ask you things that you explained in a way but yet you didn't. I'm trying to gather all the information to make my own assessment."

"Like you did yesterday when you disregarded the word of a survivor that another person was murdered by her attacker?"

"I did not disregard Lila's word. What I mentioned was another alternative."

"A message aimed at her was carved into the man's body."

Agent McCall blinked. "Dr. Remington-Thorpe, I can understand that you might be close to Deputy Dayne, but in the course of an investigation, you must keep an objective mind. This is especially true of a woman in your position."

"When I need a lecture on how to behave as a medical examiner, I'll be sure to request your presence at that symposium, Agent McCall."

He frowned. How the hell had Lila ever been involved with this man?

"Is something about me bothering you, Doctor?" he asked.

Yes! Something damn well did bother her. He could be the culprit behind her missing forms and tampered phone. How, she had no idea. And worse, his probable actions had made her look at her own husband in suspicion, which cranked her temper. His attitude bordered on narcissism. Olivia dealt with enough gaslighting in her life to see it when it was being flaunted in front of her. She'd be damned if this Agent McCall would degrade her in her own morgue.

This agent was irritating the hell out of her.

She stood, sick of allowing this man to stand above her. "Why do you keep showing up in my morgue?"

"This is where the vital information comes from. Once I have the full picture, I can move forward with my investigation."

"An investigation you originally wanted no part of. Why is that?"

"Have you discussed your findings with Sheriff Benoit?" he asked.

"I have not, because she's been busy. If it didn't pass your notice, we are dealing with catastrophic flooding."

He gave Olivia a curt nod. "Let us keep it that way. When the time is right, I will fill her in on everything." He moved away from the counter and toward the door.

"Agent McCall, I think you forget, I don't answer to you. You have no authority here in Iowa and thus have no say in how I do my job."

He hesitated in the doorway and looked back. "True. I ask this favor of you out of courtesy. As you so firmly reminded me, the sheriff has a lot on her plate at the moment. If we can alleviate just a little of her stress, all the better."

"In the meantime, you manage to stay two steps ahead of her in this investigation. And what of Lila? Do you plan to keep her in the dark as well?"

He tapped the doorframe. "Lila will be told what she needs to hear in due course. I remain firm in my concerns that she's a ticking bomb." With that parting shot, he left the morgue.

An uncharacteristic urge to throw something at the wall

overwhelmed Olivia. What was it about the man that elicited such a violent response from her? She turned from the empty doorway, stomped over to her desk, and gathered her reports, ensuring that she had everything. Agent McCall hadn't been allowed near her desk, but she couldn't take the chance.

Everything in hand, she left the autopsy room, and headed toward her regular office. She wanted to add these new victims to her "murder" board. While she did that, she'd consider Agent McCall's *courteous* request to keep Ellie out of the loop a bit longer—or not.

She was leaning heavily toward the not.

ELIZABETH HAD NO more returned to her office than she was paid a visit.

"Agent McCall." She sat at her desk. "To what do I owe the displeasure of your visit today?"

The Illinois State Police investigator took a chair, uninvited, and lounged in it with his right ankle resting on his left knee. From her perch behind him, Bentley eyed the man.

"I came by to lend a helping hand," he said.

The hairs on Elizabeth's arms rose. She narrowed her eyes and leaned forward. "Helping hand for what?"

"Your department is feeling the strain of too many work hours and not enough deputies. I can be of assistance with the murder investigations while you juggle the duties with the flooding."

He wasn't wrong in his statement—she had ordered Rafe home for a few hours of sleep since he'd pulled a thirty-plus hour shift. Everyone in this department was running on fumes. No way she would ever concede that point to McCall.

Smiling, she sat back in her chair. "Appreciate the offer, but we've got things handled. The National Guard has arrived to assist with flooding, and my deputies are managing just fine *juggling* all their duties."

"Nice to hear the National Guard is on-site." He adjusted himself but remained in the chair. "I stand by my offer to assist with the murders."

"How do you know they're murders? I have yet to hear an official confirmation from the ME."

"Before coming here, I stopped by and had a chat with Dr. Remington-Thorpe. Both are murder victims."

Elizabeth clenched her jaw, her teeth grating against each other. A knock on the door saved her from saying something undiplomatic. Georgia entered carrying two steaming mugs of coffee. She handed one to Agent McCall and set Elizabeth's down in front of her hands. When Georgia released the mug, Elizabeth saw the small, yellow sticky note stuck to the side facing her.

Cecil is here.

Elizabeth caught the dispatcher's eye and motioned to bring the man into the office. With a wink, Georgia exited. Elizabeth lifted her mug and watched McCall over the brim.

"Twice now you've visited my ME in my absence. And twice you got vital information into my investigations before I did. Tell me, Agent McCall, is this how police work is done in Illinois? I'm barely a year into this sheriff job and I'm still learning the ropes. Seeing as I've spent the majority of my adult life bouncing from one military base or another all over the world, this is a new ballgame for me. So, you tell me how this investigation thing works."

He cocked his head to the side. He opened his mouth to speak but was deterred when Cecil Waterford, a mug in hand, entered.

"I see you're up to your old tricks, McCall," the handsome retired detective said.

McCall scowled and found interest in his coffee.

Cecil stepped up to Elizabeth's desk, hand outstretched. "Sheriff Benoit, pleasure to finally meet you in person."

She stood, shook his hand, and gestured for him to take the other open chair. "Pleasure is all mine." She resumed her seat. "It's nice to put a face with the voice. When she talks about Chicago, Lila speaks highly of you."

"As you know, I do the same of her." Cecil glanced at McCall. "What have I missed so far?"

Elizabeth stared at McCall. "Go ahead, Agent. You've seen fit to conduct your own investigation without my consent. Catch Mr. Waterford up to speed."

"There really is no need for this hostility, Sheriff," he countered. "This is how I do my job, and I do it exceptionally well."

"Until someone else pays for your mistakes," Cecil said and sipped his drink.

"Is there something you'd like to get off your chest, *Detective?*" McCall shifted in his chair to face the other man.

"There's plenty I'd like to say, but the good sheriff here doesn't have all day to listen to me run you down."

The men glared at each other. Elizabeth, much to her

surprise, was enjoying the battle. But her pleasure was short-lived as Georgia once again knocked on the open door and poked her head inside.

"Sheriff, I hate to interrupt, but would you mind stepping out here?"

Before leaving her desk, Elizabeth grabbed a quick sip of her coffee. "Please refrain from bloodshed. I need a clean and tidy office," she said to the men.

Five men stood along the bullpen railing dividing the deputies' workspace from the entry for the general public. Five men of whom Elizabeth was not ready to deal with—the mayors of the five incorporated towns of Eckardt County.

She wanted to groan.

She nodded to Jason McKinnley, the mayor of Three Points. "Gentlemen, how may I be of service?"

"Perhaps we should conduct this meeting in your office?" Randall Abbott, mayor of Juniper and the older of the five, said.

"Fortunately, my office is currently having another meeting and it would not fit all of us. How about we meet in the conference room down the hall?" Elizabeth glanced back at her dispatcher. "Georgia, if you would kindly escort them."

Lila chose that moment to enter the room. She halted in the entryway and eyed the men before her. All five stared back at her.

"Sheriff Benoit, I think it best that Deputy Dayne join our meeting," Jason said, sympathy lacing his statement. He had a soft spot when it came to Lila, due to the unfortunate circumstances of Lila finding his dearly departed mother.

Gauging by his request, Elizabeth knew it in her bones that Orville and Jim had squealed what Bo Cullen drunkenly blabbed about last night.

"Deputy Dayne, if you would step into my office."

The five mayors frowned, or glared in the case of Mayor Abbott, at Elizabeth as her deputy followed orders. Once she was out of sight, all five men broke into protest. Elizabeth jerked her hand up.

"Not a word out of any of you. If you are here about the flooding situation, I am happy to sit down with you and update you on the progress so far." She crossed her arms and leaned her weight onto her left leg. "If it is about any rumor or gossip spread about by a pair of Sheehan party-liners, then march yourselves right out of this department."

Each man glanced at the others, twitching and shifting. Elizabeth had her answer.

"We do need to coordinate on the flood efforts," Jason said.

"Then I suggest you all go take a seat with a cup of coffee in the conference room. Wait." She about-faced. "Georgia, if you would do the honors."

Elizabeth marched back into her office, slapping the door shut in her wake. Lila had chosen to stand in front of the trio of windows, her eyes fixed on Agent McCall.

Elizabeth cut a path between the woman and her adversary and sat at her desk. "Now that all three of you are here, I'm going to lay down the ground rules. Things are getting out of hand. There are procedures and chain of command being flagrantly violated." She zeroed in on Agent McCall. "And it will stop now."

"Sheriff—"

Elizabeth motioned for her to remain quiet.

After taking a healthy dose of coffee, she set her mug down on the desk, then placed her hands on each side of the ceramic container. "This is my county, Agent McCall. You answer to me. Or I'll see fit to call your superior and have a nice long chat with him or her about your lack of professional courtesy."

"Won't work," Lila muttered.

Elizabeth shot a heated look at her deputy. Lila tilted her chin in that stubborn way and stared back. There was a weight of meaning in that one expression that Elizabeth didn't have time to unpackage.

"Fine." She swung her gaze back to Agent McCall. "Step out of line again and Deputy Dayne has my permission to see to it you leave here permanently."

"Is that a threat, Sheriff?"

"It's a promise," Lila said from her perch.

"What she said." Elizabeth gripped her mug once more. "Is there something you need to relay to me, Agent McCall?"

McCall resumed his previous lounging position. "With the autopsies on the two bodies nearly completed and the ME almost certain that each victim belongs to the I-80 killer, it's time I bring you up to speed on these cases."

"You didn't tell her everything, did you?" Cecil asked.

"Why doesn't that surprise you?" Lila asked.

"I didn't find it necessary to concern the sheriff with an overload of case files," McCall shot back.

Elizabeth set her mug aside and leaned toward the men. "Mind filling me in on what it was that you didn't find *necessary* to concern me with?"

As the state police investigator revealed the extensive body count across the country, Elizabeth, for the first time since taking office, regretted her decision to be sheriff. Along with her regret came the humble pie. No wonder Lila was freaking out. As far as anyone knew, she was the only person who had ever survived this diabolical killer. With a body count of forty-three victims—and rising—that could be definitively contributed to the I-80 killer, the man was truly hellish.

Elizabeth slumped in her chair, staring at the still-talking Agent McCall. Her ears picked up at what he was saying, but her brain was still reeling. She raised her hands and waved. "Enough." She pointed at Lila. "You knew about how much of this?"

"Most. The only thing we don't have is the newer cases that occurred in the time after my attack." Lila's eyes narrowed. "And he won't cough up the files."

"Agent McCall?"

"She could have asked Iowa DCI for them at any time. The bodies were discovered in Iowa."

The blood drained from Elizabeth's face. She sagged forward onto her desk. "What?"

"Why wait for them to get around to sending them down? We both know you have the files with you," Lila snapped.

"There is a chain of custody that needs to be—"

"Screw your chain of custody bullshit," Lila lashed out.

Elizabeth pound a fist against her desk. "Enough!" She pushed to her feet. "Give us the files, Agent McCall. Once

I've been thoroughly brought up to speed from Dr. Remington-Thorpe, we will *all* go over the files and evidence thus far provided. And I do mean all of us."

McCall stared at Elizabeth, his face a blank slate. Here she thought she had the only law enforcement officers in the whole Midwest who looked at her like that and balked at her orders. At least her crew was respectful—well, except Fitzgerald on occasion—toward her. McCall's CO must eat a case of Tums on a daily basis.

Elizabeth turned to Cecil. "Detective Waterford, it has been brief but a pleasure, and I'd like to spend more time chatting."

Cecil nodded. "I'll keep an eye on them."

"See that you do." She backed from her desk. "I have a meeting with the mayors of this county. If you'll excuse me."

Elizabeth vacated the office, Bentley hot on her heels. From one hot frying pan into another.

CHAPTER SIXTEEN

L ILA IGNORED TATE'S glare and hurried after the sheriff down the department hallway. She caught Elizabeth's arm halfway across the hall.

"Sheriff, what's going on with the mayors?"

Elizabeth's star-bearing shoulders drooped. She gripped Lila's elbow and ushered her toward the restrooms. Bentley sat in place and watched them.

After glancing up and down the hall, Elizabeth leaned in closer. "For your ears only. During lunch today, Rafe and I learned that Bo Cullen got drunk last night and let it out what happened yesterday. Knowing the two men who questioned me on it, they spread it around before I heard about it. Now the mayors are going to play the concerned men ploy on me." Her gaze hardened. "I'm going to make them eat it."

Lila avoided her boss's gaze, her brows furrowing. "About me pulling my service weapon? Or about the body?"

"Probably both, but I'm leaning more toward the weapon incident."

She met Elizabeth's steady eyes. "I have a right to defend myself to them. I'll lay out the whole bloody details if that twists their balls."

Elizabeth shook her head. "No. As much as I'd like to see

you do that, let me handle this. Besides, Jason means well. I'm fairly certain he's on your side, but he has to do the political thing." The corner of her mouth kicked up. "And do I know how to do political."

"You're sure?"

Elizabeth gripped Lila's shoulder and squeezed. "Most certainly. Now go do what you do best. I mean it. If Agent McCall pulls any more crap, you twist his balls."

"With pleasure." Lila headed back to the sheriff's office. At the door, she turned and watched Elizabeth stride into the conference room across the hall.

"Gentlemen, where were we?"

Lila slipped into the office and pulled up short. Cecil and Tate were no longer alone. In the office was Kyle— Lundquist. She had to start calling him that again. Shaking from her mental lapse, Lila closed the door behind her.

"What's going on?" she asked.

"We have a big problem," Lundquist said.

LILA FOLLOWED LUNDQUIST to his desk, Cecil and Tate right behind her. Laid out in a strategic manner—the deeply trained portion of him that screamed navy—were photos he'd taken as he worked through the evidence. Lundquist had a nifty room at the hospital to run tests and samples before passing the evidence he'd gathered along to DCI.

Lila picked up one photo of women's clothing. "What's the problem?"

"It's not a problem per se, but this woman's ID might be

solved more quickly than our John Doe with the message," he said.

Lila caught Cecil's eye. Their prediction of the I-80 killer's victims being IDed faster because of missed details might be played out right here and now. It would give them a chance to corner Tate on the other cases she and Cecil had yet to see.

"You felt this garnered a hysterical reaction?" Tate sniped.

"Where it could *lead* to a problem," Lundquist interjected, "will be up to your determination when I tell you what I know."

"What is it that you know?" Tate's voice dripped of disdain.

Tamping down the urge to punch him again, Lila put her back to him. "Ignore him. Details."

After giving Tate a particularly cold stare, Lundquist focused on Lila. That spark or chemistry—hell, call it a thing that always happened between them when they worked a case—flared to life. It was like her brain was syncing with his to the same wavelength. The power of it pulsated through Lila, reviving her from the stupor she'd been wading through for the last forty-eight hours.

"You recall four months ago, we got a be on the lookout for a young woman from Coal Valley, Illinois? She'd gone missing three days before they put out the BOLO about her and her car?"

Lila squinted at him, racking her brain. "I vaguely recall something about it. Keep going."

"Is there a point to this?" Tate broke in.

"Shut your trap, McCall, or I'll shut it for you," Cecil growled.

With a glance at the irritating agent, Lundquist moved on. "I dug up the info on the BOLO, and that's why I'm here." He laid a printout of the BOLO next to the image of the woman's clothing.

Lila grabbed up both and read the details on the missing Martina Perez. Martina was a beautiful twenty-three-year-old woman with long, dark brown, wavy hair. Her smile was brilliant, her eyes twinkled. Her family had been thorough with the details of what she had been wearing the last time they saw her. It was the exact set of clothes in the photo. And the description of the car matched the one where they found the victim in the trunk.

There was more.

"Oh my God." Lila dropped the pages on the desk. "That's the problem." She met Lundquist's steady gaze. "Isn't it?"

"What is it?" Cecil asked.

"The woman was a few months pregnant when she went missing."

Lila's legs quaked. She grabbed the back of Lundquist's chair and steadied herself. "Did Dr. Remington-Thorpe find signs of a pregnancy?"

"She didn't say. From what I gathered from her when I picked up the evidence bags, she was still deep in the middle of the autopsy. As bad as the decomp was, I don't know how'd she be able to determine it."

"If this Ms. Perez was denied food and water before her death, it's likely she miscarried the baby before she was killed," Cecil pointed out.

Lila gritted her teeth at a flutter low in her abdomen. The muscles in her torso twitched at the ghost of a knife slicing through flesh and sinew.

"Or she was killed outright," Tate said. "Attacked the same way Deputy Dayne was."

She whirled on him. "Shut up."

Smug satisfaction passed through his eyes before he shut down. Lila pushed away from the desk chair and closed the gap between them. Tate backed as fast as she advanced until he smacked into the wall separating the sheriff's office from the rest of the bullpen. She kept four inches of separation between them, and her hands fisted at her sides.

"Speak again and I'll put you on the floor," she said through a clenched jaw.

His pupils dilated, but that was all the reaction she got from him. Backing away was the smartest move. Despite the urge she had to throat-punch him.

"Lila." Cecil placed a gentle hand on her arm and guided her back. "I think you and Deputy Lundquist need to take this new information to the ME and work from there. I'll inform the sheriff when she's through with her meeting."

Without taking her attention off Tate, she nodded. "Make sure you get those files from him."

"Don't worry. I will."

The rage leached from her body, leaving her more exhausted than she had been so far. But she refused to allow her bearing to sag or droop in any way. The moment Tate saw or even sensed her falter, he'd continue with the barrage. God, how she wanted to just turn his smug face into ground beef. She put her back to him.

"We'll take your vehicle," she said to Lundquist.

He gathered the photos and records and slid them into a file folder. With it tucked under his arm, he gestured for her to go first. As she departed, she gave into her baser self and gave Tate the middle finger salute.

She and Lundquist were partway down the hall when he took hold of her elbow and eased her to a halt. Low conversation drifted from the closed conference room three yards away.

"What is going on in there?" he asked, nodding at the door.

"Sheriff going toe-to-toe with the mayors."

"Over you?"

"Over everything." She freed her arm and continued walking. "I need to get out of here."

A blast of hot, muggy air hit her when she stepped outside. She took a few deep breaths of moisture-laden oxygen and winced. It smelled and tasted like muddy fish.

"That's what happens when the Mississippi floods," Lundquist said as he passed her.

They hurried to his car. Lila strapped herself in as he cranked up the AC. Before he left the parking lot, Lundquist grasped her hand and held it. She stiffened under the tender hold.

"Now that I see what he's really like, I don't understand what brought you two together."

Relaxing against the seat, she sighed. "He wasn't like that at first. The fissures started after he got me in the sack the second or third time. I was naive and apparently easily manipulated. Cecil was warning me, but I refused to listen." She looked down at their joined hands. "People like me are usually messed up in the head when it comes to love, because we've never known the reality of true love."

"Are you still that way?"

Lila slipped her hand from his and clenched it in her lap. Closing her eyes, she lowered her head. "I don't know."

He sighed. Seconds later, the gearshift moved and the car was in motion. Lila lifted her head and stared out the passenger-side window at the overly green and wet landscape flashing by.

Was she still that naive and easily manipulated woman of three years ago? Could she see real love if it stood right in front of her face?

Or was she forever doomed to be a walking disaster? Blowing up one good thing after another because she hadn't been able to hold onto the one thing that she thought mattered.

She pressed the knuckles of her clenched hand against her abdomen.

CHAPTER SEVENTEEN

ELIZABETH SAW TO the mayors' departures. That little BUB (battle update brief) went exactly as she expected. Mayor Abbott was like a drill sergeant with a stick up his ass, badgering Elizabeth left and right about Lila's slipup and what she planned to do about a rogue deputy. He could whine and moan all he wanted, but no way in hell would she ever air a person's dirty laundry to the likes of someone like Randall Abbott.

The man was a throwback to Sheehan's days, and how he kept his elected position was anyone's guess. He walked a thin line, hoodwinking the voters into believing he, too, was trying to clean up the town and, by default, the county. Elizabeth suspected Abbott was feeding intel to Sheehan, but she had no proof.

Assured that the men were well and truly out of her hair for the time being, she returned to her office via the side door. Halfway through the more than hour-long meeting, Bentley had escaped the conference room and was probably curled up at Georgia's feet, enjoying some long-desired loving. Lucky dog.

Elizabeth closed the door and turned for her desk. She let out a startled cry, her hand flying to her chest. "Damn it, Sheehan! What the hell?"

"You've certainly turned this little place into your bunker," he said, settling his right ankle on his left knee. The foot was encased in what looked like rattlesnake skinned boots. Only the devil would appreciate the irony.

"What are you doing here? And how the hell did you get in?" Elizabeth made her way behind her desk but refused to sit. Her guard was never relaxed around this man.

"I'm a concerned citizen who has every right to be allowed entry into these hallowed halls." He held up a blue file folder and tapped it against his bent leg. "I felt it vitally important to bring you this."

Elizabeth jutted her chin at the file. "What? You decided to come clean with the rest of your transgressions and came here to ask me to arrest you?"

His snake-like smile made her skin crawl. "Not likely." He tossed the file onto her desk.

Elizabeth stopped its steady slide toward her. "What is it?"

"Where's your illustrious detective?"

"Doing her job. Don't sidestep the question."

"When it comes to sheriff's work, you have a lot more to learn," Sheehan said as he examined his fingernails.

She glared at the crooked ex-sheriff, then grabbed up the file and shook it at him. "Have you been spying on us?"

"In a manner of speaking."

A chill crept through Elizabeth's veins. Was one of her own turning traitor? "You are out of line. You've seemed to have forgotten that you're no longer the sheriff."

"Once an LEO, always an LEO." He buffed his fingers on his jeans. "Or does that concept slip your grasp?"

"You're treading razor-thin ice there, *Kelley.*"

He snorted. Elizabeth's ire for the man jumped two notches.

"How did you even get this in the first place?"

He paused in cleaning his nails. "That information is confidential. Look at the bright side, Sheriff, you've just been handed a gold mine—well, maybe it's more like a copper mine for you."

The more he opened his mouth the stronger the cold built inside of her. It would be just like him to pick at the frayed edges of her deputies' loyalties to her and their positions. After all, it still had to burn that Fitzgerald and Rafe hadn't aligned with the sidewinder after Sheehan was overthrown. She still harbored a niggling suspicion that Ben Fitzgerald was living a double life.

Elizabeth narrowed her gaze, staring down Sheehan. Had he cornered the deputy and dragged their secrets out of him? To be frank, it was Ben who had been with Lila when she pulled her gun and nearly shot him and Bo Cullen. Given the right circumstances, Ben could gossip with the best of them.

What am I doing? This was not how a sheriff thought about her people. Damn Sheehan for making her go there.

A low chuckle thawed her bones.

She scowled. "Why should I trust you?"

"Now you're getting the knack of being an investigator." Sheehan stood, adjusted his black blazer, and smoothed down the neatly trimmed beard. "Happy reading."

"That's all you came here for. To give me this and lob another warning that I should listen to you?"

"A man knows when he is not welcome." He sauntered to the door exiting into the hall. "If I were you, I'd not leave that file where certain eyes might catch sight of it."

"For someone who was zealously vocal about his opinion on a woman's place in the world, you sure seem hell-bent on working with me."

Sheehan paused with the door opened wide enough for his escape and looked back at Elizabeth. "Give Deputy Dayne back her badge and gun." With that parting bit of wisdom, he disappeared behind the closed door.

Frowning at the varnished wooden barrier did little to ease Elizabeth's indignation. The sane side of her said to read the file and be done with it. What could Sheehan have possibly found to twist her into a million knots? But the petulant side of her said to hell with it. This was Kelley Sheehan. Nothing good ever came out of the man's mouth. God forbid he ever do anything out of the goodness of his heart.

"Georgia!"

The curly-haired dispatcher entered the office. "You bellowed?"

"Why was he allowed entry in here?"

"It was either sequester him in here or allow him access to your other guests."

"My other guests?"

Georgia stepped back, swinging to door open wider. Right beside her stood a National Guard solider—more precisely, a captain and her lieutenant.

Georgia introduced the two guard soldiers. "They're here with the guard unit seeing to the flood efforts."

Her composure regained and the file slid into a top drawer, Elizabeth gestured for the two to enter her office. "Georgia, no more visitors for today."

"Yes, ma'am."

With the door firmly closed behind the two officers, Elizabeth offered them a seat. "Apologies for my unprofessional voice. It's been a cluster from the moment the rain started."

The captain smiled. "I can see that."

"Let's coordinate how to attack this flood situation."

OLIVIA RETURNED TO her office to a pair of surprise visitors. Lila and Kyle were pouring over her murder walls. At least it wasn't that gaslighting agent this time.

"How long have you two been here?" she asked, dropping her lab coat and tablet on an empty chair.

"Since about the time you ran out of here to answer an urgent page from the clinic," Kyle said. He pointed at her desk. "We have a pretty solid ID on the car trunk victim."

Olivia picked up the missing flyer and scanned the contents. "How are you sure this is her? We haven't gotten a hit on DNA yet. We're at least another day away from being able to examine the bones."

"The clothes," Kyle stated, his attention never wavering from the wall. "What could possibly be so important to decapitate a human?"

"Special dental work that a simple teeth pulling won't resolve. Plates in the skull. Massive scar tissue to indicate surgery. Reconstructive surgery. Just about anything, right down to fury over being outwitted," Olivia said as she examined the evidence photos he'd included.

"Has anyone found the heads?" he asked.

"No," Lila answered. "That's probably the easiest thing to dump far from the interstate and have animals drag off."

Olivia looked up from her examination. "She's right. So why not do it with all the victims?"

Kyle's phone rang, pulling him away from the two women as he answered.

Lila wandered over to Olivia's desk. "Because he likes to be the one in control. The I-80 killer wants us to know he's the one in charge, and he'll do what he damn well pleases." She picked up the flyer. "Martina was pregnant when she went missing."

"Both I and the forensic anthropologist didn't see any indications of that."

"I was pregnant."

Olivia jolted at the admission. Lila's soulful eyes met her own. The grief buried deep inside this woman was glaring back at Olivia.

"He might not have known it at the time, but he made sure my baby never stood a chance. I, however, survived." She set the paper down and ran a finger over Martina's smiling face. "She and her baby were never going to be that lucky."

"Has anyone contacted the Coal Valley police to ask them for a DNA sample?"

"Already done," Kyle said as he returned his phone to a pocket. "DCI is running the sample right now. They called to tell me they have a match for our John Doe."

"So soon?" Lila asked.

"People are getting wiser," Olivia said. "If for one minute they suspect a family member is dead, missing, or on the run, they give the police DNA samples in the event anything might pop up over the databases. It's becoming more of a fascinating phenomenon in this day and age, because of true crime documentaries and those ancestry DNA kits."

Lila's lifted eyebrow and twitching mouth made Olivia grin. She truly did get carried away.

"Who is he?" Lila asked.

"Jordan Davis, thirty-eight, married, father of three. He was from Wichita, Kansas, went missing when he was on a trip to see his mother in Nebraska before she died from cancer." Kyle's voice cracked. He took a breath and sat in Olivia's office chair.

"She died never knowing what happened to her son," Lila said softly.

He nodded.

"I want to nail this bastard to the wall and do to him what he's done to countless families," Olivia said.

"You can't strip someone of their humanity if they never had it to begin with in the first place," Lila said. She moved to place a hand on Kyle's arm.

Olivia gave them a moment of privacy. There was an obvious connection between the two that needed cultivated, not scrutinized.

"Where's Agent McCall?" she asked a few minutes later.

"Hopefully, tied up with Cecil and out of our hair for the time being," Lila answered. "He has more files on other victims that we were not told about. Cecil is getting them from him."

"He relayed to me that there is a total of forty-three victims attributed to the I-80 killer," Olivia said.

"Two of those were left here in Iowa," Lila said. "He's never had a body drop in Iowa until after I moved here."

Olivia caught the stricken look on Kyle's face. This was news to him.

"Tate will have the autopsy reports and any other information Cecil wasn't able to get access to after he retired," Lila offered. "The sheriff ordered Tate to hand them over."

"Do you think he will?" Olivia asked.

"Yes, while pitching a hissy fit. Those victims were IDed as quickly as we've IDed these latest ones. That's not the I-80 killer's MO."

"You don't think it's him," Kyle blurted out.

"No. Cecil and I firmly believe it is him." Lila shrugged deeper into her hoodie.

"But?" He gestured for her to go on.

"But there might be an acolyte. And they might be working together."

Olivia clapped her hands together. "Oh, this makes a lot of sense." She hustled over to the murder wall with the more recent victims. "I don't mean to sound callous, Lila, but when were you attacked exactly?"

Lila gave her the date two years prior. Olivia poured over the information on her walls and found the last victim discovered a week before Lila was attacked.

"Why do you have more here than what the sheriff gave you?" Kyle asked, interrupting Olivia's ongoing inner monolog.

She turned to the deputy. "Because the state police agent was arrogant enough to reveal to me about the other victims, and I exploited my connections to get these reports. We don't need to wait for him to cough them up. I have everything here we need."

Lila smiled. "Should have known."

"Now, let's get cracking here." Olivia removed her notes from under each victim's profile. "We've got a lot of work to do."

CHAPTER EIGHTEEN

ELIZABETH SPENT THE afternoon with the National Guard unit captain, making sure flood relief work continued. For the remainder of the day, she got caught up on long overdue paperwork and other administrative duties. She'd checked in with Olivia twice, glad to hear that Dayne and Lundquist were working with the ME on cases. However, Olivia did relay that neither Cecil nor Agent McCall had shown up with the requested files. But it didn't matter, as Olivia had worked her magic and had all the information they needed. Elizabeth should have known better, and yet she wasn't surprised that McCall had not done as ordered.

The trio of her two deputies and the ME were staying mum on their findings, saying they weren't ready to relay what they were cobbling together. If the three of them could finally nail down a legit suspect, Elizabeth could deal with being left out of the loop for the time being.

Seven p.m. rolled around too fast. One minute she was signing off on equipment requisitions and firing range qualifications, the next Rafe was strolling into her office.

"Trying to do another all-nighter?" he asked, leaning a shoulder into the doorframe, his thumbs hooked into his duty belt, gunslinger fashion.

"Not really. It's been a hellish day. Between that state

police dick pulling rank, the mayors bitching at me, and waiting for new developments on our victims, I've reached my limit. Oh, yeah, Orville and Jim flapped their gums enough that the mayors caught wind of Lila's incident yesterday. I really need to track down Bo and chew his ass." She tossed down her pen and rubbed her aching fingers and wrist. "On the plus side, the National Guard took over flood control duties. I let the captain know you're our go-to guy for all things flood related."

"Great," he grunted.

"She's agreeable, won't walk all over you."

"You'd know. I'll trust you on that."

"They came at the right moment. There's more rain heading in overnight, and Red Rock and Saylorville are planning to release more water. I don't have the mental capacity to cope with everything going on and the flooding at the same time."

"I'll check in with her and make sure we're all on the same page. We may need to have more people evacuate." Rafe strolled into the office and headed for the chair across from her. "Speaking of the state police dick, where is he?"

Bentley scrabbled off her throne and wiggled her way in between Rafe's knees, her bushy tail wagging as he paid attention to her.

"I'm not sure. I haven't seen him since noonish when I had to rip him a new one. He left here with Lila's retired detective friend, and I haven't heard a peep from either of them. And according to Olivia, neither of them has shown up with the requested files. McCall, I can see pulling that, but not Cecil."

"Maybe they're chasing a lead?"

"Maybe, but you'd think he'd call. Is Georgia still here?"

"Nope. Alexis is on her way in."

Elizabeth shuffled through the small stack of missed call slips and notes Georgia had given her throughout the afternoon. There was nothing from McCall or Waterford. "Odd."

"Has Dayne heard from them?"

"She didn't indicate she had. She's been with Lundquist and Olivia all afternoon."

Bentley placed a paw on Rafe's knee when he hesitated in scratching her ears.

"I could head out to the Miller B and B and see if both men are there," he said.

"No. Don't bother them. I like Cecil. He's an asset to Lila. That being said, the less I have to deal with that asshat state cop, the better I feel. If something comes up, one or both of them will make their presence known." Elizabeth rubbed her face and rocked back in her chair. "Who's on duty tonight?"

"Fitzgerald, Young, and me. I'm pulling Meyer in to-morrow. You have his re-quals scheduled?"

She held up the signed sheet. "Right here. The state should give me a date and time by end of day tomorrow or Wednesday. Mentally, is he ready to go back to full duty?"

"Not my call. That's for the head doctor to decide. But from personal observation, yes, I think he is."

Elizabeth sighed. "Good. I need to talk with Olivia again. I think I'll just mosey on over to her office and see what the three of them are up to."

"Actually, maybe you should head to the bar. I think Bo Cullen should take priority tonight."

"How do you know Bo is at the bar?"

Rafe smiled as he gave Bentley one more good head rub and stood. "Have my sources. I think the sheriff cornering him and lecturing him is going to go off better than a lowly undersheriff."

"Maybe. And then again, maybe not."

THE BAR IN question was not The Watering Hole, Marnie's establishment, but an antique place called the Dew Drop Inn located in a little unincorporated town known as Soap Creek, just north of Three Points. Soap Creek consisted of the Dew Drop Inn, a handful of houses, and an ancient one-room schoolhouse. In its heyday, the Dew Drop also served as a true inn, a general store, and the post office. During Prohibition, the Dew Drop did steady business selling illegal moonshine and cheap, watered-down beer while the inn portion and the post office floundered. Once Prohibition ended, the Dew Drop was back and running, with a few extra under-the-table perks of the illegal kind. Over the years it got a few upgrades, but for the most part, the bar still looked like a throwback to the 1870s.

During her teen years, Elizabeth, along with a good majority of her classmates, spent a lot of time throwing cow-pasture beer parties on the fringes of Soap Creek. They bought the beer, and on occasion liquor, at the Dew Drop, always supplied by one of two legal adults who kept the rowdy teens well-oiled with booze and acted as lookouts for parents. Three-fourths of the time, the deputies during those years joined in on the parties. Elizabeth suspected, although she never participated herself, that there were plenty of drugs floating around those parties as well.

Today's teens were most certainly trying to keep up the tradition. Elizabeth usually had Rafe or Fitzgerald patrol this area, checking for the parties. However, since she took office as sheriff, the gatherings seemed to disappear. Whether this was because the kids were getting wind of the patrols and found new places to hide out or the urge to drink and get high was going down as more kids got smarter about the repercussions, she didn't know. Either way, the recent rains and flooding had most likely dampened the kids' spirit of illegal mischief.

Elizabeth guided her Ford Interceptor into the Dew Drop's gravel lot and parked it near the entrance. The Interceptor's headlights lit up Bo's truck. Rafe was right again. Elizabeth killed the engine and exited the SUV with Bentley on her heels.

Thunder rumbled from the darkened sky. The next round was on its way. She hoped it would hold off until after she completed her task.

The murmur of voices hesitated momentarily when she and Bentley were spotted, but once the patrons of the half-filled bar figured out who had entered their sanctuary, they went back to their conversations. Where Marnie's bar catered more to a younger crowd and a more upscale type of clientele altogether, the Dew Drop was the locals' bar—farmers and factory workers, bums and the unemployed preferred to come here. If the owner of the Dew Drop was still into the drug trade—which, by the looks of some of the half-stoned gazes in the room that was true—it was the main reason people came out of their way to visit the bar.

Three HD TVs hung above the bar, all three playing a different baseball game. Some of the men were watching the games, but mostly people were drowning some problem or another in their beers. Which was what it looked like Bo Cullen was doing. With his head propped up by both hands, he sat alone at a small table, staring deep at the top of a beer bottle, six other bottles standing at attention next to his left elbow.

Sighing, Elizabeth marched over to his table. She grabbed a nearby chair and plopped right beside him. Bentley rounded the chair and sat on Elizabeth's left side.

Bo lifted his head and blinked at her. His eyes were dilated, and he acted like he couldn't control his head as it wobbled around. "Sheriff?" he slurred.

"Bo." She took the bottle and set it aside with the others. "Does your daddy know you're here?"

"He's still in the hospital." How he got that full sentence out was a miracle.

"I know. I called to check on him. He tells me you haven't been in to see him. Why's that?"

"I've got to ..." He settled his cheek on his hand and slumped. Through his half-closed lids, his eyes did an odd shake.

"Bo, did you take something?" This was not typical drunk behavior.

"No," he said but nodded. The exaggerated head bob

threw him off-balance, and he tipped forward.

Elizabeth caught him as he tumbled toward her. She hoisted him up and back into his chair, leaving a hand on his chest to steady him. "I'm going to have someone come get you."

"No-no-no-no …" He trailed off as his head rocked back and connected with the chair.

Elizabeth jerked her cell phone out of her uniform pocket and put in a call to Alexis, then ordered a patch-through to Rafe.

"Yes?" he asked.

"Make your way to the Dew Drop. Bo needs to dry out in the tank."

"Halfway there," he answered and signed off.

As she was returning her phone to the pocket, Bo lifted his head and leveled his gaze on her. Though his pupils were still extremely dilated, there was a clearness to his eyes. In that second, Elizabeth's hackles went up.

"Sheriff, why are you here?" he asked with a clarity that hadn't been there moments ago.

"I came to talk with you, Bo."

He frowned. "Why?"

"Because you broke your word to me. You were speaking out of turn about the events of yesterday."

He sniffed. "I don't know what you're talkin' 'bout." His head bobbled again, and the clarity was beginning to fade.

She reached out and grasped his callused hand he'd laid on the tabletop. "Bo, look at me." When he did, she squeezed his hand. "You do know what I'm talking about. When you've been drinking and abusing drugs, things can easily be said and spread around. What would your daddy have to say about that?"

He mumbled something that Elizabeth missed, but she thought it was the verbal equivalent of the middle finger about Bill. The younger Cullen jerked his hand from hers and tried to rise, succeeding only in losing his balance and plopping down on the seat.

"It appears that we're not going to get anywhere." Elizabeth rose as Bo tried again and settled a heavy hand on his shoulder. "Stay seated." She pushed him down.

A low growl from Bentley gave warning. Elizabeth looked over her shoulder and swore she felt her blood pressure hit an all-time high. What the hell were Orville and Jim doing here?

"Sheriff, what's all this hubbub about?" Orville, the spokesperson, hooked his thumbs behind the straps of his overalls and stuck out his protruding gut. "Are you harassing young Mr. Cullen here?"

"Orville, so help me God, if you interfere, I'll have you arrested." Elizabeth shoved Bo down again as he struggled to rise. "Bo, keep your ass in that seat."

"I need to piss," Bo whined.

"Can you hold it?" she pressed. Where the hell was Rafe?

"Sheriff, you better let him use the men's facilities," Orville said.

Jim snorted. "Yeah, ya better. He done pissed all over himself last night."

Elizabeth rolled her eyes. "Oh, for the love of God."

"I did not!" Bo yelled at Jim.

The older men sniggered. That was enough for Bo. With

an ungodly strength honed by hours of farm work, he bolted from that chair, shaking loose of Elizabeth's hold, and charged at the two men. Bentley barked and rounded the table, putting herself between Elizabeth and the men.

The hours of work, stress, and lack of sleep held her in place, as, dumbfounded, she watched Bo deck Jim in the jaw. While Jim reeled from the blow, Bo moved on herky-jerky legs and slammed his fist into Orville's ample gut. There was a brief pause as the air was sucked from the room, the only sounds coming from the TV baseball games.

Someone let out a shout, and all hell broke loose.

"Ah, shit!"

Elizabeth ducked a flying beer bottle. She caught movement behind the bar and watched, aghast, as the bartender hid behind the bar. So much for law and order.

Feet away, Bo and Jim were slugging it out while Orville remained bent over, gagging and gasping for air. The bigger the mouth, the harder they fell. Elizabeth circled the table and managed to grab Bo's hand as he brought it back for another punch. She tossed him aside, at the same time deflecting Jim's sloppily thrown fist. She slammed her boot heel down on his foot, earning a howl from the bastard. With Jim out of the mix, Elizabeth turned her focus on the raging Bo.

All around them the fight continued, but Elizabeth ignored it as she slung Bo around and slammed him face down on the table, scattering his beer bottles. He bucked against her hold, and she was thrown back, losing her grip on his arms. As he went to push off the table, a hand settled on the back of his head and smashed his face into the wood. Flecks of blood splattered across the top.

Elizabeth glared at Sheehan. "What the hell are you doing here?"

"Apparently, helping you out." He nodded at the squirming Bo. "Cuff him, Sheriff."

She hurried to do so, but a beefy hand on her arm intercepted her. To her shock and dismay, Sheehan's free hand shot out, a pistol in his grasp.

"Unhand the sheriff, Orville."

The man did as ordered and backed off with hands raised. Elizabeth quickly cuffed Bo. She'd no sooner done that when the bar door slammed shut.

"Enough!" Rafe bellowed.

Silence descended as the brawlers stopped mid-fight. Sheehan quickly holstered his weapon. From behind the bar, the bartender popped up and pointed an accusing finger at the trio of men under Elizabeth's and Sheehan's watch.

Rafe's gaze met hers, one of his eyebrows lifted in question. She shook her head. This was one situation she wasn't sure how to explain. With a huff, Rafe began barking orders at the dissenters.

Elizabeth took hold of Bo's cuffed arms and lifted him from the table, grimacing when she realized he'd passed out. The odor of urine assaulted her at the same moment. "Aww, damn it."

She noticed the wry smile on Sheehan. "Not a word from you."

"Perhaps a thank-you would be in order."

Flinching at his point, she sighed. "I appreciate the assist ... Kelley."

"Close," he said and sauntered to the door. "By the way, I usually stripped them of their pissed-on clothing before throwing them in the back of the squad vehicle. Not sure if that would grate on your woman's sensibilities."

"Oh, not one bit."

With a two-finger salute, Sheehan exited.

Rafe joined her, looking at the now-snoring Bo. "Do you want me to take him?"

"Watch yourself. He urinated."

While Rafe found a way to get Bo out of the bar, Elizabeth directed her attention on the two who had caused the fight. Jim kept his head down, letting the blood from his nose drip on the floor. Orville massaged his gut.

"Would either of you care to press charges against Bo Cullen?"

Jim lifted his head enough to peek at Orville. Something unspoken passed between the two, and they shook their heads.

"Good. I thought not." Elizabeth inched closer to the two. "If I see hide or hair of either of you for the rest of this week, I will make it a point to have Bo or the bar's owner press charges for harassment. Get your shit. And get out."

Both nodded and scurried out of the bar.

Elizabeth assessed the carnage, noting with glee that Rafe had put the brawlers to work cleaning up the bar. She crossed the floor in a few strides and hit the bar top. The tender flinched and shifted closer to her.

"If I were you and I wanted to stay in business, I'd be getting rid of your little side business. Don't and I'll be making your life a living hell until this mess is cleaned out of here. Get my drift?"

"Yes, ma'am."

"Good. Make sure these delinquents get your bar back in order." With that final order, Elizabeth exited.

She drew in a huge breath of hot, humid air and shuddered. Bentley trotted over to the Interceptor and sat, waiting for her. Rafe was gone. Good. Hopefully, Bo would dry out and/or detox from whatever he had and tomorrow she could get somewhere with him. Poor Bill. That son of his was turning out to be a disappointment. Which was a crying shame, as Bo had never shown any inclination toward drug abuse.

As she took a step toward her SUV, a shadow emerged from the dark side of the bar. Elizabeth jolted when Sheehan blocked her path.

"Why do you keep doing that?" she demanded.

"Why are you so shocked to see me?"

"I thought you left. But you're still here. Whatever for?"

He reached inside his blazer pocket and withdrew a plastic-wrapped toothpick. He took his sweet time unwrapping it, flicking the plastic sleeve into the wind and then placing the pick in his mouth.

"Patience is a virtue, Sheriff." He smiled around the toothpick. "I see you've gained your wings."

"I'm leaving." She sidestepped him only to have him move with her. "Damn it, Kelley. I will not be ambushed by your crap."

"Have you given Deputy Dayne back her service weapon and badge?"

"Why do you care so much?"

He stared at her. The fall of shadows over his eyes made them look like the pits of hell. "Have you read the file?"

"I didn't have time. After you left, I had a meeting with the National Guard unit commander. Then I came here."

Sheehan rolled the pick to the opposite side of his mouth. "You might never have approved of my methods, but if you disregard my warnings, there will be hell to pay. *Sheriff.*"

"I never said I wouldn't heed them. I haven't had time. Nor have I seen Deputy Dayne lately." Elizabeth crossed her arms and regarded the man. "Why are you so hell-bent on me taking your bits of wisdom seriously?"

"Do or don't. That's up to you. But don't say I didn't warn you." He walked around her and strolled back into the bar.

Elizabeth took a step to follow Sheehan when Bentley let out a whine. Sighing, she turned back to her faithful companion. Yeah, they needed to go home and get some sleep.

Sheehan's dire warnings would have to wait.

CHAPTER NINETEEN

L ILA CALLED IT a night around eleven-thirty. Their trio had pulled together a lot of new information and managed to cobble it together into some semblance of order, but as the night dragged on, things were getting fuzzy. Dr. Remington-Thorpe locked her office and headed home.

Kyle drove Lila back to the department to get her vehicle. Silence accompanied them the entire drive. Lila was feeling every minute of her three long days and lack of sleep. Her body ached in a way that reminded her of being sick with the flu. The constant rumble of thunder warned that sleep wasn't going to come easily for her again tonight.

She dragged her gaze from the window and looked at Kyle. The dashboard lights showered his stoic and stern features in green and red lights. He was focused on driving. A different kind of ache took over Lila, one that came from her heart.

He pulled into the department lot and parked his vehicle next to hers, right under the single light. Lila didn't move to exit. Kyle turned to her, a frown marring his handsome face.

"I'm sorry," she whispered, her voice cracking.

She grabbed the handle and bailed from the car.

"Lila!"

She was halfway around the back end of her car when he

caught up with her.

"Whoa, wait." He drew her around. "What do you mean?"

With her lip firmly tucked between her teeth, she stared at him. Heat was building in her eyes, and she refused to let him see her like this. She bit down on her lip, the pain stemming the tide.

Kyle cradled a callused hand against her cheek, his fingers threading through her hair. "You can't leave me hanging like that."

Lila closed her eyes and leaned into his hold. Against her will, she lifted her hands and placed them against his chest. The feel of his heart beating into her palm made her shiver.

"Talk to me," he whispered, leaning closer.

She couldn't. If she did, she'd lose what small thread of control she had on her emotions.

Thunder rumbled, and she flinched. Kyle cupped her face in his hands. She stared at his face, searching for something to give her reason to push him away and leave. The only thing she saw were deep worry lines. She dropped her gaze and closed her eyes.

"You shouldn't be alone," he said.

Lila shook her head, freeing her from his hold. Drawing in a deep breath gave her more sense of control. She let it out slowly. "I have to be."

She was pulling from him when he grasped her head again. She opened her mouth to protest, but he claimed her lips. His kiss was equal parts tender and possessive. Lila melted into it, her hands fisting his shirt and drawing him closer.

A sharp crack of thunder jolted her. She retreated from Kyle, her chest rising and falling in rapid succession. He went to reach for her again, and she held up her hand, putting more distance between them.

"I need to think." She hurried to the driver's side and unlocked her car. She made the mistake of looking at him as she started to enter the car.

The stricken expression tore at her.

She placed a hand on the car roof. "We'll talk in the morning. Please, Kyle."

He gave her a hesitant nod and returned to his vehicle.

Before she lost her resolve, Lila slid into the car and locked the doors. She started the engine and backed out of her spot.

Kyle watched her leave.

Out on the street, Lila pointed her car for home. Once she was far enough down the road, she struck the steering wheel.

"Damn you! Damn you, Tate, for ruining me!"

OLIVIA ENTERED THE house, hung her keys on the hooks over the entryway table, and set her things aside. Dim lighting was coming from the living room area. Dominic should be in bed, so she went to investigate.

Her husband was not tucked up in the master bedroom. He was crashed out on their living room sofa, charts scattered all over the glass coffee table and his chest.

Olivia smiled. A soft snore escaped Dominic's lips as she

removed the patient files from him. She was closing the opened one when a name caught her attention. Assuring herself that Dominic was truly and deeply sleeping, Olivia brought the file closer to read.

Marnie had been Dominic's patient? She'd had a hysterectomy. Why?

"Liv, what are you doing?"

She slapped the chart shut and dropped it like it was on fire. "Nothing."

Dominic, through sleepy eyes, glared at her. "You can't lie. Why are you reading my charts?"

"I didn't mean to. It just …"

With a growl, he pushed to his feet. "You and I both agreed that we'd never cross patient and doctor privileges. Ever." He gathered his charts.

"We did agree to that. However, you crossed the line when you told me about Lila." Olivia jabbed a finger at Marnie's file. "Tit for tat."

Dominic stared at her slacked jaw. For a single heartbeat, Olivia regretted her childish retort. Then his features hardened, and her regret disappeared.

"What I shared with you about Lila pertained to the cases you are working on. This"—he wagged Marnie's file—"has nothing to do with those cases." He slapped the chart down on the pile in his arms. "I thought you better than this, Olivia."

"Same could be said for you."

"And what is that supposed to mean?"

"You're the only one who has constant access to my phone, maybe you're the one who turned off my notifications. Copies of my test requisitions are missing. You were the last one in the morgue, and they're now gone."

The shocked expression on Dominic's face set Olivia back on her heels. What had she done?

"I'm not even going to grace any of that with a comment. I'll sleep in the spare bedroom." With his charts in arm, Dominic left the living room.

Olivia gulped down the despair clawing at her throat and sank onto the sofa. She stared at the empty coffee table, reliving her disastrous conversation. Dominic was right. Where had that come from? Hadn't she assured herself that it wasn't possible for him to have done any of what she accused him of?

Maybe she hadn't really. She groaned and buried her face in her hands.

What was wrong with her?

Olivia dragged her hands into her lap and flopped against the sofa back. She was tired, mentally worn out, and walking a razor's edge. Her accusations should have been lobbed at Agent Tate McCall. So why hadn't she done that the last time he paid her a surprise visit?

Because Ellie's unintentional mention of Dominic's involvement weighed more heavily in Olivia's mind than some outsider. Because Olivia felt the need to glean more information from the arrogant agent outweighed her suspicions.

She was a fool.

Sleeping this off was the best course of action. She stood and turned off the chair-side lamp. She'd apologize to Dominic in the morning.

Hopefully, he would be in a willing mood to accept it.

LILA DECIDED A long drive before going home was in order. She had to clear her head. Twenty minutes after leaving Kyle at the department, she was on a county road north of Juniper when there was a loud *whap* and the steering became difficult.

Muttering a few choice words, she manhandled the car to the side of the road, managing to get it off the pavement and into a field accessway. She turned off the engine and popped the hood, exiting the car with flashlight in hand.

"I just had this damn thing in the shop," she railed as she thrust up the hood. "How the hell did they miss this?" Whatever *this* was.

She directed the beam at the place where a belt should have been. It lay slack on the closest pulley to her. She grabbed the belt and pulled it out until a frayed end appeared.

"Shit." She flung the useless belt back at the engine.

Lila stomped to the open car door and took her phone out of the cupholder. No *G*s. No bars. No damn reception. Which meant no call. No texts. No way to contact someone for help. So much for a good coverage plan.

"Damn it!"

She tossed the phone at her seat and sagged against the car roof. How was she getting home? She couldn't drive this thing back safely; it would damage too many internal parts to the engine. She rocked back and studied the road in both directions. Walk to the nearest house? Or sit here and wait for someone to come along? That could take a while. Walk it was.

A ripple of light made her jerk. She looked to the sky just as a loud crack of thunder shook the earth.

"Are you freaking kidding me?"

After all the noise and light show for the last three hours, it was finally going to rain. The first drops hit the car roof. Grumbling, she slid back inside the car and slammed the door shut. Well, no walking anywhere.

Lila twitched with each crack of thunder, but for the most part she maintained her composure. The rainfall increased until a sheet of water hit the car. The drops were so big and heavy it sounded like hail whacking against the car body.

Looked like she was waiting on someone to drive up the road. Who that would be at this time of the night was anyone's guess. She turned the key to the battery and dialed in a radio station playing old rock songs she'd heard as a kid. Lila watched the light show in the sky. She wasn't panicking or reliving the attack. Odd. It still made her tremble, but she wasn't losing her mind.

As the storm continued, she let her eyes drift shut. She could still feel the urgency in Kyle's kiss. See the expression on his face when she left him. It tore her to pieces all over again.

Had he fallen in love with her? God, she hoped not. She accepted that a relationship with him was okay for her. But love? Her fling with him was never about love.

A slew of commercials distracted her. She changed the stations until she landed on one playing that hillbilly country most of the folks around here liked to listen to and left it there. She checked up and down the road for any travelers. Empty.

Lila leaned her seat back and stared at the fabric-covered ceiling.

She liked Kyle. A lot. She liked working with him. Partnering with him on cases. But she could never love him. Hadn't she explained why that was true? He crossed her as the type wanting a huge family. Little Lundquists running around calling him Daddy.

When they first hooked up and he saw the scars, she'd warned him, begged him to understand. This hookup could be only that.

Tate had stained her soul. But her attacker had taken it.

A loud bang jolted Lila upright with a squeak. That crack sounded like it was right on top of her. She adjusted the seat and hunkered her shivering body down inside her hoodie. This was getting ridiculous. She checked the clock. She had been sitting here for nearly thirty minutes.

"Ugh!"

Damn engine belt.

A halo of light appeared in her rearview mirror. Lila turned the radio down and twisted around. Someone was coming. Could it be true? A pair of headlights, sitting high off the ground, drew closer. Over the sound of the downpour, she made out the noise of a diesel engine. Rescued!

She turned off the battery, palmed her keys, and hopped out of the car. Through the deluge, she waved at the oncoming semitruck and trailer. The driver applied the brakes and the air brakes, slowing the big rig and dimming the headlights.

"Yes."

The semi would have a radio she could use to hail Alexis and get help out here for her car.

The driver pulled the rig to the side of the road behind her car and parked. Lila hurried over to the driver's side, hand shielding her eyes from the heavy rain. The cab door opened and the driver, wearing a raincoat with the hood up, jumped down. Lila couldn't make out any of his features.

"Having problems?" he asked over the sound of the engine and rain. Through it, Lila picked up the Southern drawl.

"Yes. A belt broke in my car. Can I use your radio to call for help?"

"Sure," he said and stepped aside for her to move past him.

"Thanks. I can't tell you how glad I am to see you. Thought I would be stuck out here all night." She grabbed the handrail on the cab. "I'm an Eckardt County deputy. I'll just radio the department."

"No problem, darling."

Lila froze at the endearment. Her raised foot slammed into the puddle forming on the roadside. She turned to look at the driver. "What did you say?"

The raincoat hood obscured his face, leaving him in deep shadows. Fear pulsated through Lila. He took a step toward her. She released the handrail and retreated.

She reached for her sidearm and found nothing. Where was it? Shit! She'd left her backups at home and her issued weapon was surrendered to the sheriff.

"Stay back."

His hand disappeared inside the hood. Lila heard the shushing sound.

"Hush, my darling."

She bolted, running for the rear of the trailer, looking for anything to use as a weapon. The slick gravel on the shoulder tripped her up. She went down on a knee. The impact rattled her.

He was advancing but not as fast as she'd expect. He was stalking her.

Lila scrambled to her feet and ran into the middle of the road, circling him until she got into the beam of light from his truck. Her chest heaving with each breath, she faced him. He would not take her without a fight. This time she was better prepared.

He came out onto the road with her. He jerked his hand down and a long baton appeared.

No knife this time.

Lila settled into a fighter's stance. Water poured down her face, but she wouldn't let it get to her. He kept the raincoat hood up, giving him the advantage of keeping the rain off his face and making sure she never saw him.

"You don't get to take me down twice," she yelled.

No response from him. He circled to his left, and Lila countered, maintaining a safe distance from him. He continued going until she had her back to the truck.

"Why me? What the hell did I do that made you want me?"

He canted his head to the side. "You were damaged goods."

Her hands dropped. "What?"

The prick of something on her neck startled Lila. But she didn't have a chance to react as waves of electrical energy lanced her body. Her legs buckled, and she went down but didn't hit the pavement. Someone grabbed her.

She stared at the hooded man yards away, her brain unable to wrap around what was happening to her.

"Hush, my darling. It will all be okay."

That voice. That was the voice! She wanted to scream, but she couldn't get her mouth to open or force the air from her lungs.

Something warm and tingling filled her. Her muscles unlocked and her eyelids grew heavy.

"I will take you away from all of this," he said.

No! Lila tried to utter the word. Instead, she sank into oblivion.

CHAPTER TWENTY

Day 3: Tuesday Morning

ELIZABETH HAD SLEPT. It wasn't the sleep of the dead, but at least she could be thankful for some rest.

Her morning started out with Bentley taking her for a jog in the dark. Back home, Elizabeth enjoyed a cup of coffee in the peace and quiet while Bentley ate her breakfast. They got ready for work and left just as the gray skies were lighting up. For one day, she'd love to see the sun again.

An eerie silence greeted her at the department. Bentley crept along the hallway, her nose plastered to the floor, drawing in all the scents. Elizabeth bypassed her usual entry into her office and headed straight for the bullpen. Georgia was at her station, and Rafe was bent over his desk.

The undersheriff tilted his head to the side and regarded Elizabeth. "He's still sleeping it off."

"You're certain he's sleeping?"

"I just checked on him twenty minutes ago. Still breathing."

Elizabeth poured a fresh mug of coffee and snagged a chocolate-frosted chocolate cake donut from the pastry box. "Georgia, if you keep bringing these in, we're all going to fail to pass our physicals."

"One does not need to eat the whole box to themselves,

Sheriff." Georgia continued to type at her computer.

Elizabeth bit into her donut and made a face at the dispatcher.

"I saw that."

"Did you get any sleep?" Rafe asked.

She washed down the donut with a sip of coffee. "I did."

Elizabeth turned to her office, Sheehan's warnings echoing in her head. Abandoning the two for her inner sanctum, she went behind her desk and pulled open the drawer where she had stashed the file.

It was gone.

Elizabeth set her mug down and ransacked the drawer. Gone!

"Georgia!" She stalked to the doorway.

The dispatcher rose from her chair, her features pinched. "Something wrong?"

"Has anyone been in my office since you got in?"

"No."

"Call Alexis. Now."

Her eyes wide, Georgia did as ordered.

Rafe wandered over. "What's wrong?"

"Sheehan gave me a file yesterday. I didn't have a chance to read it because the National Guard commander came in. I put it in a drawer, and now it's gone."

"Why would Sheehan be giving you a file?"

"Because apparently it had some vital information about whatever the hell has been going on around here."

"Why would he give you something like that?"

"I don't know. It's Kelley. Why does he do half the things he does?"

"Are you sure you put it in your drawer?"

"Yes. It was a blue folder. You couldn't miss it. And it's gone."

Georgia lowered the phone and placed it against her chest. "Sheriff, she says no one ever set foot in your office all night."

"She's certain? Someone could have slipped inside while she was using the restroom."

"How?" Rafe and Georgia asked.

How was right. Entry into the department at night was restricted to those on duty and department personnel with keycard passes. Elizabeth had a state-of-the-art security system put in after she took office. In fact, the whole building had been upgraded to prevent unauthorized entries.

"Rafe, pull the security video. Let's see if my thief was aware they were caught."

"Uh, Ellie." Georgia pointed at her computer monitor. "Bo is awake."

"I'll go talk with him. You two find out if we had a B and E last night."

"Is that file the only thing missing?" Rafe asked.

Elizabeth returned to her desk and went through the drawers. Everything seemed in order, except for the file. She changed course direction and unlocked her metal filing cabinet. The first two drawers didn't appear to have anything missing. At the third drawer she nearly threw up her coffee and donut.

"Oh my God."

"What?" Rafe asked.

"Lila's badge and gun are gone."

"Impossible."

She slammed the drawer shut. "Footage. Find this bastard."

THE HEAVY SCENT of loam penetrated Lila's muddled brain.

Oh God, her head hurt. Scratch that. Everything hurt. She shifted and something crumbly brushed against her cheek. She was belly down on whatever she was lying on. Curling her fingers inward brought up a pile of that crumbly stuff. She blinked her eyes open only to be met with blackness. Closing them, she remained in her horizontal position.

She was tired. So tired. Why the hell was she this tired?

Lila gave into the pull of sleep.

When she next became aware, she felt jolts of pain rippling through her neck and shoulders. Groaning, she rolled onto her back and laid there, listening. Silence. No raindrops. No wind. Not even the sound of the bubbling water in Gerry's tank.

Her senses cleared more, and the scent of earth enveloped her. Where the hell was she? She peeled her eyelids open and blinked in the darkness. This was not her bedroom.

She patted the solid surface under her, stirring loose dirt. That explained the earthy smell. Lila touched her clothing. They were damp. She found the end of a string, her hoodie string. She was still wearing it? Getting her hands under her was a fumbling mess, but she eventually did it and sat up. She felt … drugged.

Light-headed, she remained sitting as the world inside her head tilted on its axis. When it was righted once more, she peered through the blackness, trying to get a handle on where she was and what she was doing here.

A memory of headlights flashed through her mind. Lila squeezed her eyes shut. Rain pounded the pavement. A shadowy figure stood on the edge of her sight. She opened her eyes.

"No," she croaked.

This was not the time to be doing this. She had to figure out where she was. Memories could wait.

She pulled her feet under her and froze. Her boots were gone. She was barefooted. Ignoring that thought, she rolled onto her knees and went to stand only to smack her head into a solid obstacle.

"Ow." She slumped to her knees, cradling her head, and looked up. Unable to make out what it was, she reached up and her fingers touched wood. She ran her hands along it, discovering wide, thick slats covering the breadth of her reach.

Based on what she could feel in the dark, she guessed she had enough room to stand bent over. How far? How big was this place? God, if she could only get some light.

Her phone. She searched her pockets. Gone. Why didn't that surprise her? She was missing her boots and socks. Another thought crossed her mind. Her phone was left in her car. Which now begged the question, where was her car?

Obviously not here with her. Wherever here was.

Lila carefully rose until she was inches from the wood slats. Then with one hand touching the wood and the other sweeping back and forth in front of her, she moved forward until her fingers brushed against a wall of dirt. She felt her way along the wall, going about six more feet until meeting another wall. Then she went back the way she came, counting her steps, stopping when her hand met yet another wall.

"Twelve feet," she muttered.

Above her, the ceiling remained solid wooden slates. As she followed the second sidewall, she again counted her steps. In front of her, a sliver of light peeked through. She hurried forward and found a seam in the wood. Probing the seam determined it was a trap door. Lila pushed up, but the door didn't budge. She positioned her body under it and pressed her back into the wood and thrust upward. The door was heavy, but it shifted an inch and rattled something above.

Lila dropped to her knees and stared up. She was locked inside a cellar-like pit. Why? And how?

Another flash of memory hit her. Those words. Three horrific words.

Stifling the cry tearing at her throat, Lila curled into herself. He had her. The I-80 killer had found her, and he'd taken her.

Lila sat there, rocking and sucking air as she stifled the urge to endlessly scream. Her chest ached from the restraint.

How had she allowed this to happen? She had trained to protect herself. Hours, days, weeks spent honing the skills meant to be able to stop him from completing his botched attempt to end her life the first time. All of it wasted in one moment.

She choked on a sob. She buried her head in her hands

and let loose. Her screams tore through her body, ripped from her throat, and shattered her resolve.

Minutes later, spent and her throat burning, she lay on her side in the dirt and stared at the nothingness around her. This was not how she wanted to go. Not by a madman's blade. Another statistic in a growing case file of victims. She was one, but she had survived. She had been the anomaly. The one who got away. Only to turn on herself and become addicted to opioids.

It had taken her months of recovering from her drug addiction to battle through her cravings for oblivion, the need to forget everything, and the urge to live in a constant state of fog. Drug rehab turned fear and loathing, her only friends for so long, into her enemies.

She had friends now. Cecil. Elizabeth. Kyle.

Oh God. Kyle.

Lila clutched her hands and pressed them against the hurt digging deep into her heart. She had been such a wretched person to him. He'd been doing what he was brought up to be, a sincere gentleman. A man who put others before himself. And she threw it back in his face.

She would die here. Alone. And he'd never know. None of them would. How long before the I-80 killer dumped her body? Where would he dump her? No doubt far from here, where they wouldn't know who she was. How much of her would he remove so no one could ID her? How far would he take this to keep his record intact?

Lila gagged at the idea of being beheaded. Her fingers stripped of their prints. Her scars removed from her flesh. There would be hardly anything of her left after he'd finished. Nothing to be able to say *this body belonged to Lila Dayne.*

A heavy rumbling penetrated the environment. She stilled, straining to hear what was making that sound. As it drew closer, she pushed herself upright. The rumbling slowed, going deeper, like an engine gearing down. An engine like a semitruck.

Lila scooted around and stared up at the point where the sliver of light came through the wood. The truck idled nearby. Slowly, she pulled her feet under her and rose until she was close to the ceiling. A high-pitched squeal of metal on metal startled her. More light filled the gap. Seconds later, someone with a heavy tread walked across the wood. Lila followed the steps with her eyes until the person stopped, then there was a click.

She glanced back at the lighted gap and shuffled closer. Brushing her fingers along the edge, she could feel air blowing through. So, she was in a pit of some kind covered by thick wood slats. Over those wood slats was some kind of structure with a ... metal door? The way the metal squealed when it opened reminded Lila of a cargo container.

Where the hell would someone keep that without anyone noticing it?

A loud clap, like a car door shutting, brought her head around. The footsteps came back in her direction. She held her breath, listening. The person stopped right above her head. Within seconds there was a hard splash. It seeped through the gap and Lila was struck by the odor of urine. Disgusted, she scrambled backward to avoid being hit.

It was him. The killer. He laughed as he finished.

"Bastard!" Lila slammed her hands into the wood.

This only amused him more. He stomped down on the door, shaking it, his urine spraying the dirt underneath. His territory marked, he left, closing the metal doors with another squeal, and darkness came once more.

Lila flopped on her rear, staring at her only means of exit. The semitruck roared away, leaving her alone.

This was how he did it. He found a way to disable their vehicles, captured them, and took them to some hole in the ground to let them wither down to nothing. Then what? Did he just show up and slaughter them while they were defenseless? Was there more?

She wrapped her arms around her knees and drew them tight to her chest. How long before he came back and finished her off? She settled her forehead on her knees. How many days would she sit here pondering her own mortality?

When would she decide to take away his power and end her life herself?

CHAPTER TWENTY-ONE

B O, WEARING A tan jumpsuit, was hunched over, staring at the floor between his knees, his hands cradling his head. He lifted his head and squinted at Elizabeth. "Sheriff?"

Elizabeth unlocked the cell door and gestured for him to follow her.

He stood, swayed a bit, then tottered out of the holding cell. "What happened? Where are my clothes? Why does my face hurt?"

"Bo, Deputy Fontaine had to bring you in last night to dry out. You were drunk and high on something."

The young farmer halted and gaped at her. "High? I don't do drugs." He held up his hand. "I swear it."

"Let's get some coffee in you and something to eat. Then we can talk about it."

She led him back to the sheriff's department. Once she had him seated in the interview room, she brought him coffee and two donuts. She didn't want him out where he could see what Rafe and Georgia were doing.

Bentley scrabbled into the room and sat near the door, watching the man seated at the small table.

Elizabeth sat across from Bo and waited as he downed one donut and half of his coffee.

He set his mug down and didn't touch the second donut.

"Sheriff, did I do something really stupid last night?"

"You could say that."

"Does my pops know?"

"No one from this department has said anything to him. I can't speak for anyone else who was there."

Bo moaned and rubbed his face, grimacing when he touched bruises.

"Bo, what's the last thing you remember?"

He pondered her question for a moment, his features pinched in concentration. "I was drinking my second beer and this guy came up to my table, started talking baseball with me."

"Okay. Let's go back to why you were at the Dew Drop in the first place."

"To watch the Cubs play."

"Why not do that at home? Or in the hospital with your daddy?"

"Didn't want to be alone. And you can't drink in the hospital."

Viable answers. Elizabeth leaned forward, settling her arms on the table. "This guy who sat down with you. What did he look like?"

Bo frowned. He picked up the coffee mug, brought it to his lips, then set the mug down. "Kinda average-looking. Just like any of the other guys who go into the Dew Drop."

"Nothing about him stands out?"

"He wore a Cubs hat. Jeans and a T-shirt."

"What did his voice sound like? Was there an accent?"

Bo shrugged.

"Forget about him for a minute. What was your last

count on beers?"

"Three. That guy bought my third one."

"Did you finish it?" Elizabeth asked.

"I don't ... No? I don't think so."

She sat back against her chair. There had been seven empty bottles of beer with Bo at the table. The big question was, how many of those were beers he actually drank? By now, the bartender probably had the bottles that had not been shattered in last night's brawl all together in a recycling bin. There would be no way to know which bottles were Bo's without checking every single bottle for his DNA. That took hours and manpower away from their current situation. She couldn't justify it, even if it was to see if he'd been drugged without his knowledge.

"Bo, shoot straight with me. Have you ever done drugs?"

He rapped his knuckles against the table. "Never. I wouldn't touch that shit in a million years." He wagged his head. "I would never do that to Pops."

"I believe you. Now it's my turn to shoot straight with you. Last night I could see that you were high on something. I was trying to get you to come to the department when Orville Patterson and Jim Thurnhall started mocking you about an incident from the night before. You started a fight."

The color drained from Bo's face. "I didn't."

"It's why you have bruises. Jim got a few punches in."

"Oh God." Bo groaned.

"I came out to talk to you about something you let slip when you were out drinking the night before. Something that affects this department and one of my deputies. A statement that Orville and Jim harassed me about yesterday morning."

"Ah, man, Sheriff. I ... what did I say?"

Elizabeth frowned. "You don't remember?"

There was a long, pregnant pause from Bo. He stretched his hands out along the length of the tabletop and bowed. "Oh my God." His troubled gaze met Elizabeth's. "Did I tell them about Deputy Dayne? If I did ... oh my God. Sheriff, I'm sorry."

Elizabeth reached across the table and grabbed his hand and pulled it toward her. "Bo, were you at the Dew Drop the night before?"

"I left the hospital and went home."

"You're sure?"

"I swear." His face puckered in panic. "At least, I think I did. Maybe I did go the bar ... Yeah, I did. Why did I go there?"

Elizabeth grasped his arm and squeezed. "Bo, look at me."

His panicked eyes wavered.

"It's okay. So, you did go to the Dew Drop. Can you recall anything from when you were there?"

He squinted, his features pinching in a way that spoke of deep concentration. "I had a beer or two. And I think I talked to ... someone?"

"Orville and Jim?"

"Probably. But I have no idea why I would have said anything about Deputy Dayne."

Elizabeth waved that off. "When you woke up yesterday morning, where were you?"

"In my truck. I couldn't figure out why. Just thought I

had gotten home so tired that I passed out and slept there all night." The blood drained from his face. "Oh God."

"What is it?"

"Sheriff, I swear I wasn't doin' anythin' wrong." His arm quivered under Elizabeth's hold. "I remember on my way home, some state trooper pulled me over. Said I was weaving all over the road."

"Were you?"

"I don't think so. This guy wasn't real friendly about it. He slapped me with a ticket and big fine. Claimed I was drunk."

"Did he do a Breathalyzer?"

Bo shook his head. "He didn't do a field test neither."

That was highly unusual. But if that was the case, there would be some kind of record of the stop and hopefully a detailed report. She could check with the trooper's office for that. "Bo, do you still have the ticket?"

"Might be in my truck." He began to hyperventilate. "Sheriff, none of this makes sense. I have no idea what's going on with me. I don't do drugs. And I don't drink a lot, neither."

"Calm down. There's no need to panic."

A knock on the doorframe startled them. Elizabeth twisted around. "Yes, Deputy Lundquist?"

"Would you join me, please?"

She gave Bo another reassuring squeeze. "Bo, we'll figure this out. Drink more coffee. I'll be right back."

As she left the room, Bentley skirted around the table and nudged Bo. He gazed down at the collie and stroked her head. Good ole Bentley. She knew when a human needed comforting.

Elizabeth closed the door to the interview room and joined Kyle in the hall. "What is it?"

He headed back toward the bullpen, gesturing for her to follow. When they stepped into the open room, Deputy Meyer rose from his chair. Rafe and Georgia were still pouring over the security videos.

"Have you heard from Lila?" Kyle asked.

"No. I've been busy with other things."

"She's not answering her phone again," he said. "I've been trying to call her for the last two hours. She was supposed to meet up with me this morning."

"Has anyone gone by her house?" Elizabeth asked.

"I asked Fitzgerald to go check on her," Rafe said.

"When?"

"Right after Lundquist told me," Rafe answered. "He should be radioing back soon."

"Did anyone talk with her last night?" Elizabeth asked.

Silence met her inquiry. The stricken expression on Kyle's face spoke of a different matter.

"Kyle?"

"I dropped her off here after we finished for the night with Dr. Remington-Thorpe on the I-80 killer cases. I watched her leave the lot. That was nearly midnight."

What he wasn't saying was something had been said or happened between the two of them and he wasn't going to announce it in front of Meyer.

Unease dallied with Elizabeth's mind. First Sheehan's file went missing along with Lila's badge and gun. Now Lila was missing. Could she have finally let the events of the last two days send her over the edge? She did have access to the department and knew how to get into Elizabeth's office without being seen or heard. Lila had been off her game from the moment McCall arrived and began throwing his weight around. She'd had plenty of time to rethink her decisions and bail.

"How was she behaving last night?" Elizabeth asked Kyle.

"She's messed up." He couldn't have been blunter.

"Okay. I need to think. First, I need you to draw blood from Bo Cullen. I think he was drugged without his knowledge last night and maybe the night before. I'm just hoping it isn't something that burns off quickly."

Her statement earned Rafe's undivided attention. He left his chair and crossed the floor.

Elizabeth faced Meyer. "I want you to help Georgia go through all the video footage from the security cameras last night and the night before. Look for someone entering this department who shouldn't have been. Even if it's Deputy Dayne."

"Sheriff?"

"Brent, please, just do as I asked."

With a curt nod, he joined Georgia, taking Rafe's place.

"What's going on inside that head of yours?" Rafe asked quietly after Kyle went down the hall.

"Circle the wagons." She met his steady gaze. "No one—"

"Sheriff Benoit."

She ground her molars at that aggravating voice. Rafe's features tightened. She turned and faced the man walking toward her.

"Agent McCall, you're still here? How unfortunate."

The man was dressed as he had been the day of his arrival. He studied the room and brought his attention back to her. "Has something happened?"

"Actually, Agent McCall, something has happened. We've got two murders in my county, flooding everywhere, and I've got a state police investigator who likes to trample all over my authority. I'd like to clear the air with you." She gestured for the agent to enter her office and waited for him to close the door.

"Rafe, as soon as Fitzgerald reports in, you patch me through."

He nodded.

"Have Deputy Lundquist take Bo's blood sample over to the hospital. Either he or Dr. Remington-Thorpe can run initial tests on it."

"Got it." He cupped the back of her neck. "Take care of him. I've got it handled."

Elizabeth drew in a deep breath and headed for her office. As she passed the dispatcher's desk, she met Georgia's gaze, her own worry reflecting in the other woman's face.

Elizabeth thrust back her shoulders and marched into her office. "Now, where were we?"

"Sounds like you've got more going on than two murders and flooding," McCall stated.

Settled behind her desk, Elizabeth gave him a deadpan stare. "Agent McCall, where is Mr. Waterford?"

He shrugged. "We parted ways about three yesterday afternoon. I haven't seen him since. Perhaps he's returned to Chicago? Or he's with Lila?" He settled his right ankle on his left knee and crossed his arms. "Speaking of Lila. Where is she? I need to compare notes with her."

"Compare notes on what?"

"The I-80 killer case. What else? Cecil and I came upon some interesting information that was not previously known. I wanted to see what she and Dr. Remington-Thorpe had come up with."

Elizabeth hooked her thumb under her chin and pressed her curled fingers to her mouth, studying the man before her. His look of detachment, so like Sheehan's at any given time, set off every nerve in her body. The electrical pulses coursing through her muscles were sending out mixed messages. Wariness and mild panic combined with her exhaustion were creating a storm in her head. Something in McCall's statement wasn't lining up.

"Sheriff."

Georgia, in the doorway, pointed to her phone. Elizabeth bolted upright and grabbed the receiver. "Sheriff Benoit."

"She's not here," Fitzgerald said by way of greeting.

"You're sure?"

"Her car isn't here. The house is locked up. I got a look through the windows and no sign of her even coming back last night. There's a lot of files and paperwork all over her kitchen table."

"Where would she have gone?" Elizabeth asked.

"How should I know?" Fitzgerald remarked.

"Is it Lila?" McCall asked from the other side of the desk. Nosey much? A polite person would wait. Apparently, the politeness train bypassed this twit.

"Fitzgerald, I'm on my way."

"What do you expect me to do?" he asked.

"Stay put. On the off chance she does return from wherever she went, I want someone there to intercept her."

"Fine, whatever. Over." He ended the call.

Elizabeth placed her handset on the receiver and rose. "Deputy Dayne is missing."

McCall bolted out of his chair. "Are you certain?"

"I'm not certain of anything right now. Georgia!"

"Who was the last to see her?" McCall asked.

Elizabeth ignored him.

Georgia entered the office.

"Get me the state troopers office," she told the dispatcher.

With a nod, Georgia went to do Elizabeth's bidding.

"Do you have a means to track her cell phone?" McCall asked.

Tilting her head to the side, she glared at him. "No, that is why I'm calling the troopers in. We aren't equipped with state-of-the-art tech."

"Does anyone have a key to her home?"

One person might. The same person Elizabeth had just sent on an errand. If Lila trusted Kyle as he claimed, he would have been granted a token of that trust.

"Troopers," Georgia called from her desk.

Elizabeth's phone rang. "If you would excuse me. I need to get a BOLO going and call in a few favors."

ELIZABETH LED THE way inside Lila's house, Kyle right on

her heels. She had been in here only twice before, never going much farther than the kitchen. Lila kept sort of a barrier between her boss and her private life. Elizabeth noted the beta fish, Gerry, floating contentedly in his tank, a blue navy T-shirt draped over the back of the sofa, and a general sense of desertion hanging in the air.

Kyle pushed past her and stalked into the kitchen. Behind him, Agent McCall slinked inside the house but remained in the entryway, staring at Gerry the fish.

Elizabeth trailed Kyle into the kitchen, but he then bolted into the back room that served as Lila's bedroom. The table was covered in files. Elizabeth picked one up and opened it. These were photocopies of the I-80 killer cases from Chicago. She laid the file down and wandered over to the counter. A half-full coffeepot sat on the counter. Clean dishes were in the dish drainer. Two dirty mugs sat in the sink. Lila had a guest, and Elizabeth put money down it was Cecil.

"Her bed is still made," Kyle said as he returned to the kitchen.

"Lila was never one to make her bed," McCall remarked.

No, but the man sleeping with her who had been drilled over and over to do so when he was training and serving would. Kyle flushed red.

Elizabeth didn't comment. She turned instead to the floor-to-ceiling cabinet doors and opened them. The washer's lid sat propped open. Elizabeth opened the dryer and discovered Lila's uniform inside.

"There's no signs of forced entry," McCall noted.

"That doesn't mean shit," Kyle rebutted.

Elizabeth closed the dryer and the cabinet doors and faced the two men, who were standing toe-to-toe. "Agent McCall is right."

Kyle jerked.

"I don't think Lila ever came home last night. Whatever happened to her, happened when she left the department."

"If anything happened to her," McCall said. "For all we know, she decided to make good on her escape now that she knows the I-80 killer was here."

"Not Lila," Kyle said. "She told me she was going to talk with me. Today."

McCall coughed. "She's a recovering addict. Addicts lie. It's their go-to method of avoiding reality."

"Are you implying she's getting high?" Kyle stabbed a finger into McCall's chest with each word.

Red infused McCall's face.

Damn it to hell! Elizabeth didn't have time to referee a pissing match. "Both of you out of here!"

Their gazes flicked in her direction. She jabbed her finger at the door. "Now!"

Seconds dragged past as the two seemed to consider her orders. Finally, Kyle, the better man in this situation, stepped back and exited the house. With a parting glance at the piles of files on the table, McCall soon followed.

Left alone in Lila's kitchen, Elizabeth let her head drop back, and she glared at the ceiling. What the hell had she gotten herself into with those two?

Boot falls over the hardwood flooring brought her attention down. Fitzgerald inched through the living room, glancing about with his hands hooked on his duty belt.

"You're supposed to be on sentry duty," she snapped.

"Those two yahoos can keep their eyes peeled for her." Her taciturn deputy paused in the arched wall separating the two rooms. "Should let Lundquist process the house."

"There's nothing to process. She never came back here."

"You don't know that for sure." Fitzgerald picked up the Navy T-shirt. "He'd know if things were missing."

Elizabeth removed the shirt and tossed it back on the sofa. "Am I seriously the only one who never figured out those two were sleeping together?"

He shrugged. "Meyer doesn't know. And Young hasn't been with the department long enough to care."

"But she knew?"

He shrugged again.

Elizabeth wandered back to the table and assessed the files. "We'll let the troopers have a few hours to see if they can spot her car."

"If she's even still in the state. She's had plenty of time to get to Nebraska or southern Missouri by now."

She headed for the open door. "She wouldn't go west or south."

"What makes you so sure of that?" Fitzgerald asked as he followed her out.

"She's a Chicago girl. She'd go east." Elizabeth paused on the porch. "She'd go to the only other place she considered home." Her voice faded with her statement.

"Yet, you don't believe that."

Joel had always said if your guts weren't feeling right, something was wrong. He would know. How many times— when he had actually revealed anything about his work in

Delta Force—had this same feeling come over him and saved his hide and those of his team? One time, one very gut-wrenching time, it had happened to Elizabeth while Joel was deployed. She later learned he'd come inches away from returning to her in a flag-draped coffin.

Trust the intestinal warning.

"No. I don't think she ran." She clenched her fist and dropped it to her side. "Something happened to her. It's not good."

"But what?"

What indeed? They needed to find Lila and fast.

CHAPTER TWENTY-TWO

L ILA LOST TRACK of time as the day dragged on. At some
point, she passed out only to be startled awake. Stuck in
the dark with only her thoughts for company led her down
dangerously morbid paths. For hours, she waited for the
driver to return. She couldn't fathom why he would bother
to come back this early in her capture, but the idea that she'd
have some form of human interaction was better than
dwelling on the possibility of being left alone until her death.

Whittling away at the hours, she measured her prison.
Assessed the earthen walls, finding them compact by dirt and
clay, a common mixture in southeastern Iowa. This was
good news, as she hadn't been taken far from her kidnapping
point. She hoped.

To keep her mind off her growing hunger and thirst, she
searched every square inch of her dirt prison for anything to
use as a tool or weapon. The place was dry, a wonder after all
the rain that had fallen in the previous days. While she had
no luck locating a tool of any sort, she did come across a few
residents of the six-legged nature. With that brought a whole
another worry. Where there were insects, their predators—
spiders—would follow. Especially the sort that had no
qualms about biting a human and leaving behind a dangerous payload.

This sent Lila into a huddle in the center of the pit.

Here she sat, her body quivering from the strain of tightly hugging her knees and listening for the sounds of shuffling dirt. It was just like those days after the attack, while she was still in the hospital recovering from the multiple surgeries to save her life. Before the lull of an opioid-induced oblivion had taken hold of her.

Cecil had kept vigil next to her through it all, letting their colleagues tear up Chicago in search of the person responsible for an attack on one of their own. He hadn't showered in days, still wearing the shirt covered in her blood.

Through the morphine haze, Lila recalled his promise to fix this. His regret at not being there for her. And his pleas for her to fight back. Stay with him.

When she'd recovered enough to be discharged from the hospital, she stayed with him. She never wanted to return to her place. It was there at Cecil's that Tate had cornered her and ended their relationship, his selfish reasons waving like a bright red flag. In an unexpected fury, Cecil threw Tate out of his home, giving him a parting gift of a bloodied nose. Lila later learned he'd broken it.

Trapped in the dark, she revisited the whole episode, shocked at how much of it she remembered through the lull of the oxy.

She closed her eyes and lowered her face. Her stomach growled. Her tongue stuck to the roof of her mouth.

Why hadn't she run the second she saw that body? She had allowed Elizabeth to sweet-talk her into staying. To reconsider her actions. All so she could be a sitting duck for the I-80 killer. It was a trap. The moment she realized what was going on, she should have gotten in her vehicle and disappeared, left everything and everyone behind. Kyle would have taken care of Gerry.

The recriminations kept on rolling, driving up her frustrations. Lila worked herself right into slamming her fist down on the dirt at her sides and letting out her fury, screaming at the trap door above.

Throat raw, she shrank back on herself and let more tears fall. She shouldn't cry. She should reserve what little fluids she had left in her body. But damn it, she needed this.

Wrung dry, she laid down on her side and curled into the fetal position. She fiddled with her hoodie strings, finding comfort in the childish act.

If only she could muster up the nerve to wrap those damn things around her neck and hang herself.

How was that idea any better than drugging herself? Hadn't it been her whole reason for letting the oxy take control? A means to an end. Then why fight so hard to beat back the drug addiction, better her chances of survival the next time around, if she'd only cave to the weaker side of her humanity when he managed to kidnap her?

Lila released the strings and rolled onto her back. She stared at the darkened ceiling. Damn it, she wasn't weak. When he attacked her before, she was ill-equipped to handle the fallout. That was no longer true today. There had to be a way out of this.

Because out there, somewhere, a handful of people were searching for her. Of that she was assured. Elizabeth Benoit was like a lioness on the defense. Hurt one of her cubs, and all hell would break loose.

Lila closed her eyes and released a soul-cleansing breath. She just had to hang on long enough for them to figure it out and find her. In the meantime, she'd plot.

He would return, there was no doubt in that, because whatever he had planned for her would mean taking her out of this pit. It might be sooner than he'd like, which gave her the upper hand if she wasn't weakened by dehydration.

Lila needed to make the first strike and make it count.

CHAPTER TWENTY-THREE

"FIND HER CAR, we find her," Elizabeth said to Rafe as they tromped down the hall to the bullpen. "She's not far."

"You don't know that for certain," he said.

Coughing from the interview room brought her to a stop. She peeked in. She had completely forgotten about Bo.

"Rafe, see what Georgia and Brent have come up with on the videos. I'm going to finish up with Bo."

Bo looked up when she took the chair across from him. At some point, someone had given him pencils, pens, and paper.

"What do you have there?" she asked.

He rotated the legal pad and slid it toward her. Elizabeth stared at the uncannily good sketch of a man in a Cubs cap.

"That's the guy who talked with me last night. I've never seen him before in my life."

Elizabeth pulled the pad closer and stared hard at the image. "Neither have I." She tapped the paper. "Bo, I didn't know you were that good of an artist."

He shrugged. "Just something I do when I have time." He cleared his throat. "Did Kyle find any drugs in my blood?"

"It takes a little bit of time to figure that. I'm not too

sure we'll find anything. It was probably a fast-acting drug that was meant to be out of your system after a certain amount of time."

"Is Deputy Dayne okay?"

Elizabeth sighed. Was her deputy okay? Was Lila somewhere safe? Had she realized just how close the I-80 killer was? Had it scared her so badly she decided to run? Or had she done the unthinkable? Her gun and badge were missing. It wasn't out of the question to wonder if Lila had been the one to sneak into Elizabeth's office and take those things and the file. The bigger question would be why.

"Sheriff?"

Elizabeth forced a smile. "She'll be fine, Bo. She's made of tougher stock than we all give her credit for." She picked up the notepad. "Do you mind if I keep this?"

"Not at all. It's why I drew it. Maybe it can help you in some way."

"I think it might. Deputy Fontaine has your truck here, and per your permission, he searched for the ticket. He didn't find it. Are you sure you left it in your truck?"

"Sheriff, I'm not rightly certain of anything at this moment. I can check my house."

"Would you, please? One more thing, Bo, and then you can head home. Do you recall how tall this man was?"

Bo's face scrunched as he thought. "He was over six feet. I do know that." His features slackened and his eyes lit up. "I remember he smelled like diesel. That stuff hangs on you."

"Maybe he drove a diesel pickup?"

"Or a semi."

There's a theory that the I-80 killer is a long-haul trucker.

Elizabeth bolted from her seat. "Bo, thank you."

Bo frowned. "Thank you for what?"

"You might have given us the one thing no one has ever been able to do before. Go home. Then go visit your daddy. I mean it."

She scooped up the legal pad and hurried into the bullpen. "We might have a big lead."

All eyes turned to her. She noted that Agent McCall had stuck around. What a crying shame.

"What kind of lead?" he asked.

She ignored him. "Deputy Fitzgerald, I need you to round up Orville Patterson and Jim Thurnhall."

"What the hell for?"

"Eyewitnesses. Go, now."

Grumbling, the deputy marched out of the department.

"Where are we on the security footage?" she asked.

"We have nothing, Sheriff. Everyone is accounted for. There's nothing out of the ordinary coming or going," Brent answered.

"Have we gone over the keycard swipes?"

Georgia held up the readout. "Doing that right now."

"Am I missing something?" McCall asked.

"Where's Kyle?" Elizabeth demanded, still ignoring the jerk.

"At the hospital, running those tests. He and Dr. Remington-Thorpe are going over something. He wouldn't say what," Rafe explained.

"Sheriff." Agent McCall's strident voice was so irksome.

She shifted her attention to the man. "Can I help you?"

He pointed at her office and then walked into it. Elizabeth trailed after him, pausing next to Rafe and handing him the notepad.

"I think Bo might have encountered the I-80 killer." She pressed a finger to her lips in a shush motion.

Rafe looked at the pad, his eyes widening, then tucked it under his arm.

Elizabeth left her bunch and entered her office. Hostility hung heavy in the room. She closed the door and faced Agent McCall, who stood there with his arms crossed and face peppered red.

"My, Agent McCall, you seem perturbed. Is anything the matter?" She wandered over to her desk.

"That stunt you pulled out there, was just that—a stunt. I agreed to cooperate with your department, and I expect the same in return."

"I beg your pardon. You have done nothing of the sort. After I laid down those rules yesterday, you and Mr. Waterford made yourselves scarce. I saw nothing of you nor heard one peep from either of you until this morning. It would be noted that Mr. Waterford is still unaccounted for, while you seem to think that you can continue to stick your unwanted nose where it doesn't belong."

"I need not remind you that the I-80 killer is someone I have been tracking and following for years. I am the only one who is capable of helping you."

"Or hinder me."

His features twisted, and the red dots fused together. "Bullshit." As suddenly as the anger came over him, it was gone. He let his arms fall to his sides and tilted his chin higher. "Lila has something to do with this. She told you things about me. Most likely lies in order to color your perception of who I am."

"You really are a piece of work, Agent McCall."

A hard knock on the door and Georgia stuck her head in. "I've found something."

Elizabeth beckoned the dispatcher into her office.

Georgia laid a sheet of paper on the desktop and pointed at the red circled timestamp and name next to it. "At 2:57 a.m. Lila's keycard was used to enter the building. I had Deputy Meyer cross-check that time on the video. There is no sign of her coming or going. In fact, there is no one on the screens at that time."

"Where was Alexis?"

"She says she was in the holding cells checking on Bo around that time. She wouldn't have been able to hear the doors buzz."

Because the holding cells were downstairs in the basement area of the courthouse. Someone knew this. Someone had been spying on Alexis outside the building, waiting for her to go to the basement. They had enough time to pick the lock on Elizabeth's filing cabinet to take Lila's badge and gun and the blue file then escape out of the building undetected. Was it Lila?

A riot of panic erupted inside Elizabeth. *Lila, where are you? And what are you doing?*

Her worry that Lila had harmed herself was beginning to decrease. But why come back for her service weapon? Lila, like all law enforcement officers, surely had extra weapons at home.

What didn't make sense was for Lila to take the file. She

had no way of knowing about that file. Not once had Elizabeth mentioned it to her. Hell, she hadn't even seen Lila after Sheehan had given it to her. The only way Lila would have taken it was if, in the course of looking for her badge and weapon, she found it and read it. That still didn't explain why she'd take it. Unless ... Unless there was something bad about Lila in that file that no one knew about.

Elizabeth wanted to kick her own butt. She should have read that file. But no, she had to let her need to stop letting Sheehan man the helm control her actions. In the end, what was she left with? A big fat zero. But that was neither here nor there. There were more pressing matters to deal with.

"How do you enter this building without being captured on video?" she asked.

"You find a way to wipe the footage," Brent said from the doorway. "I looked closer at the footage, and there's a tiny blip. Somehow, whoever entered the building was able to wipe it and get it back on track. If you didn't know to look for it, you wouldn't notice the change."

Which meant the thief had more than enough time to steal the items and get on the main server to wipe the footage. It was entirely possible this person could get remote access into the system and make the changes. Far as she knew, that was not a skill Lila had.

Elizabeth glanced over at McCall. He seemed entirely too invested in their conversation. "Do you know anything about such capabilities, Agent McCall?"

"Not my forte, but a good hacker would know what to do. Why are you so concerned with finding if someone has broken into your department?"

Part of her wanted to tell him the truth and see his reaction. But her cautionary side overruled any thoughts of divulging their secrets. She'd give him tidbits.

"We have had some things go missing. To be frank, so has Dr. Remington-Thorpe."

"Things like what?"

"Like they don't pertain to these cases and your reasons for being here. This is an in-house deal."

"Yet, Lila is somehow involved." He smirked. "I'd say that could be justified as pertaining to me."

Elizabeth smirked back. "Nice try. No dice, Ice."

"Why do I even bother with you, Sheriff Benoit?"

"I ask myself the same question every time you come in my presence."

"A man knows when he's not wanted. I shall take my leave." He headed for the door.

About time, Georgia mouthed.

"Agent McCall," Elizabeth called out.

Heaving a frustrated sigh, he faced her. "Yes?"

"Why don't you locate Mr. Waterford and send him my way. I'm pretty certain he'd like to be in the know of Lila's sudden disappearance. It would save me from sending my already strapped deputies on another task."

"Why would I do that for you?"

"For starters, the two of you are staying in the same B and B. Secondly, you know the man better than the rest of us. You would have some insight on where to look for him."

"If I do manage to locate him and, say, he's no longer in the state, then what?"

Elizabeth tilted her head. "Inform him about Lila. Then relay your information to me. *Capisce?*"

"Perfectly." With that he left.

Elizabeth waited until she'd given him enough time to leave the building. "Now. Back to the task at hand."

CRUNCHING SOUNDS WOKE Lila.

She pushed up to a sitting position and listened. Moments later, the overly long screeching sound of the outer door made her stiffen. He was back.

His heavy footfalls treaded over her head. Another door creaked, opening right above her head; she crab walked out from under him. She'd just missed getting pissed on the first time—she wasn't about to allow it to happen a second. The door clapped shut, then an engine came to life.

A vehicle had been sitting over her head this whole time. Was it her car?

Lila tracked the vehicle as it backed out of the building. She stopped right under the trap door, waiting. After a pause, the building's outer door screeched back into place, dousing the thread of light.

She listened as the crack and pop of gravel and the sound of the engine faded. Once silence reigned, Lila sank to the dirt floor.

What had she learned? It was still day. She didn't know how many hours had passed since her abduction. She was living on borrowed time. And her abductor was going to toy with her until he got his revenge.

"What else is there, Lila?" Her voice sounded rusty and raw to her ears.

What else was there?

She peered up at the trap door. *Think!*

She closed her eyes. Twice now, he'd come this direction and entered through this way. This had to be the front of the building, whatever it was. It was large enough to fit a vehicle in, but not a semitruck. The entire thing sat on a well-constructed wooden floor. From the inspection of her holding cell, there was no signs of concrete of any kind for support.

The floor above her, while firmly placed, spoke of haste. A temporariness to the whole thing. She frowned. There would be no need to use concrete. Not that it would have been able to set properly with all the rain.

Wait.

Lila opened her eyes and stared into the dark straight ahead. No concrete. Just dirt.

She scrabbled to all fours and crawled to the opposite side of the pit. If that was the front of the structure, and it was the only way in and out, then perhaps the backside wasn't visible from whatever driveway was created.

Lila ran her hand over the dirt wall, some of it giving way into her palm. She rubbed the dirt crumbs between her fingers, noticing the dampness. With all the rain, the ground had been overly saturated. Unfortunately, she didn't know where she was exactly. If she was still in Eckardt County, the soil was made up of a thick mixture of clay, which made a mess of everything. Yet wet clay was easily wiped away.

Lila scratched at the dirt, and it kept coming away. She

dug her fingers in and pulled out a chunk, some of it sliming her fingers. She plowed both hands into the soil and dragged rich, loamy chunks out of the wall. An erratic cry-laugh erupted from her chest.

She could escape. She had to dig her way out, but there was a chance.

With renewed vigor, she tackled the wall like a madwoman.

The I-80 killer had grown careless. Lila would exploit it.

CHAPTER TWENTY-FOUR

"SHERIFF?"

Elizabeth held up her hand at the inquiry. "One of my deputies and I will be out to assist. Thank you, Trooper." She ended the call with the state trooper and gave Fitzgerald her full attention.

Behind him, battered and bruised, looking for all the world like they'd rather be somewhere else, stood Orville and Jim. They wore the same clothes from the night before, and the clothing appeared to have been hastily donned. Jim's graying hair stuck up at odd angles, and the whole left side of his face was purple. Orville had missed getting his arm through one of his overall straps, and his body odor was tipping the scales to the reeking side.

Elizabeth smiled. "Good afternoon, fellas."

"Am I needed for anything else?" Fitzgerald asked.

"No, not right now. Get some sleep. I'll alert you when we have confirmation."

The weary deputy nodded and exited the department.

"Hey, wait," Orville whined. "He's our ride."

"We'll get you home by other means." Elizabeth pointed into the conference room. Hell would freeze over before she allowed either man in her office or in the small interview room. The smell coming off Orville would stink up her office space for days.

Once the two were seated at the table, she circled around and leaned against the bank of windows.

"What's this all about?" Orville asked. Still ever the spokesman.

"Just out of curiosity, does Jim ever talk first?"

The men glanced at each other, frowning. Jim avoided her gaze and shook his head.

"Well, guess that answers that. Anyway, can you confirm that Bo was in the Dew Drop two nights ago? And if he was, do either of you recall seeing another man with him?"

Orville crossed his arms and slumped in his chair, making his protruding gut stick out more. "What's in it for us?"

"Nothing much, just the satisfaction of knowing that you might have had a hand in bringing someone to justice who has been long overdue for it."

He snorted. "That's hogwash."

"It is what it is, Orville. I don't have time for theatrics. If you're willing to stall on me, thinking you can get some kind of preferential treatment, you're in for a big fat surprise." She pushed off the window casing. "I can let you two stew in here for however long I want, seeing as you need a ride home and it's an all hands on deck kinda day."

She made tracks to the door.

"Wait," Jim barked.

Elizabeth halted.

Jim peeked at Orville, then shifted to face her. "Yeah, Bo was there. That's how we heard about the female deputy almost shooting him. And I saw a guy with Bo. He was wearing a Cubs hat."

Sweet mercy! Yes!

Elizabeth returned to her previous post. "Anything else you can tell me about this Cubs hat-wearing guy?"

"Every time he'd get some beers for Bo, he'd slip something in the bottle as he was taking it back."

So, Bo was drugged. Kyle had informed her that the tests he ran came back inconclusive, which meant the drug was long out of Bo's system by then, or Kyle, without knowing exactly which drug it was, wasn't testing for it. The larger question remained; why drug Bo at all? What was the purpose? Was this how the I-80 killer took his victims? If Bo was a potential victim, why hadn't the killer taken him already?

Elizabeth brought her rambling thoughts to a screeching halt. This wasn't the time to dwell on those. "Okay, now we're getting somewhere. Was this man at the bar last night?"

Jim's face screwed up, then he flinched. Painful bruises tended to do that. "I don't think so. I got up to go take a leak and saw Bo. Looked like he had company, but no one was at the table or the bar that wasn't already there when we got there."

"Do you remember how many beers Bo had at the table then?"

Jim opened his mouth, but Orville whacked him.

"Hesh up!"

Elizabeth advanced on the table and smacked her hands down, jolting the men. She leaned forward, glaring at Orville. "Interfere again, and you can sit outside in the rain."

"That won't matter to me," he snipped.

"I'm sure it won't, especially if it gives the rest of us a reprieve from your stench. However, it will matter if you're cuffed to the railing for all the world to see."

"This is harassment," Orville croaked.

"And so is what you're doing to Jim. What you two did to Bo last night." She stared hard at him. "Maybe I should let word slip that the pair of you have been flapping your gums in the sheriff's office. How happy do you think that will make some people?"

Orville's features went ghost white.

Elizabeth nodded. "My thoughts exactly. Now, Jim, where were we?"

"I don't know how many beers he had at that time. It was a lot. I think you came in not long after."

Elizabeth stepped back from the table, and she pulled out Bo's sketch. She unfolded the sheet and laid in front of Jim. "Was this the guy you saw?"

He jabbed a finger at the image. "Sure was. Man, that's some good likeness."

"Orville, did you happen to see this man or any other with Bo two nights ago or last night?"

He went to shake his head when Jim whacked him. The men glared at each other.

"Tell her," Jim said.

The moment of sulking on Orville's part grated Elizabeth's fraying nerves. He sighed. "Fine. I saw some old Black guy talking with Bo when we got to the bar last night."

Every cell in her body froze. "Black guy?"

"Yeah, couldn't miss him. Ain't like we got a lot of ..." His mouth froze.

"I'd thank you kindly to keep your remarks to the facts," Elizabeth ground out. "What was he wearing?"

Orville's features reddened. "He was wearing clothes like some lawyer or salesperson."

"Dark-brown slacks, blue shirt, and a dark-gray blazer? Look kinda like a movie star?"

He nodded. "Sounds 'bout right."

What was Cecil doing at the bar talking with Bo?

"Did he happen to have any beers? Give Bo a beer?"

Orville shook his head. "Not sure. I didn't pay them much mind. Didn't want to look like I was suspicious or nuthin'."

Elizabeth drummed her fingers against the table. None of that made sense. Cecil had no reason to be questioning Bo. Unless he heard something going around town. Or Agent McCall learned something and put Cecil up to it. Bo was one of the men involved with Lila's discovery of the body in the cow pasture.

Was that why the I-80 killer was interested in Bo? Picking his brain to see what he remembered and why? If the drug used was the equivalent to a truth serum, it might be a good reason to get Bo talking. Loose lips sank ships and all that jazz. Maybe the drug was also used to keep Bo from remembering what the killer looked like. Which made sense in a way. But what about the other patrons in the bar—case in point, Orville and Jim. None of this added up.

"What time did you two get to the bar last night?" she asked.

"Uhhh, six? Seven?" Orville didn't sound too sure.

"Jim? You have any idea?"

"I think it was about seven."

Well, this placed Cecil in the bar at that time. He was still in town. Where had he gone since then? Come to think of it, she still hadn't heard back from McCall.

Elizabeth snatched the sketch from Orville's inquiring fingers, stuffed it back in her uniform pocket, and headed for the door. "You two sit tight."

"Why can't we go home?" Orville whined.

"Because I might still have need of you. We're not going to track you down again." She exited the room and strode to her office. The better reason was not to put those two on the street where they could blab to all at large that they had seen the sketch. Somehow, Elizabeth sensed she had to keep this under wraps as long as she could, especially from McCall. The way people talked around here, he'd eventually get word. Call her petty, but Elizabeth wanted him to have a taste of his own bitter medicine.

She cut through her office and entered the bullpen. "Kyle, with me."

Kyle's head snapped back at her command. He left his desk and crossed the floor. "Where are we going?"

"Troopers called me a little while ago. They think they've got Lila's car."

Hope flashed across his face. It was so fast, Elizabeth wasn't sure if she'd read it right. His features settled into that indifferent mask. Man, he was having a hard time trying to prove he wasn't emotionally invested in Lila.

"Where?" he asked, a touch of hoarseness in his voice.

"Coleman Road."

After a few ticks, Kyle nodded.

"Georgia, keep an eye on our guests. Call Deputy Fontaine and relay our position. I may need his assistance. Check in with everyone else and update me."

The dispatcher nodded as she scribbled down Elizabeth's instructions.

"Deputy Meyer."

Brent looked at her with raised eyebrows. "Sheriff?"

"Any updates from you?"

He shook his head. "Still working on it."

"Let me know when you've got it. We're out." She turned on her heel and marched back through her office and into the hall with Kyle on her six.

"Do I need my kit?" he asked as they stepped outside into a steady rain shower.

"You can take it, but I'm not holding out any hope there is evidence left behind for us to track her."

He grabbed her arm and dragged her to a stop. Elizabeth looked into his soulful eyes.

"You think he's got her. Don't you?"

"I think he does. And I don't think he's done playing games with us. For some reason, he's pulled Bo into this mess, and I can't figure out why."

The scowl on his face left deep lines. "If he sticks with his MO, he's going to keep her for days until she's weakened. We have no idea where to start looking. He's probably not even in the state."

Elizabeth touched the pocket concealing the sketch. "I don't think he's gone. He's still here. Watching us chase our tails. He's banking on our ignorance. What he's not stopping to realize is that Lila's made of tougher stuff than before. If he's got her hidden away somewhere, she will fight hell and high water to get free." She pressed a finger into Kyle's name strip. "You bank on that."

Raucous barking jolted Elizabeth. Bentley danced in the doorway, pawing the glass.

"Guess she's coming with." She hurried back up the steps and let the dog out. "Let's roll."

CHAPTER TWENTY-FIVE

TWENTY OR SO inches into her dig, Lila hit a wall of exhaustion. She gave a frustrated yell and sat back to assess her options. Her fingers were battered and bleeding. They could use the break.

So, the pit and structure weren't as hastily pulled together as she thought. The dirt was littered with gravel that cut and tenderized her fingers and ripped and tore her nails. It was either a product of the area this place was staged for or to prevent the idea of digging free. He wanted a barrier. A thwart to any ideas she might have. That was why she was bootless. The boots would have given her a tool and, when she escaped, protection.

He believed she'd be wallowing in her terror, be a mental wreck unable to pull herself together and think. Tenacious he hadn't planned on.

Lila fingered her hoodie strings, rolling the fat cord between her thumb and forefinger. The gravel was loose enough in the soil, but as she got closer to a thicker clay mixture saturated by rain it was becoming tiresome and difficult to move. Her fingers ached from the idea of continuing the work to make a hole big enough for her to wiggle through. Even as she dug away the dirt from the bottom of the wood slats, she'd made no progress finding light. She clenched the string. She needed some kind of protection on her hands. Something that would give her another hour.

The rumbling of a diesel engine echoed through the structure above. He was back.

Lila scrabbled around and rolled to her knees.

The truck was left running right outside. The squeal of hinges announced his entry into the building. Lila peered up at the flooring, catching the faint sounds of grunts and shuffles. She jumped when something thunked against the floor. Then a pair of footfalls left.

Two! Two sets of feet.

She sat back on her heels and slammed into the dirt wall, causing a tiny avalanche of crumbles to fall on her. Two of them. There had been two last night. One to taunt and chase, the other to capture. His words spoken in her ear. She convulsed.

Lila was right! She had been right from the get-go. There was the master and an apprentice. They were working together. But who were they? Men, obviously. Why change the MO? Why work with someone after being a one-man show all this time?

The door squealed shut. Moments later, the rumbling engine faded.

Lila stared at the flooring. What had they dropped in here? Earlier there had been a vehicle removed. Now something heavy was left in the building.

A stifled groan made her stiffen.

They had someone else.

Seconds ticked past before the other captive made a sound. She lunged forward. Her objective had been upgraded. She had to free not only herself but another as well.

She tackled the dirt wall, crying out when gravel bit into her damaged fingers. Her hoodie. She could use the hoodie as makeshift gloves.

Free of her lone barrier to the pit's damp chill, she wrapped it around her hands, leaving a gap to keep her hands mobile. With at least two layers of cloth between her hands and the gravel-littered dirt, she attacked the top of the wall with new vigor.

Three good, deep swipes gave way to a tiny patch of light. Lila swallowed a cry of triumph and kept going until she had a hole large enough to reach her arm through.

A thump above her warned that the other captive was there.

"Hang on," she whispered. "I'm coming."

COLEMAN ROAD RAN parallel to a four-lane state highway cutting across the northern portion of Eckardt County. For the most part, one could see the majority of the road from the highway, except for the sections that dipped down below the four-lane overpasses. It was one of those places where the state trooper cars were parked.

Elizabeth pulled the Interceptor up behind the first closest car and parked, leaving her lights flashing.

"That's not her car," Kyle said.

"No, it's not," Elizabeth conceded.

The car positioned between the two trooper cars was a dark-gray, four-door sedan. Two of the tires were flat, and the plates were missing.

"It's close enough to her vehicle. I can see why they would want to make sure," she said.

They exited the SUV, Bentley hopping out behind Elizabeth. While the collie made a beeline for the car, Elizabeth and Kyle met up with the troopers.

"Sheriff Benoit." The first trooper gripped the wide brim of his hat and nodded.

The second trooper hung back, staying near the abandoned car. Elizabeth caught Kyle's eye and tilted her chin toward it. He nodded and headed over.

"Hey, Vance, thanks for calling." She shook the other man's hand.

"Lee spotted it and asked me to come down and check. I thought it best to have your people out here to confirm." Vance turned and together they walked to the car. "Is this your missing deputy's vehicle?"

"Unfortunately, it's not. I'm not sure whose this is. Hey, real quick, I keep forgetting to put in the request to your main office. I need to pull records on traffic stops made the other night by a state trooper. Would you be able to pass the word along?"

"Should. You know who did the stop?"

"Nope, but I know who was stopped."

"Give me that info and I'll radio it in when we're done here."

"Thanks." Elizabeth halted mid-step when Bentley, who had been sniffing around the car's trunk, sat and placed a paw on the bumper. "Vance, have you noticed any odd odors or weird liquids coming from the car?"

He looked at her with a cocked eyebrow. "No."

"We need to open the trunk."

Kyle's attention snapped directly to her. A look of panic flashed over his face. The other trooper retreated from the abandoned car and inched closer to his unit.

"Sheriff, is there a reason we need to do that?" Vance asked.

Kyle was heading back to the Interceptor and no doubt the crowbar.

As Elizabeth drew closer, the other trooper backed away, keeping a goodly distance between himself and her. The counter steps gave her pause. She tried to see the trooper's face, but he kept the wide brim of his hat at an angle, blocking portions of his face.

"Vance," he said, "if you're not needing me, I'll get back on the road. We can't both stay here."

Before Vance could answer, Elizabeth held up a hand. "Trooper Lee, did you tell him exactly what you did when you found this?"

His mouth turned down, a slight twitch in the corner. He was not happy at being questioned.

"He did. It's good, Sheriff," Vance answered for his fellow trooper. "Head out, Lee."

Lee gripped the brim of his hat and strode to his unit.

"Is he new?" Elizabeth asked as she watched him go.

"Yeah. Sorry about that. He transferred in two weeks ago from Nebraska. Kinda quirky, but a stand-up cop."

Once Lee had driven off, Elizabeth shifted her focus on Vance. "Quirky how?"

"You know how it is out here. Sometimes there's long

stretches of boredom, and we're usually riding alone. Can you imagine what it was like for him having to patrol Nebraska?"

She smiled. "Yes, I can. Drove those stretches of road many times in my day. Nothing but flat earth."

The creak of metal and then the pop of giving fiberglass pulled them back to the abandoned car. Kyle lowered the crowbar. Bentley had scuttled off to the side and was watching the humans. With a nod from Elizabeth, Kyle lifted the lid.

Elizabeth rolled onto the balls of her feet to peer inside. Relief coursed through her. No body!

It dissipated quickly.

Nestled among the usual paraphernalia of a car's trunk—a spare tire, a cheaply engineered car jack, an emergency roadside kit, and random pieces of junk—was a small, black suitcase.

"Maybe the case has the owner's information in it," Vance suggested.

Elizabeth swallowed down the lump forming in her throat. She wagged a finger at the luggage.

Kyle slipped on a sterile glove. He didn't bother to take it out of the car trunk, just pulled the zipper back. When the top slipped free of the base, he grimaced.

"What is it?" Elizabeth asked.

"I smell blood."

Vance shifted, gravel crunching under his boots.

"Do it," Elizabeth urged when Kyle hesitated to lift the top.

With a flick of his wrist, the top flew to the side.

"Shit!" she and Kyle said as one.

"What the hell is that?" Vance blurted.

A severed hand, encased in a surgical glove, blood staining the bottom of the case, sat between a gun and a badge. Other than the raw edges of flesh and bone peeking out of the end of the glove, there was no way to tell who it had once belonged to. By the size, Elizabeth guessed it was male.

Kyle reached in and lifted the badge out by the edges. "It's Lila's."

"Sheriff, mind telling me what is going on?" Vance asked.

She stared at that piece of metal stamped in the form of a five-point star, Deputy Detective imprinted on the ribbons. Her gaze met Kyle's troubled one.

"He's got her."

"And someone else," Kyle added, placing the badge back in the suitcase.

"Who's got who?" Vance pressed.

Red seeped into the edges of Elizabeth's vision. She turned her focus on Vance. "Lee—I want all the details on that man."

"Are you thinking he's the I-80 killer?" Kyle asked.

"Oh shit," Vance said.

"You know about the I-80 killer?" Elizabeth asked.

Vance's features flushed red. "I worked the Davenport corridor two years ago. We had a body dumped along there. Some schmuck from the Illinois State police swooped in and ripped it right out from under us."

"McCall," Elizabeth said.

"That's him. Never met the guy—he'd only associate

with the investigators—but from what I heard, he liked to throw his weight around. Brass didn't want to get into a pissing match, so they let him have at it. Never could understand why the FBI was never involved."

Elizabeth scowled. "Should they be?" Here's where her ignorance in some law enforcement matters tended to rear its ugly head.

Vance looked at her, confusion all over his face.

"They should have been from the start," Kyle said. He left his post and joined her and Vance. "Lila told me and Dr. Remington-Thorpe that McCall would never allow it during his investigation into the victims left in the Chicago area. Said he could handle it. From what we gathered in our research yesterday, he suppressed the information so state agencies wouldn't catch on too quickly. I have no idea if anyone did blow the whistle and bring the FBI in. Lila said she wasn't ready to pursue that avenue yet."

"Did she give you a reason?" Elizabeth asked.

Kyle didn't meet her inquiring gaze. "No."

"Thank you, Deputy Lundquist." Elizabeth's hand was head bumped. She scratched Bentley's ears. "Trooper Vance, I'm serious about Lee. I want information. And I want it now."

He nodded and hustled over to his unit.

While she kept up the ear scratching, Elizabeth stared at the contents of the suitcase. The I-80 killer wanted Elizabeth and her deputies to know he had Lila and there was nothing they could do to stop him.

"He's taunting us."

"This is out of character for him. His profile never suggested this."

A niggling of something Lila said the day before was toying with her. "Did Lila say anything about that? Or anything about her attack that made her second-guess his MO?"

"She told us Agent McCall always believed that the person who attacked her was a copycat, by the chaos of his attack and how it didn't fit the others. Lila was never so certain, until yesterday. She said she was beginning to believe there were two of them now. A teacher and an apprentice."

"Two of them. God help us. Did she say anything else?"

"She and Cecil were beginning to think that the actual I-80 killer might have partnered up with the one who attacked Lila."

Elizabeth narrowed her gaze. "And they've been cleaning up the mess left behind. Lila is unfinished business. And whoever this hand belonged to was another problem they needed resolved. Who are we missing?"

Kyle stared at her, lines deeply engraved on his forehead. "Both McCall and Waterford are in the wind."

"And each of them has a stake in what happened with Lila. Call Olivia. Get her out here. I want BOLOs put out on McCall and Cecil."

"Then what?"

"Then we go hunting for a pair of killers."

CHAPTER TWENTY-SIX

B Y THE TIME Lila had made a hole big enough to wiggle her body through, the hoodie fabric gave out. She managed to fashion a layer of cover over her feet with the tattered remains; something was better than nothing. Sweaty, muddy, and exhausted, her hunger and thirst raging, she escaped her prison.

Free, Lila surveyed her surroundings. She was deep in a timbered area. Here lay all kinds of threats aside from the two-legged kind, which included barbed plants to fanged slithering and crawling things. She would have to tread carefully. Whether this was still Eckardt County remained the unanswered question. Her assessment of the building covering the pit had been correct. A shipping container, long and wide enough to conceal a hole and hold a vehicle. The ground was littered with gravel; the sharp points poked through her makeshift socks.

She crept around the edge of the metal container and checked her options. From her position she couldn't see the front side of the building. She peered up at the thick canopy. The gray skies were tinged with a hint of darkness. It was evening. In the last few hours of her work, the pair had not returned. That didn't mean they weren't on their way back. She had to make this fast.

Checking the ground as she went, Lila slinked along the side of the container to the front side. She paused next to the edge and assessed her options. A gravel lane led away from the container and disappeared somewhere past the trees. There had to be a road or path of some kind down there wide enough for a semi to pull in and out. Logic dictated she take this route to escape. Common sense said hell no—take a direction her captors least expected. That meant traveling through the trees parallel to the lane.

It wouldn't be out of the question for one of the two captors to have remained behind, hidden and watching. But why bother? The whole setup reeked with the knowledge that they thought they had her outsmarted. Just in case, she scanned the trees for cameras or video surveillance but couldn't make out anything. If they had this place rigged for electronics, she didn't see it. At this point, what was the use in worrying about it? If they were monitoring this place, her time to make good on a clean escape was dwindling.

First, she had to find something to better protect her feet, then see who else they had brought to this hellhole. She waited long enough, listening for any approaching vehicle or footfalls. Satisfied she was alone for now, she inched along the front side of the container.

The entry was the same as every shipping box placed on the docks. She lifted the long, vertical bar latching the door in place and shoved it up, releasing the bolt from the bottom slot. The door swung out, squealing on rusted hinges. Lila cringed. She double-checked for any change in scenery. Nothing moved save the leaves in the breeze.

The clock was ticking.

Lila squeezed through the small gap and hesitated. It was too dark. The door didn't creak as loudly when she gave it a light push. More ambient light filled the space but didn't go any farther. Captive number two was somewhere in the dark recesses of the container. Her eyes, having been subjected to pitch blackness for so long, were able to make out a shiny truck bed toolbox up against the sidewall. There might be hope tucked inside the box.

She cautiously slid her foot across the floor and tapped the heavy end of something metal. It was a dead-bolt lock to the trap door. Grimacing—God, he had pissed here—she sidestepped the whole thing and padded deeper into the container.

"Hello?" she whispered.

No reply came. Maybe the captive had passed out? Moving forward was best. She inched up to the edge of the light and from there could make out the shape lying on the floor. It was at that point the scent of raw meat hit her. Her fellow captive was wounded. Or dead.

Lila got down on all fours—why she put herself in such a vulnerable position was beyond her—and crawled forward. Her brutalized fingers brushed cloth. Emboldened, she continued to pat upward, her seeking hand meeting a warm leg. Still alive maybe. She was moving along, coming to grips that this was a man, when a pain-laced groan escaped his lips.

"Lila."

Though ragged, Lila recognized the voice.

"Cecil?"

She scrambled forward, finding bare shoulders. He was

left in only his undershirt and slacks. She was certain he, too, was barefooted.

"Lila? Is that—"

Choking back the sobs threatening to strangle her, she managed to find his face. "Oh God, Cecil. How?"

"Don't ... know." His breathing increased. "Cut ... cut."

"Cut? Cut what?"

His arm shifted under her hand. The movement brought on a fresh scent of blood. Her brain spinning with images of stabbed bodies, she probed his body, finding wet, sticky places, until her fingers brushed what should have been his right wrist and hand, except it was the ragged edges of flesh, bone, and hot blood.

She had thought she'd spent the last of her tears. It was not so. Wetness coated her eyes and trailed down her cheeks. "What did he do to you?"

Cecil gripped her arm with his remaining hand. Despite his declining state, there was power there. "Go. Get out of here."

"Not without you."

"I'm ... dead. Leave."

"No," she cried. She rubbed away her tears on the sleeves of her shirt. "He doesn't get to win. He didn't last time, he won't this time."

Lila grappled with Cecil's weakened body and managed to get him into a sitting position as he feebly protested. It took everything in her already spent body to get him to his feet. With him draped against her, his good arm slung over her shoulders, she half dragged him back to the door. There, she eased him down into a seated position, and he leaned on the container wall.

"I saw a toolbox. Let me see what's in it."

"Lila … just … go."

"Argue with me later when we're out of here," she said and headed to the box.

It wasn't secured, thankfully. She opened the lid and squinted at the contents. She didn't have enough light and was losing what little she had fast. The box was too heavy to slide closer to the door. Lila dove in, letting her fingers do the investigating. There was rope and things covered in plastic wrap. When her tender fingertips hit metal, she rejoiced. A weapon. She hefted the thing out and held it closer to the fading light. A wrench.

Another check of the contents gave up a small flashlight that worked. The light nearly blinding her, she searched the toolbox. It had a tray, which she lifted out. Underneath she hit the jackpot.

"Cecil, he left clothes in here."

But he didn't reply. She swung the flashlight's beam on her mentor. He was slumped over, eyes closed. He'd passed out again. The light fell on the empty space where his hand should have been and Lila had to stifle more sobs. He was still losing blood.

Caustic words danced on her tongue, but she held them at bay. The killer didn't need to stab Cecil in the kidneys or liver, he could let her friend bleed out this way.

She took the rope and a white T-shirt and fashioned a torniquet and bandage around the stumped end, then using more rope, a sling to keep his arm pinned to his chest and stop the flow of blood. Satisfied that this should help, she went back to the box. She dug out a flannel shirt and draped it around Cecil's upper body. Another one she covered over herself. The rest of the contents didn't yield any shoes, but there were socks.

After placing a pair on Cecil, she slid into her own. Lila stood in the open doorway and listened. Silence reigned. Not even the birds were chattering their good nights. Could more storms be on the way?

No time to worry about it. She went back to the toolbox and pocketed the wrench. After a few agonizing minutes, she was able to get Cecil to regain consciousness. In the murky darkness, she could see him watching her through half-lidded eyes. How much of this situation was reminding him of how he rescued her?

Lila squeezed his arm draped over her shoulders. "I've got you. I'm not letting go."

With him once more relying on her small frame to aid him, she led him out of the shipping container. Before she left, she closed the door and slid the bolt home. No sense in giving them any fair warning the two of them were gone.

With the echoes of the past dogging her heels and a tiny beam of light leading the way, she headed straight into the thick trees. The pair of them faded from sight.

CHAPTER TWENTY-SEVEN

"IT'S CECIL WATERFORD'S hand," Olivia confirmed as she laid a set of papers on Elizabeth's desk. "The prints match ones on file with Chicago PD."

Elizabeth gnawed on her lips. The I-80 killer actually left Cecil's prints. What was his end game? *Hey, look, simpletons. I've got your girl and her savior and there's nothing you can do about it!* This whole thing was getting out of hand, no pun intended.

"Ellie, there's more. I was able to ascertain the timeline for when Cecil's hand was removed. It was about two hours before discovery. If he doesn't get medical intervention, he's going to bleed to death."

Elizabeth grasped her friend's hand. "Olivia, is everything all right? You look … bad."

"Same could be said for you." The ME slipped free of her hold and waved her off. "It's nothing. Just tired. And worried about Lila."

Elizabeth sensed that Olivia was telling a half truth. However, she wasn't about to push the issue. Outside darkness creeped in. They were about twenty-four hours behind the power curve. Somewhere out there, her deputy was fighting for her life. Lila's mentor and friend could also be fighting for his life—or dead.

"Has anyone found that walking, talking cluster?" Elizabeth yelled into the bullpen.

Georgia, who refused to go home until she knew all her chicks were back in their coop safe and sound, stepped into the doorway. "No word yet. What are you doing about two of the three stooges?"

"They're still here?"

"Whining and moaning about wanting to go home."

The phone rang and the dispatch radio went off at the same time. Georgia disappeared.

"I need to cut Orville and Jim loose," Elizabeth said as she headed for the side entrance door.

"Kyle needs to talk to you," Georgia called out.

Elizabeth did a one-eighty with a groan.

Olivia stepped toward the side door. "I'll send the guys home. Get this call."

Once her friend was gone, Elizabeth took her radio in hand. "What do you have for me?"

"He's gone." Kyle punctuated his words in a way that would make any army drill instructor proud.

"What do you mean, he's gone?"

"That prick McCall packed up, checked out, and left town. So Mrs. Miller tells me."

"Damn it to hell!" Elizabeth slammed her fist into the desktop. "Did she say what time he checked out?"

"This afternoon. By the sounds of it, right after you gave him that stripping down."

"He's running," she said. She turned to her second door as an unwanted figure stepped in.

"Why would he do that? If he's so hell-bent on catching

this killer, he'd stay," Kyle said.

"That is the million-dollar question. We have confirmation on the hand. It's Cecil's."

Kyle uttered a blistering oath.

"Lundquist, I've got to go. Head back to the department and we'll circle the wagons."

"Copy."

Elizabeth set the radio down. "You just keep showing up at the most inopportune times, Sheehan."

He pointed at her, then the exit, crooking his finger for her to follow.

"Sheriff!" Georgia hollered. "I've got Trooper Vance on line one."

"You'll just have to wait," she told Sheehan and picked up the phone. "Vance, thanks for calling me back."

"No problem, Sheriff. I have some information for you on that request you made. You said the traffic stop was for a Bo Cullen, correct?"

"Yes. Did you find anything?"

"We did. It seems it was Trooper Lee who made that stop, but he never issued a citation."

From his corner, Sheehan tapped his wrist. Elizabeth scowled at him.

"You're certain there was no citation?" she asked Vance.

"That's what the reports say. And, Sheriff, Lee hasn't returned to post. In fact, he's completely off the grid. My superiors are looking into him harder."

All the heat in Elizabeth's body pooled at her feet. "Thanks, Vance."

When she set the handset down, Sheehan gestured at the

door and walked out of her office. She was going to regret this, but Elizabeth followed him, down the hall, and outside. Thunder rumbled in the distance. More rain was coming. Would it ever stop?

Sheehan sauntered down the steps with the ease of a thirty-year-old. The man did not act his age, and for someone who liked his whiskey, it was surprising.

Drawing in a breath, Elizabeth trailed him halfway to the parking lot. "Why are we out here?"

"You've bumbled this investigation long enough. I'm tired of waiting for you to quit stumbling around and figure it out."

"What the hell are you talking about? We've gotten further on this damn serial killer case than anyone has before."

He shook his head like he was talking with a fifth grader. "I practically handed you the keys to apprehending the guy. Instead, you let it disappear. Shit, this is what the folks of Eckhardt County voted for over me."

If this ass kept talking, she was going to lay him flat. She took a step closer to him, realizing that, for the first time, he didn't smell like liquor. She leaned in.

"What are you getting at, Sheehan?"

"Are you armed?"

"Yes."

"Then you come with me, *Sheriff*."

"Why should I?"

He turned on his boot heels. "Because I know where your deputy and her friend are and we don't have much time."

"Hold on one damn minute here. I can't be leaving my

deputies behind. We need to tell—"

"Elizabeth. If you want your woman back alive, we go now. We don't have time to call in the cavalry. March."

Stunned by his use of her given name, she took two seconds to consider his words and the consequences of her coming actions. To hell with it. She could always call them in as they were heading to this place. "Lead on."

She glanced back at the department. No one at the door to see her go. Why was she putting her trust in this man again? The reasons were unthinkable. With Lila's life dangling on the edge of a cliff and Cecil's life fading away, Elizabeth was all too willing to make choices that went against her typically rational personality. Such dangerous territory when it came to Kelley Sheehan. There was no price Elizabeth had to pay that was too great to prevent the death of a woman she now considered friend, and an honorable man.

She climbed into Sheehan's truck and had just enough time to buckle in before he peeled out of the lot.

"I can't believe you lost that file," he groused as he sped through the darkened streets.

"What was so all-fired important about that damned file? More importantly, how and why the hell did you even get the information?"

Sheehan drummed a steady beat on the steering wheel, his focus lasered on the road before them. If he thought he was going to ignore her and not answer, he had another think coming.

"You should have read it when I gave it to you."

"I was planning on it, but I had a job to do."

"It was part of your job." He smacked the steering wheel. "That's what being the sheriff is about. You have deputies to do your dirty work."

"Like you did? They did all your *dirty* work and you let them take the fall when they were caught?"

Sheehan's features twisted in the green and red glow from the dashboard lights. "You seem to think you've got me all figured out, dontcha?"

"I'm not the only one. Every single person who voted for me had you pegged."

"That right there is where they went wrong."

Red, hot fury roiled through her. Why had she ever allowed him to talk her into this? Elizabeth tore her gaze off him and back to the road in time to see a young buck bolt from the ditch.

"Kelley!"

He hit the brakes, sending the truck into a skid; rubber squealed and chirped against pavement. The deer froze a fraction of a second, then darted across the road in front of them, but he wasn't fast enough. The truck's right front bumper slammed into the buck's hindquarters. Fiberglass and plastic crumpled and shattered, the headlight wiped out. The airbags deployed, slamming Elizabeth against the seat.

Once the truck came to a complete stop, the bags deflated, leaving behind the stench of burnt powder. Elizabeth fumbled with the seat belt and managed to get the clasp to release. Coughing, she grasped the door handle and tugged; the door popped and creaked open. Fresh air rushed inside the cab.

She batted down the nylon bags and reached for

Sheehan. "Kelley? Are you okay?"

He shook his head as if to clear the cobwebs and coughed. He must have let off the brake, as the truck began to roll forward. Elizabeth tapped his leg and he pressed down, stopping the vehicle's movement.

"Get us to the side of the road," she said.

Sheehan guided the wounded truck off the pavement and killed the engine. Elizabeth slid out of the cab and winced as her bruised muscles protested. Better to be black and blue than bloodied and dead. She carefully navigated the slim strip of ground between the truck and the ditch and wandered to the rear end.

In the ditch a few yards away, the buck struggled to flee. He grunted and bleated as he tried to claw the ground with only the front half of his body still functioning.

"You should have gone back the way you came." Elizabeth sighed and reached for her sidearm.

"Let me," Sheehan said. "You call one of your guys out here to get us."

"Kelley, we're running out of time."

"Elizabeth." The red glow of the taillights reflected in his eyes as he stared her down. "I know. Stop woolgathering and call for backup."

"Why is it you always seem to come in at the last minute to save the day?" she demanded.

"Call Fontaine. Now." He took hold of her shoulder and pushed her toward the disabled truck.

Anger fueling her, she did as he commanded. The moment Rafe answered, the crack of Sheehan's pistol echoed through the open roadway.

"What the hell was that?" Rafe blurted.

"I need you to pick up me and Sheehan. Now." She gave him the location.

"Ellie?"

"Rafe. Just do it. And hurry. He knows where Lila is."

CHAPTER TWENTY-EIGHT

LILA WAS LOSING steam, fast. She couldn't keep up any kind of pace with Cecil leaning on her. His weight was draining what little fortitude that remained. To make matters worse, he was having a difficult time staying conscious.

"Leave me," he rasped.

"For the last time, no." She adjusted his arm around her shoulders.

The change was the final straw. Cecil's legs buckled under him, and he went down, pulling her with him. Lila collapsed on him, resulting in an agonized yelp. She scrambled off his body and sat down hard on her rear. The flashlight had landed on the ground with the beam pointed at them. Cecil flopped onto his back. Blood was seeping through the makeshift bandage.

"Cecil," she whimpered.

Panting, he rolled his head toward her. He just stared at her.

"I can't ..." she choked.

"You ... can." He lifted his lone hand and settled it on her knee. "You ... are ... strong."

"Not without you."

His hand slipped off. "Navy will ... be there."

"You don't know that," she whispered.

A rumble sounded in the distance. Lila lifted her head and scanned the trees. If she was correct, they were about a hundred or so yards from the road leading to the holding cell. She wasn't sure how far they had traveled from that hellhole. She looked up, grimacing when she couldn't see anything through the leaves.

The rumble came again. Thunder. A downpour was going to make this harder to get out of the timber.

Lila rolled onto her knees and crawled to Cecil's side. "I'm not leaving you."

"No ... choice." He grappled with her hand and held fast. "Go. Come back ... with help."

"How will I know where to find you?"

He tilted his head to the penlight.

There was another sound echoing through the trees. Lila's muscles stiffened as the rattle registered in her exhausted brain. Diesel engine.

She grabbed up the penlight and turned it off. She hunkered down next to Cecil as the semitruck drew closer. Headlights flashed through the trees, bouncing off the trunks and underbrush. She held her breath as the truck growled past. They were closer to the road than she thought.

"Go," Cecil whispered. "Get help."

Lila laid her head on his chest. "Don't leave me." She lifted her head and stared at the place where his face should be. "Please."

"I won't."

Before she took off, she helped him sit up against a tree. She pressed the flashlight into his hand, then kissed his forehead. She stuffed down the sobs rising in her throat as she climbed to her feet. Without looking at him, she jogged for the road.

If her captors were at the shipping container, she had no worries about them coming on her running alongside the lane. She only hoped she wasn't that far from a well-traveled road.

Her socked feet met gravel, and the screech of metal hinges echoed through the timber. Lila spun at the sound. Seconds later a decidedly angry male roar reverberated, scaring the birds from their roosts.

Fear pounded through Lila's veins. He knew she was gone. He would come for her. She patted the pocket holding the wrench. Still there. Her sole weapon against two angry men with knives.

She always had her wits.

Behind her, she could sense Cecil urging her on. She had to do this. For him. She wasn't going to lose him.

Lila broke out in a run, ignoring the sharp, piercing sting of rocks biting through the fabric. The diesel engine revved up. He was coming. She willed her legs to move faster.

The lane began a gradual descent. Lila had to slow her pace or she'd end up ass over teakettle. A bright flash of light from above blinded her. Squinting against the glare, she kept going. Thunder cracked, making her want to jump out of her skin. But it was the roar of a diesel engine behind her that scared her more. Headlights cut across the night.

Lila cried out and veered left. The semi bared down on her. She darted back into the trees and crashed into an incline. Behind her, the truck skidded to a stop, gravel flying.

She slipped and scrambled up the hill, topping it as the truck door slammed closed.

"Bitch!"

Breath seesawing, Lila pitched forward. Lightning rippled across the sky, illuminating her path. She weaved between the trees, looking for a good place to hide. Droplets pelted her head. An enormous tree trunk surrounded by a fat, leafy bush beckoned. She swerved that direction and slid to the ground, pulling herself under the low hanging limbs and pressing her curled body tight to the trunk. The rain picked up momentum; the drops beating against the leaves drowned the sounds of his pursuit.

Lila strained to hear. Had he seen her bolt for this hiding place? Her hand went to the pocket, and she slid out the wrench. The slick metal handle gripped tight in her fist, she waited, trying to calm her breathing.

Through the splattering of rain, she heard his boots pass over the wet undergrowth. She peered up as lightning flashed, and through the leafy undergrowth watched him creep past. Her wrench-wielding hand trembled when she spotted the gleam of metal. He held that knife like an expert.

He paused ten feet away. Lila seized, her jaw clenching painfully.

"I always knew you would make it a good hunt," he said.

She shrank down as he turned, looking directly at her tree.

"The more you run, the better it gets."

Where was the other one? Lila resisted the urge to look to her right. If she moved even a fraction, he'd see her. Her instincts prickled with the urge for her to check, but she controlled them with an iron will.

Eventually, her current pursuer rotated, putting his back to her. She waited. He walked away from her, farther ahead. Once she could no longer see him, she shifted and scanned the entire area behind her. She didn't see or hear any sign of the second man. With a quick check—the first one was far from sight—she slithered out of her hiding spot. She stayed in a crouch and waddled her way around the tree trunk. The lightning was becoming infrequent, but the rain was coming down harder.

Wrench lofted and ready for an attack, she made the risky decision to go back the way she came and hope she could get to the truck. As she rose, movement to her far right caught her eye. She ducked down. There was Number Two.

Her heart slammed against her rib cage. They were crowding her in. Two hunters, stalking their prey. Her. Just as they had done on the road last night.

Lila leaned into the trunk, the bark biting her cheek. How was she going to get past them? One she could do. But two?

The second hunter was approaching her hiding spot. She slunk down and carefully backed around the trunk. Her wet socked foot slipped in the mud, and she bit her tongue as her knee slammed into the ground and her cheek hit the tree. She cringed. Had he heard her?

Underbrush rustled from the left. Number One had returned. She cowered. They were mere inches from her. All they had to do was reach out and one of them could touch her. It would all be over for her if they did.

"That bitch. We shouldn't have waited."

"She can't get far." That voice. The voice that haunted her. Stirred her nightmares. The one who had shredded her happy little life to bits. Lila had more to fear from him than the first man. "Where's the truck?"

"Out on the road. Think she went back to camp?"

"You check it out. I'll get the truck."

Lila watched them head in their respective directions until they faded into the darkness and rain. Alone, she sagged to the ground. It was time to get out of here. The road was out of the question. She drew in a ragged breath and faced the direction she had been running when Number One chased after her. Help was that way.

Her breath caught in her throat. Cecil! He was in Number One's path.

Lila rose. He would not take Cecil's life. She shoved down the fear pulsating with every beat of her heart. It was time to turn the tables. She was over being the prey.

They didn't get to decide her fate.

It ended here. Tonight. With her.

Neither of them would see the sun rise.

A death grip on the wrench, she followed Number One. He would be the first to go. Then she'd face down the man who stalked her dreams. She was done with running.

They both died tonight.

CHAPTER TWENTY-NINE

E LIZABETH, ENVELOPED IN a long, yellow slicker, was out of the car the moment Rafe put the Charger in park. The headlights illuminated the rumbling semitruck parked in the middle of the gravel lane. Long-haul trucker. Lila had been right. So had McCall. That thought left a bitter aftertaste in Elizabeth's mouth.

Rain sheeted down around her; streams of water cut a path through the ground. She stepped over the gullies and hopped up on the semi's running board. "Locked!"

"Same over here," Rafe hollered over the sound of the engine and the rain beating against the truck.

"Son of a bitch," she muttered, stepping down and backing from the rig.

Sheehan joined her. "Looks like their plan was interrupted."

She looked at him. "Meaning what?"

He lowered his chin. "Your woman got the better of them." One corner of his mouth tilted up. "I knew I liked that girl when I met her."

Elizabeth rotated, taking in the area. Sheehan had directed Rafe to the northeastern most part of Eckardt. It was nothing but timber, acres of open pasture and hunting ground, and rocky bluffs that dropped into tributaries feeding into the Mississippi. Out here, if someone did not know where they were going, they would get lost. Travel farther north and you ended up in a state park known for its geodes.

"How did they know about this?" she asked.

"Research, Sheriff," Sheehan replied.

"If Lila is here, it's possible they have Cecil here as well," she said.

"That's saying he's still alive," Rafe pointed out. "If that's the case, she might have sprung him."

"Without his hand, most likely bleeding out, he doesn't have long for this world," Sheehan said. "He's a liability to her, and he'll know it. It's what they wanted."

"We find both of them," Elizabeth stated.

Sheehan pointed at the Charger. "You and Fontaine drive up the road and see what's there."

"Not on your life. I stay out here. You and Rafe go."

"You can't take on two men alone."

"Why, because I'm a woman? You do realize they've murdered men who are just as capable of defending themselves as you are."

"We don't have time for you two to bitch this out," Rafe snapped. "If this rig is here, then no one is back wherever they were keeping Dayne."

"He's right." Sheehan flicked his flashlight at gouge marks in the side of an incline. "Someone went up that way."

"Then so do we." Elizabeth drew her weapon and turned on her flashlight.

Before they made the climb, Rafe grabbed the shotgun out of the Charger. They headed up the incline one at a time. Once on top, they spread out. From here, it was difficult to see a path of any kind.

"We're going to have to separate to cover more ground," Sheehan said.

"I don't like that," Rafe countered.

Elizabeth didn't like that idea either, but what choice did they have?

"Dayne is out here," Sheehan continued. "She probably has them separated looking for her. They're hunting her, which means they're trying to circle around her. This is how he plays the game."

"Which means we can hunt them," Elizabeth said. "Radio contact only."

"Ellie," Rafe pleaded.

"He doesn't get to win this time." She lowered her head, and rivulets of water poured over the edge of her hat brim. "We stop the threat. Tonight."

LILA CAREFULLY PICKED her way through the timber until she caught up with Number One. Her instincts to run were wreaking havoc on her brain. She fought it off with sheer will. She'd lost a child and the ability to have kids, but she damn well refused to ever lose a friend.

Number One paused and started to turn.

Lila darted behind a tree and blended into the shadows.

He rotated and stopped, facing the direction he'd come. Had he heard her? Sensed her stalking him?

Lila had a clear view of him, while he couldn't see her as

she hid in the tree's shadow. Her nerves jangled, sending a vibration through her muscles. She wanted to charge at him. Bring that wrench down on his head and wail on him. But the direct approach wasn't the way to take on a viper.

Precious seconds ticked past as he stood there, staring into the dark. Finally, he put his back to her and continued forward. He faded into the distance, and Lila stepped out of her hiding spot and trailed after him.

She had long since discarded the socks because she spent more time losing traction with the ground. Her feet were slimy and chilled, twigs and roots cut and scraped her skin, but she pushed past the pain. She would not allow Cecil to become another case with the I-80 killer.

After a few more yards, she pulled up. By now she should be able to see him just ahead of her. Lila shrank back toward a tree and reached out with her senses. He had to be right in front of her. The rain wasn't coming down as hard. The foliage was thicker in this area and canopying the ground. Lila rotated slowly.

There was a shift in the atmosphere behind her and she moved, ducking at the last second. His arm slammed against the tree. Lila slipped past him, bringing the wrench down on the back of his knee. He let out a furious yell as he buckled forward and connected with the tree. She danced aside and settled in a fighter's stance.

He pushed off the tree and faced her. Something in his hands moved from one to the other. The knife, most likely.

"Where's the cowering girl?"

"Gone." Lila clenched the wrench handle. "You ruined her life once before. You won't again."

He laughed. "Bold. I like it." He came at her.

She darted to the right as the knife blade came at her, and she swung the wrench down on his arm. There was some give in the connection, and hopefully, she had broken bones, or at least made him lose the knife. She spun behind him and slammed the wrench into his side. He jerked.

As she raced forward, her feet slipped on the wet ground, her legs went out from under her, and she flung her body to the side. Her motions saved her as he barreled past her. Lila hit the ground and flopped into a tree.

Adrenaline coursing through her, she never felt the pain. She scrambled to her knees and on to her feet. He was coming at her again. She gripped the wrench, realizing it was gone. She'd lost it when she fell.

"To hell with it." She let out a war cry and dove at him.

Their bodies collided. Her sudden counterattack stunned him, and he fell backward. She heard the air rush from his lungs when he hit the ground. She reared up and straddled his body and rained down punches to his face. She connected hard three times before he was able to buck her off. He rolled up with her in a move that would have landed him on top of her body, but she kicked off his torso, her heel catching him in the chin as she slid away.

Lila brought her feet under her and crouched low to the ground. A few yards from her, he lumbered to all fours. They squared off.

"Scrappy little fighter. Makes this all the better when I kill you."

"You're not going to get that chance."

He coughed. "He shouldn't have taken so long to finish

you off."

"He should never have come for me in the first place."

"That we both agree on. But he just had to have you. Said you were the trophy."

"I'm no one's trophy." Lila's battered body was protesting her cramped position.

"You'll be mine." He bolted upright and came at her.

Quick as a cat, Lila dashed to the side. She scissor kicked, tangling her legs with his and tripping him. He flew to the ground. Lila untangled her legs from his and crawled to her feet. She didn't get far; he grabbed her ankle. She slammed into the ground, water and mud spraying her face. As he dragged her toward him, her hand grazed against metal. On instinct, she gripped it, the razor edge biting into her fingers.

It was his knife.

He was crawling up onto his knees and advancing on her. The knife handle was in her hand, and she sat up, slashing the knife at his face. The blade ripped through his flesh. He shouted and reared back.

Lila scrabbled away, taking another swipe at his upraised arm and slicing through sinew and bone. His shriek hurt her eardrums.

Free of his reach, she hopped to her feet, the knife dangling in her hand. She backpedaled, watching him.

"All those people. For what?!"

His arm cradled to his chest, he rocked back on his knees, and let out a cruel laugh. "For whatever the hell I pleased."

Lila inched closer, adjusting her grip on the knife handle. "You're sick."

"That's what they all said right before they bled out."

"You've killed your last."

He bowed his head. "And you think you're the one to stop me?"

"That's the plan."

His head snapped back as he lumbered to his feet with a roar. Lila blindly slammed the knife into his chest, the blade stopping only when the hilt met flesh. She released the handle as he staggered back. He seemed to hang suspended by strings before he collapsed to his knees. Lila lingered a few heartbeats, hearing his gurling breaths, and then broke out in a run toward the place where she believed she'd left Cecil.

Through the darkened timber she could make out a spot of light. She veered toward the tiny pinpoint. As she drew closer the beam grew. Yet it never moved.

"Cecil?"

He didn't answer.

Lila slowed and crept toward him. "Cecil?" She dropped to her knees next to his slumped body. She grabbed up the penlight and reversed the light. A jagged cry ripped from her throat.

A knife was plunged in his heart. His eyes were wide, his face frozen in shock.

"No-no-no-no-no." Lila grabbed at his face. "No, you can't be dead." She clutched at his limp body. "Cecil. No!"

She grabbed at the last person who had meant something to her. He was gone. Taken from her just as her child had been. Her hopes and dreams. The last thing she loved.

Gone.

Gasping grunts rose above the sounds of her crying. She

lifted her head from Cecil's corpse and swung the penlight around. The beam lit up the I-80 killer's blood-streaked face, that deadly knife raised in his hand, looming above her. Lila had a split second to imprint his face in her mind.

"Lila, down!"

She flattened her body against her dead friend as a slew of gunshots rent the air. She peeked under her arm in time to see the killer's body crumple to the ground. He would never rise again.

A hand on her shoulder startled her out of her stupor. She jerked back.

"Lila. It's me. Ellie."

The name registered into her war-torn mind. "Ellie?"

Elizabeth threw back the ball cap from her head and reached for Lila. "Yes. It's me."

With grateful cry, Lila wrapped her arms around her boss. Elizabeth dragged her close and pulled her away from Cecil's body.

"It's okay. I've got you. You're safe now."

CHAPTER THIRTY

E LIZABETH STOOD OVER the I-80 killer's body. Her aim had been true, killing the monster instantaneously. Joel would be proud of his ex-wife's shooting skills. It might have been her bullet to finally stop him, but the vertical slash just below his clavicle would have ended his life, eventually.

"Do you recognize him?" Sheehan asked.

"He's the man in Bo's drawings. Once I talk with Trooper Vance to confirm it, I'm sure he's also the man going by the name Lee and posing as a state trooper." She turned her back on the corpse, resisting the urge to kick it. "We'll probably never learn who he really was. He would have made sure of that."

It had taken some time to pry Lila from Cecil's body, and when she did leave him, she couldn't walk. Rafe had picked her up and carried her to his car.

Elizabeth had no sooner joined them in the back of an ambulance than Lila convulsed under her hands. The warming blanket draped over Lila slid down. Elizabeth settled it once more around her deputy and rubbed her arms. She was so cold. Dear God, don't let Lila seek solace where she had before.

Once an addict, always an addict.

Elizabeth's gaze drifted from Lila to the sight before

them.

Chaos.

Everywhere.

The rain had long stopped coming down, but there was another round of storms headed their way in another hour. Around them an eclectic gathering of law enforcement officers, from DCI to state troopers, combed the area for evidence and the second killer. Olivia and her bunch were taking care of the I-80 killer and his casualty. Elizabeth had no desire to join the fray, not when she had a wounded deputy to care for.

"It's not over," Lila rasped. "He's still out there."

Lila had been adamant to Rafe that the second man was in the woods with them. But no one seemed to find him. Even now, search teams were combing the area.

"We'll find him," Elizabeth assured her deputy.

Lila just shook her head and hunched over. She no more believed Elizabeth's assurances than Elizabeth did herself. They had nothing to go on with the second man. He was a ghost more so than the dead man.

Sheehan crossed the road and joined them. "You won't find him. He's probably halfway through Illinois by now."

"Let them finish what they came here to do," Elizabeth said. "Maybe they will find a clue that will lead us to him."

"That's some mighty fine wishful thinking you have there, Sheriff."

Elizabeth stared at the ex-sheriff. At every turn, he surprised her. His instance on helping, guiding her—it was out of character for what she'd believed, what she had learned about him. It was causing turmoil in her own mind when it came to Kelley Sheehan. Who was the real man?

She tightened her hold on Lila. "Kelley, thank you."

He tilted his head to the side, his features remained smooth. "That had to burn coming out."

"I mean it." Elizabeth lifted her chin. "I'm not saying I'm wrong in my initial assessment of you. However, you were ... are a good cop. When we get back to the department, I want to hear how you pulled this all together."

He chuckled. "You won't like what I have to say." With a dip of his chin, he turned and walked away.

Elizabeth watched him meld with the bevy of LEO vehicles and disappear. A walking, talking enigma. That was Kelley Sheehan.

The former sheriff's figure was replaced by a frantic one emerging from the chaos. Kyle had been waylaid on his way here and must have just arrived. He spotted them and rushed toward the ambulance.

"Lila!"

Her head snapped up. "Kyle," she croaked.

The trembling woman melted away and Elizabeth felt the change in Lila's demeanor as he approached. She shrugged out of the blanket and bolted from the back of the ambulance, running into his arms. The decidedly shorter Lila was hefted up by the taller Kyle, and they clung to each other.

Elizabeth relaxed against the open door. Was it just two days ago she'd learned about their relationship? She rubbed her forehead. So much ... too much had taken place in the days following. If she was honest with herself—Elizabeth prided herself on that fact—having Lila and Kyle together was not a bad thing. If anyone could help Lila, outside of a therapist, it would be Kyle.

The two shared a kiss. Yes. These two needed each other.

"Kyle."

Sheepishly, he lowered Lila to the ground but kept a firm hold on her. "Yes, Sheriff?"

"Take her home. Keep watch. Don't come back to the department until I call you. Those are your orders."

He gave her a crisp salute.

Lila peeked past her shoulder and gave Elizabeth a tentative smile. Her deputy detective would make it. She had done the impossible. She was no longer a victim. And she had her support group.

Kyle wrapped a protective arm around Lila and escorted her through the mess.

Elizabeth hopped off the ambulance's back end and stretched. It was going to be a long night.

A tall figure in a wide brim hat stepped out of the brush yards away. The man looked about and paused when he saw her. As he headed her direction, Elizabeth made out the familiar form of Trooper Vance.

"Sheriff," he said coming to a stop before her. "Your undersheriff said you wanted to see me."

"Yes, I did. Come with me." She led him over to the ME's van where Olivia's team had sequestered the I-80 killer's body. "I want to verify something with you."

"I still can't believe you caught the bastard after all this time."

"His first mistake was coming after one of my own. His second was thinking that we hicks are easily fooled." She gripped the backdoor handle. "I think he was at this for too long. He was getting sloppy."

"I wouldn't know, Sheriff. Chasing killers isn't my thing."

"When I started this job, I didn't think it was going to be a reoccurring theme for myself." Elizabeth popped the handle and swung both doors open. She stepped up inside the van, motioning for Vance to follow.

She flicked on the overhead battery-operated light Olivia kept in the van. Laid before them, encased in a black bag on a stretcher was the body. Elizabeth pulled the zipper back.

"Would you verify for me that this was the man claiming to be Lee and acting as a trooper?" She pried the sides apart to expose the dead man's face.

Vance stared at the face. "If you disregard the bullet hole in the middle of his forehead, I can say this isn't the man calling himself Lee."

"You're sure?"

He shrugged. "It's possible he could have worn some kind of facial prosthetic or something to disguise himself, but this guy looks nothing like the man I know as Lee."

Elizabeth closed the body bag. "You might be right about the disguise thing. I don't know if we'll ever figure out who this I-80 killer really was."

"What makes you say that?"

"According to our ME, he has no fingerprints, and it looks like he had special dental work to alter his jaw and teeth. That's just scratching the surface of how he erased his existence."

Vance winced. "How do you do something like that in

this day and age of technology?"

"Who knows? Thanks for doing this."

"No problem." He gripped the brim of his hat and exited the van. "I need to get back to HQ, give them the heads-up."

She jumped down from the van. "I'd like to know if that Lee character is still there. If not, more information on him would be nice. I think he has something to do with this I-80 killer."

"I'll have my lieutenant contact you about that," Vance said in parting.

Elizabeth closed the doors. Her hands lingered on the cool metal. Somehow, she doubted that Lee was legit. His sudden appearance and finding that abandoned car just didn't add up. If Lee wasn't the dead man behind these doors, was he the second man, the I-80 killer acolyte? Was he the one who got away?

From the corner of her eye, she caught movement. She turned to Olivia as she approached. The wrinkles in her friend's forehead were worrisome.

"Ellie, I need you to come see something."

She followed Olivia. "What is it?"

"I'm not 100 percent certain. DCI is working on it, but we might have something to pinpoint who the second killer is."

Floored, Elizabeth stopped walking. "What is it?"

"Please don't get your hopes up."

"Olivia, I promise I'm keeping a level head here."

The ME gnawed on her lower lip. Sighing, she grabbed Elizabeth's arm and pulled her along. "I think Cecil left us a message before he died."

"How?"

"He carved something in the ground under his leg. I don't know what exactly. DCI poured a quick mold in it so we can see."

Elizabeth's pulse thundered in her ears. Could it be? Could it truly be a miracle?

"I'm praying that the rain didn't damage the carvings to the point we can't make it out," Olivia continued.

"He was dying. He had to be weak from blood loss, but he was a resilient man."

"You barely knew him."

Elizabeth ducked her head under low hanging limbs. "I talked to him enough to get a good read on him. His death is tearing Lila to pieces more than her abduction and the fight for her life."

They approached the spot where Cecil's life had ended. His body was gone, replaced by two DCI techs.

"What did you discover?" Olivia asked one.

He rose, his raincoat crackling as he stood. He turned and held up a tray with clumps of the quick drying plaster laid out. "Any idea what this word is?"

Elizabeth stared at the name glaring back at her and she swore hard. She turned away and ran toward the vehicles.

"Rafe! Lila's! Now!"

CHAPTER THIRTY-ONE

L ILA STRUGGLED TO process that she was free. She was safe. She was with Kyle. As he drove her home, she kept her hand on his arm or twined with his. The feel of him, his strength, was grounding her. She feared that she was dreaming this and when she woke, she'd be back in that hellacious pit again.

As a precaution against her listening in on the radio chatter, Kyle had turned his off. He also put his phone on airplane mode. His reasoning—he needed to decompress.

"I still think we should be connected," she said.

"They know where to find us if they need us," he answered, giving her a slight squeeze before releasing her hand. "Open the glovebox."

"Why?"

"Please."

Sighing, she popped the lid and let the box fall open. Nestled among the car's owner's manual and other information were her badge and gun. She brushed her fingers over the metal.

"How did you ..."

"Someone stole them out of the sheriff's office and left them as a calling card with ..." Kyle gripped the steering wheel. "Lila, I'm really sorry about Cecil."

Her lip quivered. How would she ever get over his death? Cecil had stood by her when no one else would. Rescued her from her own devices and set her on the straight and narrow. Even while he was in Chicago and she lived here in Juniper, he had been her anchor, stabilizing her in the chaos. That anchor was no longer there, and she was left adrift.

The man beside her shifted in his seat as he flicked on the turn signal. Lila glanced over. Maybe she wasn't as adrift as she thought. Cecil had liked Kyle. Actually impressed on her that keeping him in her life wasn't a bad thing. That Cecil liked the navy man was a bonus. He had hated Tate, warned her away from him, and in the end he'd been right.

She narrowed her gaze on the badge. Between the man next to her and the pair of items sitting there in the glovebox, she had her answer on how she would heal from Cecil's passing. She kept on moving forward. Staying the course. Lila had overcome an insurmountable mountain once before. Nothing said she couldn't do it again.

She grabbed the badge and held it cradled between her hands. Deputy Detective. That was her. She, Lila Dayne. Badge gripped in one hand, she removed her service weapon, still strapped in its holster.

"Does Elizabeth know you have these?" she asked.

"Honestly, I don't know what she knows right now. She's been on the go ever since we announced you were missing. She never gave up. Swallowed her pride and allowed Sheehan to lead her to you."

"I'll never understand that man. Twice now he's stepped in and helped save me."

Kyle grunted. The sound warmed another spot on her

cold heart. She peered at him through the dark, loving how the dashboard lights lit up his grizzled features. How had she ever thought she could second-guess this relationship brewing between them? During those long hours before she made her escape, she had mulled and picked apart why she had grown fond of Kyle. It all boiled down to one simple answer—she liked him. She couldn't say it was love. Not yet. But something was sparking in the background.

She'd take it slower with Kyle. Give herself time to get to know him, let him get to know her. There would be no rushing in like she had with Tate.

She clipped the holster and her badge to her filthy jeans, reassured by their combined weight pressing into her hip. Being a cop had always been her goal. Even in the midst of her addiction and recovery, it remained her top priority. With the I-80 killer's death, she could move forward with no fear of his return.

Except her actual attacker was still free. He'd been thwarted twice now. He wouldn't stop. Lila had to remain vigil. No getting comfortable.

Kyle guided the car down her street and pulled into the short drive.

"Did you find my car?"

He shook his head and turned the engine off. "We don't know where they took it."

"It might be inside the trailer. There had been one on the semi last night."

"If we find it."

Her shoulders sagged. She was now vehicle-less. "I know how he got his victims, and what he did with them after. It makes me sick."

Kyle took her hand. "He'll never do it again. You and Ellie made sure of that."

"I want the bastard that snuck off. He's my biggest threat. But I don't know how we're going to stop him when the only thing we have to go off is the sound of his voice."

"Give yourself some time. Maybe you saw something out there that can give us a clue."

"About the only thing I have is gauging how tall he was, and even that is circumspect. I was scared out of my mind, and it was dark and raining."

He gave her a squeeze. "Don't sell yourself short. It'll come."

"I want to go inside and take a long, hot shower, then soak in my tub with the jets on."

A knowing smile lifted the corner of Kyle's mouth. "Want company?"

She returned the smile. "Maybe tomorrow." She cupped his cheek, rubbing the damaged pad of her thumb against the soft beard. "Thank you for never giving up on me. I'm sorry I pulled away."

He grunted.

"Okay, Mr. I-Don't-Show-Emotion."

"Blame the navy."

"I do." She exited his car.

He met her in front of the hood, pulling her to him for a deeply satisfying kiss. When he released her, Lila could barely stand.

"Not fair," she whispered.

"I'll carry you."

"No. I don't need the neighbors gossiping even more than they already do."

He let her lead the way into her house. Lila sensed his vigilance. He wasn't about to let anyone sneak up on them from behind.

"You got my spare key?"

He pulled it from his pocket and unlocked the door.

Lila entered the house before him and went straight to Gerry's tank. The beta floated just above his Easter Island home. "Hey, Gerry boy."

Kyle closing the door made the fish flare his fins. Gerry darted into the mouth of a statue.

"Love you too," she sneered at her reflection.

She straightened and rotated away from tank. Movement around the edge of the wall separating the kitchen from the living area caught her attention. She headed toward it, breeching the divider, and saw a man sitting at the table.

"Hello, my darling."

Her brain registered too late what was happening. He lifted a pistol and fired.

Lila cried out, jerking back as Kyle twisted and fell to the floor.

Her attacker was on her before she could react, shoving the gun under her chin and forcing her mouth shut. "Hush."

That voice. That voice didn't match the face glaring back at her.

"Looks like we get to finish exactly how we started. Eh, Lila?"

From the floor, Kyle writhed and groaned.

He pulled the gun out from under her chin and aimed it

at Kyle. "Doesn't look like he'll be pulling the hero act this time." His gaze slid back to her. "No coming between you and me again."

Lila had no idea where it came from, the surge of adrenaline hit her full bore. She brought her arms up between them, broke his hold on her, and she slammed the heel of her hand into his nose. Blood spurted, hitting her hand and arm. She took a step back, kicked up her right leg and bashed it into his chest. He reeled away but kept his feet.

Lila's hand dropped to her gun and found her hip bare.

Maniacal laughter stilled her.

"Damn, you're so predictable. And easy." He held up her holster and his weapon, leveling it on her. "Though, I do have to say, after your little ordeal, I'd figured you wouldn't have much energy left. You do have a few surprises."

Kyle flopped onto his back. Lila chanced a look down at him and felt her heart hammer against her ribs. His right thigh was soaked in blood. God, he was going to bleed out, right here on her floor. She moved to help him.

"Don't you dare."

She snapped upright and faced him.

"Come away from him. He's not getting any help from you."

He beckoned her forward with her gun.

Lila met Kyle's tortured gaze. If she could take the attention off him, he'd be able to fashion a tourniquet and slow the bleeding. It wouldn't be that impossible. She stepped over Kyle's body, blocking him from view and directing all his attention on her.

He pointed at a chair at the table. "Let's have a little

chat, Lila." He switched back to his normal voice, the one she was so used to hearing.

With a ragged breath, she entered her kitchen and slipped up to the chair. He gestured for her to sit; she did so carefully. Once she was settled, he, too, sat in the chair across from her. A blue folder sat on the top of the pile of files on the table, a folder she had never seen before.

"Isn't this cozy?"

She avoided looking directly at him, instead checking over her home.

"Not much to say?"

With a slight tilt of her head, she looked at him indirectly. "What's with the voice change?"

"This," he flipped back, "is my normal voice. The other," switched over again, "is the one I let the rest of the world think is me. A device I've been using for a long time. All those acting classes really paid off."

"It was you? You were the copycat?"

He grimaced, then did a little head bob. "Copycat is the wrong word, though I do say using it to throw you off was a good ploy." He drew in a slow breath and let it out. "No, admirer is a better description. Until he started to slip up. I couldn't hide his mistakes any longer, so I decided to help him out. When he realized what I was up to, he approached me, asked if I wanted in on the game. But he had a stipulation. I had to get rid of you."

"All that time together, you were coaxing him out?"

"Didn't intend to, it just worked that way. It was a perfect partnership. Couldn't have you screwing it up."

"I was in the way of your ultimate plan?"

"Pretty much."

"I was only in the way because you put me there. You didn't have to drag me into your scheme." She shook her head. "You slept with me. Remember?"

"I'll admit, it was a step out of the norm. There was something about you. Broken. Unloved. Needy. Easily manipulated." He slipped back into that hideous voice on that statement. "Satisfying all the same." His smile faded into a scowl. "Then you got knocked up. Didn't see that one coming. What the hell, I got to kill two birds with one stone, as they say."

"You're sick."

"Been accused of that. No one has been able to prove it though."

"Why? What was it all for, Tate? Or is that even your real name?"

Kyle let out a horrendous moan.

"Oh, shut up and die already." Tate turned, lifting his service weapon.

Lila slapped his face. His attention and his gun swung back to her.

"Bitch." He cracked her across the face with the butt of the gun.

She jerked forward and careened into the table. Her cheek was on fire, and a trickle of heat slid along her skin. She brought her focus back quickly. She lifted her head and spotted a figure outside the window beyond the kitchen sink. Tate's back was to the sink—she had to keep him from pivoting.

"You're not going to save him. Or yourself," he said.

She turned from the table and drew his full attention. "You underestimated me twice before.".

"Two times too many."

She glanced at the folder. "What is that?"

He patted the top, amusement playing with his features. "Some old battle-ax thought he could get the better of me with your sheriff. Once I've finished here, he'll be next, and maybe your sheriff too. After that, everything will be as it should. I can continue on as before." Tight lines drew on his forehead as a darkness filtered into his eyes. "No thanks to you, I'll be on my own."

He set her weapon on top of the folder and left it there—a clear taunt. He adjusted his chair to angle it so he could look at her straight on.

"Tell me, Lila, how does it feel to know you were sleeping with the enemy?"

She angled herself to face him squarely, settled her elbows on her knees and leaned forward. "Why don't you tell me how it feels knowing that you made a fatal mistake in sticking around to come after me?"

He scowled. Lila jumped.

She swept his gun hand aside, grabbed hers as his chair toppled over. Lila shifted her body in time to land her knee on his gun arm when they crashed onto the floor. In a matter of seconds, she pulled her weapon from the holster, flicked off the safety, and aimed it at his chest.

Tate's reaction was slowed by his head slamming onto the floor. He had enough time to go for her gun with his free hand before she fired into his heart, but that was all he had time to do.

The front door flew open. Elizabeth and Fontaine spilled into the house.

Lila glared down at the dead man beneath her. "Third time's the charm."

CHAPTER THIRTY-TWO

Wednesday Morning

E LIZABETH PICKED UP the blue folder. Beneath her lay the body of the man who'd orchestrated this whole ordeal, his wide eyes staring at nothing. She peeled back the flap and read the first page of the report.

Tate McCall is not an active member of the Illinois State Police.

She closed the folder. "You had everyone fooled."

"Don't beat yourself up over this," Rafe said.

"I'm not. I take solace in knowing it was my team that stopped him. For good." She threw the folder on the table and put her back to the dead man. "He can rot in hell."

Kyle had been loaded on a stretcher and was being wheeled out of the house. Lila was right on the paramedic's heels.

"Rafe, take Lila to the hospital."

He gripped her shoulder, then followed the group out the door. As he passed through, Olivia entered.

"Dominic is waiting for them to arrive. He'll take care of Kyle," she said by way of greeting.

"I expected as much." Elizabeth sagged onto the sofa. Her sigh came from deep within, draining her of what remained of her energy.

Olivia sat next to her, wrapped an arm around her waist and settled her head on Elizabeth's shoulder. Elizabeth leaned into her friend's comfort.

"I want to sleep for eternity."

"Once we process this scene and DCI has all they need, you can."

Elizabeth lifted her head. "We still have a flood to deal with."

"Let the National Guard handle it. They've got everything in hand. You've been through enough as it is."

She didn't think she could. Relinquishing leadership in time of crisis was not in Elizabeth's DNA. She had already allowed too many slipups that nearly cost the lives of those closest to her. Worse, she was beginning to second-guess her judgment when it came to Kelley Sheehan. All in all, this investigation was a mitigating disaster.

Olivia tightened her hold. "I can sense what you're thinking. And stop it. You are human, and as such, you are allowed mistakes."

"Not when others' lives are on the line." Elizabeth looked to the kitchen and the corpse cooling on the hardwood floor. "He took full advantage of my pitfalls and exploited them."

"It was how he operated." Olivia stood. "You weren't the only one he manipulated. Remember that."

"Speaking of manipulating." Elizabeth pulled her cell phone from her uniform pocket and put in a video call to Trooper Vance.

He answered after four rings. "Sheriff Benoit, is something up?"

"Yeah, Vance, there is. Would you mind having a look at another body and tell me if that was the man calling himself Lee? Just disregard the bloody mess on his chest."

"Sure."

She held out her phone to Olivia, who obliged by carrying it over to McCall's fallen body and showing him to Vance. After a moment, Olivia returned with the phone.

"That's him," Vance reported. "I'll let my superiors know what happened. Damn, Sheriff, what's going on in your county?"

"A whole lot of shit, that's what. Thanks, Vance. If any of your higher-ups need to chat, tell them to contact me. Tomorrow."

"Will do."

They ended their video call on a goodbye. Elizabeth dropped her phone in her lap and flopped against the sofa back.

"So, the I-80 killer acolyte was posing as an Iowa trooper and as an Illinois State Police officer to get close to Lila," Olivia said.

"It appears so." Elizabeth's eyes drooped. "I'm too damn tired to sort this mess all out."

Olivia patted her thigh. "Then don't. We have plenty of time to make sense of it all."

A knock on the doorframe announced DCI's arrival. Olivia took charge. Elizabeth remained on the sofa, letting the activity go on while she stared at the fish tank. The blue beta had emerged from his hiding place and observed all the commotion, darting back and forth as people passed his tank.

Elizabeth's eyes grew heavy. She felt her head tilt, and she jerked upright. The blue fish ceased his frantic motions and floated in the center of the tank, staring at Elizabeth. He dipped down like a bow, as if to say thank you. Elizabeth smiled and closed her eyes.

She vaguely sensed someone hovering over her, then felt something being draped over her body.

"Sleep, my friend."

LILA HAD FALLEN asleep in the most uncomfortable seat in the hospital room and slept hard. She was awakened by the feeling of warmth on her face. Peering through slitted eyes, she spotted sunlight coming through the slatted blinds.

Sun!

She forced her aching body upright, clutched the soft blanket to her chest, and stared at the big, bright marvel.

Lila thrust the blanket aside and got up from the make-shift bed. She tiptoed over to the window and raised the blind. The world lit up. The plants seemed to lift their green leaves to the sky, hungry for the rays breaking through the clouds. Lila closed her eyes and basked in warmth on her face.

Free.

Never again would she ever look over her shoulder and wonder would he come for her today? He was gone. Her nightmares vanquished by her own hand.

She smoothed her bandaged fingers over the pair of cheery pink scrubs one of the labor and delivery nurses had given her last night. After Dr. Thorpe had whisked Kyle off to surgery, Lila was sucked into the grasp of her favorite nurse. Israel Jones saw to it that she got a shower, clean clothing, and food. After Kyle was out of recovery and wheeled into a room, Lila was allowed to stay with him. Israel stood guard the rest of the night until his shift ended, which she had missed as she slumbered away. If anyone had visited, she was unaware.

The reassuring sound of the pressure cuff keeping tabs on Kyle's BP pulled Lila's attention from the scene outside the window. He slept with his head tipped to the side.

The bullet had ripped through arteries—not the femoral, thank God—and missed his femur. Dr. Thorpe couldn't explain it, and Kyle was unconscious, so he couldn't give an explanation on how he managed to keep Tate from killing him. Lila's best guess was, somehow, Kyle saw what was coming and twisted his body just right, so the bullet entered through the fleshy, outside part. Or he was already turned that way and Tate was a piss-poor shot. Either way, he would live, and with a few months of recovery and rehab, would be back on the job.

Lila padded barefoot over to the bed. She ran her hand the length of his bare arm and up, stopping on the exposed anchor tattoo. The bandages got in the way of her feeling his skin. One by one, she peeled off the blasted tape and gauze, chucking the bits into a nearby trash can. The instant her roughened tips traced the anchor, his eyelids fluttered.

Slowly, those blue-green eyes came into view. Lila gnawed on her bottom lip.

"Hey," he croaked.

"Hey."

He lifted his hand and she took it. His gaze drifted behind her. "Is that sunlight?"

"Yes."

"Finally."

Lila slipped free of his hand and lowered the handrail along the bed. She sat on the edge and scooted close to his body. Kyle settled his hand on her bent knee, his fingers brushing her thigh.

"What time is it?"

She shrugged. "Morning?"

"Is he dead?"

"Burning in hell if there is any justice in the afterlife."

A comfortable silence filled the space between them. Lila stared at him, soaking in this moment. Even when they'd been sleeping together, she'd avoided watching him sleep or looking at him in the morning when she woke before he did. In her mind, Kyle was the stoic, fierce protector. Even when still, his mind was racing, and it showed in the ticks and twitches in his face. This relaxed, partially drugged Kyle was something new for her to explore and cherish.

"Are you okay?" he asked.

She leaned forward, pausing inches from him. "I will be." She kissed him.

His hand spasmed and gripped her knee.

"Oops, too soon."

Lila pulled away and looked to the doorway. Olivia hid her smile behind her hand and found a spot on the ceiling to study. Georgia winked and bustled into the room, her hands loaded with a cup carrier and a brown pastry box. Elizabeth, with a lilting smile, propped her body against the doorframe. Olivia joined Georgia in handing out to-go cups of hot coffee.

"We got the okay from the top man for you to have some decent food." Georgia handed Lila a gooey pecan roll. "And Mrs. Miller was more than happy to reward our heroes."

Kyle shifted to sit up in the bed, wincing as he moved, and then eased back against the pillows. "This is as far as I get."

Olivia took up residence on his other side, holding out a smaller to-go cup. "You didn't need to move."

He grunted and sipped his coffee. "Are all you females going to mother-hen me?"

"Maybe," Olivia said slyly.

From the doorway, Elizabeth pointed at Lila, then crooked her finger. Lila left the bed. Georgia filled her empty space.

Elizabeth led Lila into the hall, a few feet from the door. Around them, the soft chatter of nurses and doctors was joined by the sounds of machines and clattering wheels. They pressed up against the wall to stay out of the way.

"It's over," Elizabeth said. "Both men are dead."

"They still took Cecil."

"He got his revenge. He was the one who told us it was Tate."

Lila stepped back. Even if Tate had succeeded in killing her and Kyle, the department would have known and, in the end, he would have met the same fate.

She gave a weak smile. "He always did outsmart everyone." Tears burned her eyes.

Elizabeth gripped Lila's shoulder. "He made sure the one person he cared about more in this world had backup. We'll always be there for you."

Lila nodded.

"I just need to know one thing."

She met Elizabeth's steady gaze.

"Do I still have my deputy detective?"

Before walking in to find Tate waiting to end her life, Lila had made her final decision. For the barest moment, she'd wondered if it would be taken away from her. But now, on the other side of the horrors she survived, that decision seemed more important than she had given it credit for last night.

"You do."

Elizabeth reached behind her back and pulled out a badge. She held it out. "Found this lying on the floor under Gerry's tank."

Lila took her badge and clenched it in her hand. "What about Kyle and me? It's not—"

"Don't you dare tell me to break the two of you apart. This is a small enough department, I don't need friction. Besides. I'm the sheriff. Who's going to tell me how I can or can't run my department?"

"Uhh …"

"Don't answer that." Elizabeth winked. "I've got a meeting with the National Guard captain in a few. You are officially on medical leave for the rest of the week. I do not want to see you back until Monday."

"What about a psych eval?"

"It'll come. Don't worry about it." Elizabeth turned and started to walk away.

"Sheriff." Lila swallowed the word. "Ellie."

Her boss hesitated and rotated. She cocked her head.

"Thank you. For not giving up on me."

Elizabeth gave her a crisp salute and did an about-face that would have made every army drill sergeant nod in appreciation. Lila watched her go until she disappeared around a corner. It was going to take some adjustment on her part getting used to seeing her boss more as a friend than a superior.

She returned to Kyle's room and lingered at the edge of the doorway, observing the activity inside. True to their promise, Olivia and Georgia were mothering him. Or was it *smothering* him? Seeing the hulking Viking red-faced and helpless to their whims made Lila grin.

He must have sensed her presence, because his head swiveled her way and he glowered. Lila felt a little sorry for him, but she wasn't about to intervene. Not when those same two women would turn on her and sweep her under their fussy wings. Nope. Not happening.

She inched out of sight and slid down the wall to sit on the floor. She leaned back against the wall and hefted that large, glorious roll to her lips and tore a huge chunk out of it.

As she savored that sweet, caramelly goodness, a growl came from inside the room.

"You owe me, Dayne."

With a wide grin, Lila bit into the roll once more.

THE END

Want more? Check out Elizabeth and Lila's adventures in *The Killer in Me*!

Join Tule Publishing's newsletter for more great reads and weekly deals!

If you enjoyed *Hush, My Darling,*
you'll love the other book in the…

BENOIT AND DAYNE MYSTERY SERIES

Book 1: *The Killer in Me*

Book 2: *Hush, My Darling*

Book 3: Coming soon!

ABOUT THE AUTHOR

Winter Austin perpetually answers the question: "were you born in the winter?" with a flat "nope," but believe her, there is a story behind her name.

A lifelong Mid-West gal with strong ties to the agriculture world, Winter grew up listening to the captivating stories told by relatives around a table or a campfire. As a published author, she learned her glass half-empty personality makes for a perfect suspense/thriller writer. Taking her ability to verbally spin a vivid and detailed story, Winter translated that into writing deadly romantic suspense, mysteries, and thrillers.

When she's not slaving away at the computer, you can find Winter supporting her daughter in cattle shows, seeing her three sons off into the wide-wide world, loving on her fur babies, prodding her teacher husband, and nagging at her flock of hens to stay in the coop or the dogs will get them.

She is the author of multiple novels.

Thank you for reading

HUSH, MY DARLING

If you enjoyed this book, you can find more from all our great authors at TulePublishing.com, or from your favorite online retailer.

TULE
PUBLISHING

www.ingramcontent.com/pod-product-compliance
Lightning Source LLC
Chambersburg PA
CBHW020951030726
47496CB00005B/1461

* 9 7 8 1 9 5 8 6 8 6 5 8 4 *